FENCING THE SKY

FENCING THE SKY

a novel

JAMES GALVIN

A John Macrae Book

Henry Holt and Company   New York

Henry Holt and Company, LLC
Publishers since 1866
115 West 18th Street
New York, New York 10011

Henry Holt® is a registered trademark
of Henry Holt and Company, LLC.

Published in Canada by Fitzhenry & Whiteside Ltd.,
195 Allstate Parkway, Markham, Ontario L3R 4T8.

Library of Congress Cataloging-in-Publication Data
Galvin, James.
Fencing the sky: a novel / James Galvin.
        p.   cm.
"A John Macrae book."
ISBN 0-8050-6220-3 (hb: alk. paper)
I. Title.
PS3557.A444F46   1999   99-13303
813'.54—dc21   CIP

Henry Holt books are available for special promotions and
premiums. For details contact: Director, Special Markets.
First Edition 1999

Designed by Michelle McMillian

Printed in the United States of America
All first editions are printed on acid-free paper. ∞

1   3   5   7   9   10   8   6   4   2

In memory of Lyle Van Waning

Life is a mixture of power and form and will not bear the least excess of either.

—Ralph Waldo Emerson

ACKNOWLEDGMENTS

Fencing the Sky is a work of fiction. Any resemblance of the characters to actual persons is coincidental. I would, however, like to thank certain individuals who loaned anecdotes from their actual lives to fictional adaptation: Richard Borgmann, Enja Borgmann, Clay Lilley, Shirley Lilley, Bertrand Honea, Tom Gage, and Roger Lorenzi.

FENCING THE SKY

I've been in jail and I can't. And I won't try to cover up what happened here."

"You gonna disappear?"

"Yeah, something like that. And don't ask me where."

"I wasn't about to. Want company?"

"No, that wouldn't work. You just go home, and when they ask you, tell them what you know."

Mike pulled a note pad from his pocket and a stub of pencil. He wrote *I did this. Mike Arans* and stuffed the note into Snipes's breast pocket.

They remounted. They said so long and rode in opposite directions. Mike rode over the top of the ridge to his truck and trailer. He loaded up the horse and drove the thirty miles home. Two miles from his house he stopped by a pasture gate. He went through and approached the zebra dun gelding. Mike put a halter on him and said, "We got one more job to do, Potatoes." He led the gelding to the trailer and loaded him with the other horse.

Back at the ranch he unloaded both horses and tied them to the trailer. He took the saddle off the one, put it on the other, turned the used horse out.

He went in the house, and when he came out he had a big pair of outfitter's saddlebags like panniers, a sleeping bag rolled in a Gore-Tex tarp, a canteen, and a black plastic garbage bag of food.

He tied these things to the saddle. He went into the barn and came out with a pair of farrier's nippers. Fifteen minutes of sweating under the horse, and he had the shoes off. He returned to the barn and came out with a set of equine boots, rubber horseshoes. He fitted the boots and clamped their steel cables shut. He loaded the horse into the trailer and drove to some ranch

FRIDAY

SOMEONE LEFT A GATE OPEN and a few of Mike's cows strayed out. Ad saw them as he was driving home. The next day Mike rode the bottom of a lush beaver-worked draw looking for them, feeling sunlight through green aspen leaves. Oscar was checking Running Water Creek.

When Mike heard Merriweather Snipes's ATV, he lunged up the side of the draw to look. There was Merry, stampeding a dozen cow-calf pairs across the prairie.

Mike pushed his horse into a gallop and let him stretch out. The horse overtook the herd and turned them. Snipes was behind them but could only follow as they curved, almost gracefully, over the rocky, sagey ground, back in the opposite direction. Mike dropped back behind them and slowed his horse and stopped, letting him blow.

Snipes was looking at Mike from a hundred yards off, idling

the ATV. Mike watched as he unsnapped the leather holster lashed to the handlebars and drew the .357. He pointed it at the sky and fired it once. Then he passed it to his left hand so he could operate the throttle and came straight at Mike fast, apparently meaning to scare him off.

Mike turned and descended back into the draw, which was a tangle of aspen trees, willows, deadfall, and bogs. The horse lowered his head and high-stepped carefully over the mess of beaver-felled aspen trunks. Mike studied the still water floating on the peat mud. Water striders jerked on the surface like a spastic cobweb. The horse thrashed through belly-deep mud to the other side. Snipes couldn't follow him there.

Instead of slipping off downstream, Mike turned upstream and made his way through dense willow growth tall enough to hide them completely. He threaded the drainage where it turned a point of rock. He recrossed the creek and stopped.

He could hear the ATV patrolling above him on the crest of the draw. Mike untied the rope from his saddle and turned out a loop. When he knew by the whining motor that Snipes had passed him, he launched out of the draw and fell in behind the man and bore down on him, swinging. Snipes never knew he was there.

Mike rifled the loop and missed. When Merry felt the stiff nylon strike his shoulder he turned, surprised. The machine hit a prairie-dog mound and bucked into the air. As he grabbed the handlebar to regain control, the pistol fell from Merry's hand.

The horse torpedoed behind as Mike remade his loop and started it swinging over his head. Snipes was going as fast as he dared, bumping wildly over sagebrush and rocks. Mike fired another loop, a good one, which settled around Snipes's neck. He threw out some slack, dallied, and set up hard. Snipes hit the

end of the rope. His neck snapped. The ATV flew o
between his legs and soared screaming into the air li
on drapes. It arched and hit the ground upside down,
once, and lay there idling.

Mike walked his horse forward and got down. He
looked at Merry. There was blood seeping from hi
tears. Mike lifted his head by the hair, removed the r
the head drop with a thud. He said, "You dumb sor
What do I do now?"

That's when Oscar loped up and took in the s
mounted and dropped his horse's reins. "What the
knelt next to Mike and looked at Snipes. "There's
his neck."

Mike said, "Is there?"

Oscar closed Snipes's eyes.

The ATV was still idling.

"Did you mean to kill him?"

Mike sat on the ground, spurs turned in, h
looking at his toes. "I don't know. I guess so. If
ing to kill him I would have roped him deep
hard."

Oscar looked at Mike. "Nobody has pe
loop."

"Yeah. Well. The reason I guess I mean
when I did it it felt good."

Oscar nodded. "What you gonna do?"

"Ain't but one thing *to* do."

"You could probably get off for self-d

"Trouble is, by the time I got the rop
defense anymore. I can't go to jail. No

buildings a mile to the east. No one lived there anymore. He unloaded his horse and tied him to a fence. He drove the truck and trailer home and unhitched the trailer. He drove back to where the horse was and parked the pickup in the shed and slid the door closed. He mounted up and rode due west.

NOVEMBER 1963

TEN-YEAR-OLD OSCAR opened his eyes to the cellar dark. The tiny room he slept in was black as the inside of a rock. Eyes open, eyes closed, he saw the same pitch. He was wide awake, though, as if he had a clock inside his head that was set for milking. He drew a deep breath to hear himself awake and make sure he wasn't just dreaming of waking, as he often did.

Without getting up he reached the doorknob to the left of his bed and nudged the door back. A dim glow entered his room: embers through the isinglass in the coal-stove door. His eyes snapped closed, open, closed, like a shutter. He said, "God, I hate that cow."

He threw back the gummy army-surplus sleeping bag he used for a blanket and swung his bare feet onto the chill of linoleum.

Seeing by grace of the soft coal glow, he yanked on his jeans, checked shirt, socks, and cowboy boots. He opened the stove door and slung in a shovelful of dusty coal. A puff of acrid smoke billowed out like devil's breath.

He climbed the steep cellar stairs, snatched his black felt hat and his horse-blanket-lined denim coat, and went out.

The stars were strewn like spilled tacks across the matte sky. The sun had not thought of rising yet. The mud under his boot soles was frozen as he crossed the yard toward the big log barn. He stopped at the corral, broke a bale of hay, threw four separate forkfuls over the rails. The smell of dank summer sagged out of the hay.

Horses materialized out of the dark and buried their warm muzzles in it. He could smell the sweet dusky smell of them. At the barn, he leaned against the big door, slid it back enough to edge through. He switched on the light.

The next thing he knew he was waking up again, his head resting against the side of the Holstein, crushing his hat brim. He had dreamt of killing the milk cow, of poisoning her with lark-spur he gathered and stuffed into his hat and boot tops. But in the dream everyone knew it was him who murdered the cow because he was the only one who hated her.

He began milking again, pulling and squeezing from index to pinky, listening to the long rips of milk on the side of the steel pail and wondering if there was any way to kill a family cow and not get caught. He decided there wasn't.

When he got back to the house, his parents were up with cups of coffee. By the time he'd had a cup his two younger sisters were up and getting ready to go. Then they all went out to the back pasture to feed the mother cows, heavy with their unborn calves.

Oscar's dad, Frank, took six-year-old Annie, bundled unto immobility, up on the tractor seat with him. Oscar's mom rode with Oscar and his other sister, Belle, eight, atop the stacked bales on the flatbed trailer.

The stars were gone, the sky brightening. Once in the pasture they broke bales and rolled them off to the cows, who, udders and bellies swaying, trotted up to feed. The first sunrays bloodied the snowy peaks as they headed home for breakfast. Then it was off to school.

The Rose kids attended one of three remaining one-room schools in the county. The one-room school was a great American institution unless you were Oscar. He didn't get along with the schoolmarm. That made it a great American institution like the milk cow. He had the same ropy old teacher for eight damned years before he was done.

Since he was the only one of the three strong enough to tighten the cinches, Oscar went out to saddle the horses. The three little vaqueros rode off across the mowed and snowy haystubble in the first November sun.

Oscar said, "I bet you can't shoot me," and spurred his horse into a lope. Belle dropped her knotted reins onto her gray's neck, made an imaginary rifle with her arms, squinted one eye, and said, "Pow!"

Oscar threw his arms up, dropping his reins, sent up a howl, and leapt straight up out of his stirrups. His bay mare ran out from under him as he flew, cruciform, into the air and crumpled on the snow-padded sod.

Annie was shrieking with laughter. Belle said, "Gosh, you'd think he thought he was made out of tires."

This was a game they played often on the spongy peat of the hay meadow. They'd gallop their horses and shoot each other, and the rule was when you were shot you had to fall off your horse.

Annie wouldn't because she couldn't remount without a boost, so she slumped into her saddle instead. Belle usually slowed to a trot and slid out of the saddle, dying slowly. But

Oscar delighted in heedless, headlong dives from his galloping horse. He couldn't get enough of being shot.

The other game they played was "counting coups," a kind of horseback tag.

Picking up the reins of his politely standing mount, Oscar vaulted into the saddle. He galloped his horse in big circles, whooping. He would have galloped the three miles to school, but the pony Annie rode had rough gaits and she bounced in the saddle like popcorn. The two older kids had to slow down for her or she cried.

They rode through the sand rocks, making up things for the rock shapes to be: a sleeping dragon, five frogs, an upside-down ice-cream cone with a bug on it.

When they reached the Sabot Ranch, where the school was, they unsaddled and unbridled their horses and turned them into the corral. Since they were the only students, school started when they walked in the door.

The girls liked Miss Holcomb better than Oscar did. Maybe she was just nicer to girls. Annie never looked at her directly if she could help it, though, because Miss Holcomb had a king-sized mole on her cheek with three long black hairs.

They were out in the yard eating their sandwiches at noon when Oscar had an idea. He knew the mailman's schedule, knew he stopped at the Sabot each day by the end of their lunch break. The three ragamuffins scrambled out to the roadside where six Quonset-shaped boxes, variously colored and tilting on their individual posts like bad teeth, red flags up or down, waited for signals from the outside world, proof of strange lives elsewhere.

Next to the motley row of boxes was a yellow fifty-five-gallon drum on a wooden frame lying on its side with a square door cut into one end. The six ranches that collected mail at the

Sabot shared the yellow drum for packages. The three Rose kids crawled into the drum, closed the door on themselves, and laid for the mailman.

Three kids inside the barrel didn't leave much room, and the dark inside was infinite. They could have been flying through space or sunk to the bottom of the sea. It was hot in there, and it never occurred to Oscar that they'd run out of air until they started gasping for breath. The door was latched from the outside.

So that's what Oscar and Belle and Annie Rose were doing the day JFK was shot.

The mailman, Joe Brine, was stopping in at every ranch house, knocking on the door to tell the news, so he was running a good deal late. Miss Holcomb had already taken a turn outside to look for them, but she wasn't worried yet, just expecting some typical Oscaresque mischief.

Joe sorted the letters into the regular boxes, and when he opened the door to the barrel, flooding it with air and light, the three kids boiled out, gasping. Joe leapt back like they were snakes. Oscar lay on the ground sucking air and finally croaked, "Surprise."

A big sob went through Joe and he didn't know what to do. If Joe had known what a metaphor was, he'd have thought he had experienced a metaphor.

FRIDAY/SATURDAY

FEELING STRANGELY EUPHORIC, with a deep sense of freedom-in-destiny, Mike rode up through his own hay meadows, leaving no tracks. He hadn't felt anything close to good since Liv died. He knew his friends would take care of his animals.

Avoiding the main road, he went through wire gates without getting off his old familiar horse. This was the easy part, while he still knew where the gates were. Later he'd be guessing. Opening the gates from horseback, leg-yielding and backing, holding the gate stick in one hand, wire away from the horse, he felt reassured. Whatever happened, he didn't much care. It would happen in the company of his most trusted and oldest friend.

Potatoes had been officially retired from sharp-end ranch work when he reached twenty. Twenty years of service was enough, besides which he had a wind puff on his pastern and tended to come up lame with overstress. Neighbor kids still borrowed him to rope from or run barrels and poles, always with strict instructions not to overdo it. Potatoes was once in a lifetime, no question. He always knew what Mike was about to think next.

Mike leaned over and slipped the loop on the next gate. The horse sidestepped away and Mike held the stick at arm's length. When the gate was open, the horse turned around the stick and leg-yielded and backed until Mike leaned down and replaced the loop. Mike thought, God, I love doin' stuff like that.

He rode up through the big meadows as they darkened. They got bigger as they got darker until they merged with everything. He hobbled his horse and camped at the upper end of the ranch. He forced himself to eat, though he wasn't hungry, to drink, though he wasn't thirsty. He popped a cube of bubble gum in his mouth and leaned back against a boulder, blowing bubbles in the dark.

He tipped his hat down over his eyes. Mike always had a weakness for certain cowboy clichés. What he had done that day was not right. It was almost right. It was, in a way, good enough, though it wouldn't change anything or stop things from happening. What would?

If nothing else, it would make a good story someday. Especially if he ended it right. Without a good ending it was just an anecdote. He'd do his best on the ending.

How did a nice middle-class kid from back east end up where he was, basking in sublime desperation? Ever since Liv, things had seemed muffled in unreality. He saw himself from a distance with authorial detachment. He blew a bubble.

When he thought of Merry's face, the bloody dead glaze of his blue eyes, he thought those eyes looked more dead when Snipes was alive, and he felt a fathomless sorrow, not for Merriweather Snipes but a larger sorrow that threaded through history like a million violins.

He never slept that night and so was moving as soon as he could see, up through the rocky canyon and big timber of the North Fork, all country he knew well. When morning was full the sky looked like a cerulean bowl turned over.

By noon he was climbing out of the canyon and crossing the saddle to Sheep Creek. He drove his horse along the ridge through thick lodgepoles and deadfall, staying out of sight even of logging trails and jeep roads.

From where he was he could look down on the county road. He was waiting for the sheriff's car to pass, for indeed he was headed straight back, returning to the scene of the crime.

He rode a little higher to a rock outcrop, and sure enough, here they came: the sheriff, a fire department rescue truck, and a van, maybe the coroner.

Traversing the slope, Potatoes churned through the deep, needly mulch of the forest floor. They crossed the county road when the law had passed, where a stand of young aspens swathed the other side. They crossed and rode up through the just-yellowing trees to the rocky ridge across the valley from where he'd been. The trees made a scrim and they rode behind it.

They skirted Lyle Van Waning's old place through ridge-top timber and dropped straight into the drainage below where Snipes still lay, now surrounded by investigation.

Mostly what a sheriff does is drive around until someone has a crime: stolen saddles or firearms, vandalism. Then he walks his sidearm and clipboard and his beer belly around the crime scene, takes snapshots, brags about what a crime-fighting genius he is, says looking for fingerprints won't help, and lets slip that there's really nothing he can do about a situation like this. He drives home satisfied.

So when Sheriff Cummins found the note in Snipes's pocket, he was elated. He had solved a crime! He felt like Richard Leakey. He had something to do.

There was, of course, the chance that the note was a misdirection. He'd talk to Arans, that hippie, find out if he had an alibi or something. After all, if Dirty Mike, as some called him, had actually offed this guy, why would he leave a confession at the scene? Usually people turned themselves in if they weren't planning on getting away.

Cummins's dark ferret eyes scanned back and forth under the brim of his Stetson as he pondered the mystery. The note was crazy any way he looked at it. But its craziness gave it possibility. He radioed for more men.

They loaded up the corpse. Just before slamming the doors on it, Cummins said, "So long, Merry. Too bad. I never got to deputize you like you wanted."

Four deputies arrived before dusk, two with horses. They found hoofprints all around the scene. They found a set of tracks coming and going to the north, and a set coming and going to the south. Both sets ended up where signs of horse trailers were clear. They reported back to the sheriff as dark came on. Mike was about a hundred yards away in the deep cover of the draw below.

He thought Potatoes might whinny to the other horses and give him away. He wasn't worried, though. That would change the ending, but not the end. He didn't care. The horse never made a sound and stood dead still. Mike was dozing before the law packed up their clipboards and left.

Cummins not only knew Merry, he knew most of the ranchers in his district. He knew Arans, the hippie. Cummins relished the idea of bringing that bastard in. The fact that there were two sizes of horseshoes leaving the scene meant that the perpetrators, or the perpetrator and a witness, were no longer in the area. If Arans had indeed left the note, being a stupid hippie, he'd probably be waiting at home to be arrested.

Cummins sent his crew home and drove to Black Thorn. It was after dark. No one answered the door. He went in. No one. The trailer was in the yard but the pickup that pulled it was gone. The criminal had clearly hit the highway.

Cummins made a call to get specs on the truck. He put out an all-points bulletin, which made him feel important. Then he went home to bed.

JANUARY 1991

SNOW GHOSTS SLAKED over the red galactic grit of the county road, the prairie a rough sea of drifts, blowing snow a blue fuzz, electric, over them. The shrinking gray Stalinist Oz of the cement plant floated toward the horizon above the words OBJECTS IN MIRROR ARE CLOSER THAN THEY APPEAR. Smoke rivered downwind from its stack under a sky so clear and cobalt it seemed ready to crack, shatter, tumble down in shards.

Dr. Adkisson Trent fought off the familiar exhaustion that, like a pet mongrel sent repeatedly away, kept slinking back to lick his hand with its foul tongue. Mostly harmless, it was just a ragged hankering for sleep the sparkling snow seemed to accentuate.

The road was piled up, thin, like a levee, and ditched out on both sides, which worked well to keep it snowless, windswept, but made it kind of deadly, too. Exhaustion and weak attention flowed from his brain down into his arms and hands and the three-quarter-ton pickup wavered.

He was driving too fast, he knew. An aberrant gust could swipe him off the built-up road and into the ditch like litter. Did he care? He wasn't sure. He tightened his grip on the wheel and resolved his gaze, but almost immediately his mind wandered off the road and out onto the oceanic expanse of basin prairie.

Nice drifts. Nice gale. Nice herd of antelope huddled asses to the wind. He thought of the rabbits and foxes and badgers and prairie dogs floating in delicious sleep beneath the visible, shrieking world, a stratum of furry well-being, a submerged city of unconscious life.

Then the right front wheel dropped off the shoulder and adrenaline coursed as the pickup fishtailed and righted. "Christ," Ad muttered, awake.

Last night in the emergency room. He assured his own spongy incredulity that it had actually happened. Clichés like "stranger than fiction" were clichés because of how true and useful they remained through time. Ad thought they were like verbal martyrs: relentless, calm, holy. But hell, fiction was stranger than fiction too, by virtue of how true it was, so where did that leave you?

He said out loud, "My mind is clearly oatmeal."

He needed holy, clichéd sleep. He needed a couple of days. For starters.

Well, he had them—and some nice bottles of wine, some books, a pair of cross-country skis.

A little shell-shocked chuckle burbled out of him as he thought back into the middle of last night. It had been like being in a tiny myth. Ovid. A woman, middle-aged and obese, had presented with a green, leafy sprout growing out from between her legs.

The nurse had led him blinking into the hospital light from the doctors' sleeping quarters. In his webby waking he'd thought it was a nurses' joke. But when he offered a drowsy quip to prove he was wise, the woman teared up again and began to mewl.

She really did have some sort of plant growing out of her, and she was understandably agitated. He imagined donning a pith helmet for this pelvic. It occurred to him, not for the first time, that Fellini was, like all great artists, a brutal realist.

It turned out that, more than several days previously, the woman had suffered a collapsed uterus and had used an old wives' tale remedy, namely a potato, to give support and relieve discomfort.

Apparently the procedure had worked pretty well because she forgot about it. Dr. Ad, as the nurses called him, delivered a seething Medusa of sprouts balled around some remaining rot.

Ad had grown up on a small ranch in northern Colorado, which was where he was headed. No one lived there anymore except for Ad, when he made the time.

His blond, linear good looks (though he was balding now) were so striking he'd been mistaken for a certain movie actor who, in Ad's opinion, couldn't act. He snapped the drifting pickup back to the middle of the road.

The snow-crowned Medicine Bow Range curved around the prairie in loose embrace, an arm around a lover's shoulders. The mountains wobbled in wind-blown heat waves, though the temperature was well below freezing. The sandstone rock formations throbbed redly out of the snow like hard clouds in sunset and, cloudlike, suggested analogs for themselves, busts and beasts.

Adkisson had driven up from Fort Collins and now was beginning to feel the mild grace specific to going home, back to the ranch, though no one would be there to greet him. Back where it was solid. Honesty of empty plains, secrecy of timber, melancholy of peaks in distance. Distance.

Still struggling to stay awake, still swerving in the occasional cat's-paw cross gust, the doctor motored steadily through the meringuelike sand rocks toward Camel Rock, a two-hundred-foot tower that stood free of a nearby rim.

He turned off the county road and drove under the rock's shadow. The first major snowdrift he came to rose up out of a cross-wind ravine and belched over the side road like lava flowing uphill. Ad killed the motor. The drift didn't look like too much to dig through, but it was only the first, and Ad thought he'd rather ski than shovel. So he put a bottle of Bordeaux, a steak, and the novel he was reading into his pack. He'd come back later on the snowmobile and haul the rest of his luxury home.

Within minutes he was waxed, loaded, clipped, and on his way, the familiar *slish-slish* of cutting new snow. Each ski tip made a kind of reverse wake in the snow, not like a boat's wake, which parts the water into an ever-spreading vee. After parting the snow, the snow heals back over, keeping all of the ski but the tip submerged. The tracks skis leave claim nothing more than their own dimension and where they've been.

He made a fast two miles uphill, then stopped on a knoll to remove a couple of layers of clothes. He could see the house from there, like an alphabet block with a roof, still a couple of miles of upgrade off, against the treeline.

Given how the country was changing, given some of the characters creeping around these days, he was always glad to see his house standing. He waxed a warmer kick onto his skis, humped his pack, and stroked out, getting pretty good glide even on the uphill without a track.

Just moving like that, expertly, rhythmically, was clearing his head of ghosts. He felt a surge of bearable joy. He reached his own drifted-over cattle guard and poled off its downside.

Before he saw it he knew something wasn't right. From two hundred yards away, he thought, *Too still*, though he didn't know quite what he meant. He never really registered the inner eclipse, the elevator going down in his chest, the change of temperature in his gut, the numbness settling over him like the return, after eclipse, of light.

The windows looked frosted over in angular patterns. He'd never seen that. He'd never seen that because that's not what it was. No, they were broken, all right, all six on the side he could see and, as he rounded the corner, two more and the door bashed in.

He said it aloud, but he couldn't hear his own voice in the ripping wind. "At least they didn't burn it down."

He planted his poles, grips in his armpits, hands on grips, and leaned on them, elbows out and breathing hard.

He looked down at the snow as though the crystalline ants rushing over themselves with such purpose could tell him what to do. His eyes blurred, and he saw furious armies flying through a luminous landscape to destruction. He hung like that for a good two minutes, reptilian, himself crystallized and blowing through.

It wasn't as though he'd never expected this. It was his worst recurring nightmare. Well, second worst. He heaved himself upright and looked around. The pines around the cabin were giving up snow to the wind like souls, boughs waving as if trying to pull them back down again. The clouds were sliding over like angelic pedestrians reflected in a shop window—not interested, bound elsewhere.

He sidestepped over to the stove-in door and tried to push it open, but some object inside prevented him. He unclipped his three-pins and kicked off his skis. He slid out of the pack straps and let the pack thud in the snow. A wave of nausea passed through him, cloudlike, cloud-shadow-like, but slower. With his feet braced into the snow, he put his shoulder against the door and pushed. Behind it the toppled bookcase slid a little and he stepped inside.

The first thing he noticed, really before his eyes focused, was unbroken wind blowing through the rooms. When his eyes began to register he saw that the wind was the only unbroken thing in there, and it seemed to blow right through him, too. A shiver. The wind was blowing through his house. Wind bearing a fine sugar of snow. Wind and snow having its way in the kitchen, the living room. Then he began to see.

Under the white powder the kitchen table was overturned and splintered. Likewise cupboards, cabinets, chairs. Axes. The floor was shin deep in rubble, rubble that had been dishes, furniture, food stores, picture frames. He looked down at one and saw his daughter's smiling face, snow-blown, slashed. Axes. They had taken axes to everything. Quite a party.

He noticed not all of the snow was snow; they had shaken out a fifty-pound sack of flour over the floor. On closer inspection he could see they had spread molasses on top of the mess. A scrawled note stabbed over a chair-leg spar said *Don't look in your cabin Ha Ha Fuck You.*

He waded and climbed through the wreckage into the living room to take in the axework on the couches, the inlaid chest, more tables and chairs whose mild resonances of comfort and security were not erased but, worse, painfully stricken. His daughter's room upstairs—her posters of horses, her teddy bears—axed.

The wind. He went back down. He thought he could get some plastic over the windows, get the cookstove and wood heater going, clear himself a place in the wreckage, and make do for the night. It was a monumentally depressing idea, but he could get a start on cleaning up. Then he saw the pick holes in the stovepipe. Both stovepipes. No way. He went out to the shop.

They had pried the doors off. Inside they had shattered the window glass and headlights on the '48 Jeep and the old Power Wagon that used to belong to his neighbor, Lyle. They'd left the splitting axe embedded in the roof of the cab. He took a roll of black irrigation plastic back to the house, along with some strips of lath and a staple gun.

Have you ever tried to tack plastic over broken windows in a gale? The black sheets he cut flapped and wagged and streamed from his grip like oil smoke. It took all afternoon, and when he was done, there was not only no wind inside, there was no light either. Like being inside a camera. So much the better. Who wanted to look? Remembering was bad enough. He was tired. Body and soul wedded in utter fatigue. Done, he hoisted his pack and pushed off in the darkening wind and skied, like a corpse, down through the gloaming of hurrying snow.

SUNDAY

THE FIRST STAGE HAD WORKED. Mike had not only asserted his existential guilt, he'd got Oscar off any possible hook and sent the hounds on a chase to the highways of America. They weren't looking where he was, at least for now, safe in the eye of the storm. That was good; it gave him control over the situation and a chance to gather his wits.

While asking questions around neighboring ranches, one deputy drove into a place where, clearly, no one lived. The reason he started snooping around was not because of some brilliant intuition, reasoning, or forensic acumen. It was because he was a snoop.

When he peeked inside the shed and saw Mike's truck he felt like all Las Vegas. When he reported his discovery, however, it still never occurred to the investigators that Mike might be horseback, riding out. After all, the horses had been loaded in trailers, and Mike's trailer was at home.

The crime fighters sent out word nationwide that the fugitive was not in his truck. As for Mike, he stayed in the eye of the storm, working on his soul.

When the sheriff went to interrogate Oscar (they had no idea who the second cowboy was) he wasn't home, as usual. His wife said she didn't know where he was, which was the truth, which was also as usual.

Mike slept on a bed of spruce boughs beside his hobbled horse. He ate sparingly from his tins and drank from the spring creek that hinged the draw. On the third day he rode out at dawn.

JUNE 1989

OSCAR ROSE SAT LIKE A COMMA on his chestnut gelding, watching the mamas and babies pass, a hundred yards or so from the drag end of his herd. His hair more sandy than red, his face iron-bound and etched, his eyes sharp-cornered from wind and piercing blue as asters. His black hat hung on his back from a stampede string.

The cows knew where they were going, no need at the moment to force them from behind. The stragglers were sore-footed, but they'd come along. No one was in a hurry.

Then he heard the gravel hissing and the horn blowing and he twisted in his saddle to look back. Of course there always had to be one jerk. He wasn't riled. He'd seen all kinds.

He wheeled the big gelding and plodded back down, against the current of the oozing herd. He told himself to keep his shirt on and be nice.

He rode up on the Jeep and took notice of the hot color of the guy's face. He noted the silver-white hair and big jaw, but mostly what he was considering was the guy's choice of vehicle. Piece of crap. Then he saw the glare and thought, Pissed-off turista.

In fact, the man was looking at him with a distillate of hatred rarely seen. He was, Oscar thought, as full of hatred as he was of shit. And he wasn't blinking, even with the dust. He wasn't about to blink.

When Oscar drew up ten feet away, about to open his mouth to (blink and) politely explain the situation, the man boomed in a strikingly deep, authoritative voice, "Get these stinking animals off this road. I'm in a hurry."

Oscar thought, You poor sucker. But he just reined in and looked.

The man spoke again. "Get them out of my way! I have an appointment!"

Oscar crossed his arms over the saddle horn and leaned on them. He spit out his toothpick. He stared. He felt like he was at the zoo, but he wasn't quite sure which side of the fence he was on.

He turned in the saddle and looked at the herd, still plugging along. He gazed up at the steep hillside splotched with sage and scrub pine. He put his hat back on. He adjusted the brim low over his eyes. Looking back at the exploding man, he pursed his lips and pulled his whole mouth over to the side of his face as far as it would go—a way of not grinning. "Where do you suppose we should put 'em?"

The man said, "Clear this road or I'm going to get the sheriff."

Oscar said, "Oh, you mean Bill? Down in Collins? That sheriff? Yeah. You could go get him. That'd be a good idea. Why don't you go do that."

The man leaned on his horn again and Oscar's horse doubled under. Oscar sat the spook.

He determined it useless to try to explain that cattle have the right-of-way. He was tempted just to sit there and look and spit until the guy maybe popped a blood vessel or something. Oh, hell, he said to himself, and then voiced, "Mister, I don't know nor much care what your all-fired hurry is, but till these girls get through the narrows here, there's not a speck I can do for you."

"Make them go faster. Run the sons of bitches."

Oscar looked up at the crown of a huge Douglas fir that held the sunlight in its branches. "OK, mister. If your pants are that much on fire we'll try to accommodate your upholstery. It's still going to take a while to get you through, but if I put my horse in front of your, uh, car here, and you keep close, we might be able to ease you up and get you on your way."

The tourist, redder than hot steel, said, "Make it snappy."

Oscar looked down at the stitching on the toes of his boots. He scratched the back of his neck. He addressed his mount—"Come on, Spook"—and touched him up. The horse stepped out smartly and the Jeep came up on his heels, ceaselessly revving.

The horse and rider reached the hindmost pairs in the herd and began wading into them, parting them like a cold fluid. The Jeep revved and crowded. They began to ease into the body of the herd. The guy leaned on his horn but Spook didn't flinch.

It was as if even the horse had this guy's bad number. Then the guy stuck his head out the window. "Hurry up, goddammit. I haven't got time."

Oscar reined in his horse and stood. He pretended to check something on his saddle. Then he heard the engine rev again, and this time the clutch was engaged. The Cherokee Chief was coming for him.

Oscar never turned around. No one would ram a mounted horse with a car just because they were in some kind of piss-fire hurry. No one.

Still, he wasn't all that surprised when the horse went straight up and finished off the buck with a kick at the grille of the car that had, in fact, just rammed his hindquarters.

Then, as soon as the horse settled and before Oscar could react, the guy did it again.

Oscar vaulted from the saddle, dropping the reins. He found himself running, reaching for the door handle. He was abjectly unglued.

He snatched the door open and threw it hard against its hinges and there it was: Oscar just stared down at the little hole in the pistol barrel. His rage drained to a kind of distant interest. He thought, You sure can't see very far down the barrel of a gun. He wagged his jaw once and closed the door.

He must have closed it a little hard, though, because all the glass fell out of the window. He pivoted on his bootheel, turned his back on the man behind the gun. He swagged two paces, stopped, and removed his hat, the stampede string dangling. He scratched his head, considering certain stupid actions. He put his hat back on and slid the rawhide bead up under his chin. He strode two more paces over to the horse, picked up his reins, and flipped the off one over the chestnut's neck. He stood into the saddle, turned on the haunches, and put his horse up the road after the cattle, at a walk.

He was looking down at his boot toe again, and from behind it looked like he'd fallen asleep in the saddle. Oscar was not asleep. He was fighting the returning surge of rage and the onset of ripping adrenaline. He was thinking hard and he never turned around to look when he heard the Jeep gears grind and howl in reverse and spew gravel into the wheel wells as the red guy made a three-point turn in the road and gunned off the way he had come. Oscar guessed he had finally thought of going around on the other—slightly longer—road nearby.

Oscar Rose had never even heard of anyone like that, let alone seen him. He sure had plenty to think about for the rest of that day as he punched his bank account up the road to summer pasture.

SUNDAY

MIKE WALKED HIS HORSE down the draw, a thick clutch of willows and aspens. It was slow, the horse picking through webs of fallen logs, while Mike pushed branches up and ducked under them or lay flat over the pommel to negotiate the thickest, most overhung spots.

Leaf shadows dazzled the sunlit grass like nervous fish. Then there was a rocky patch. The horse left no tracks. Mike was careful not to break the branches he bent out of his way.

He reached the confluence of the spring creek he was following and Sand Creek. From there, he almost reversed his direction. He'd gathered a lot of cattle out of these canyons. He knew exactly what he was doing. Later on he'd be guessing, leaning on luck.

Maybe the truck trick would work for a while. Modern American outlaws hit the highways, hid in the cities.

Sand Creek, here, had made a deep, rugged canyon. The bottom of the creek bed was throttled by apparently impenetrable willow bushes. You'd look down there from the rim and say it was impassable. But from chousing cows and calves out of that cover, Mike knew he could ride, invisibly, right up the creek bed, horse in the water, trackless.

He was headed south now, the wrong direction, but he needed to get over the pass into the National Forest. It was bound to be slow, but as long as no one spotted him there was no hurry. He'd save the hurry for when he was seen.

The canyon relented, opened into a big hay bottom, uncut, tall native grasses swaying as if with vertigo, belly high on the horse. He wove in and out of the willows, keeping hid. He came to the county road.

Riding the road, he'd have been here hours earlier. Might have been noticed, too. Not enough time to jump his horse into timber or behind a boulder if he heard a motor coming.

He had to cross here, but with thick cover on both sides it wasn't a problem. He listened. It was quiet, so he touched his horse and crossed. The rubber-booted hooves made slight tracks in the loose red road dust, tracks that would be obliterated eventually by traffic, except on the shoulders. Some rain would be nice but the sky held no promise.

He followed a long braid of pines, aspens, and willows until he topped the pass. On the west side of the pass the south side of the draw became a cliff. He had to cross the road again and make a dash into the house-sized boulders that knurled the side of Bull Mountain.

He loped his horse straight up the steep pitch. There were three boulders leaning together like inebriates in conference, where Lyle had once showed him slug scars in sandstone. Some cavalry had had some Shoshones pinned down there one afternoon, till nightfall came and fetched them out of reach. He stopped behind those rocks, where the Shoshones had stayed safe, and drank from his canteen. Potatoes Browning availed himself of the timothy grass that grew there.

Below, he could see the road for a stretch in each direction. Coast clear. He rode higher on the mountainside till it broke back and hid him. He contoured the mountain and descended into the Laramie River valley.

He came to a wire fence gate. It was the boundary of the old McLeod Ranch, where he'd gotten his first job twenty years ago, right after the bust. A few things had happened since then. Look what he'd come to. The brave cowboy. The honest outlaw. Everything he'd ever wanted. Yet he'd studied those fable formulas, how the people you saved couldn't wait to get rid of you after you'd saved them.

Mike saw himself becoming a formula, and it was a sad one. He rode into a stand of huge old ponderosas and dismounted. He loosened his latigo, hobbled his horse. He slid down the side of a big sighing tree and blew a bubble.

He had to cross the Laramie River and its big hay meadows in the dark. On the other side, in the National Forest, it would be dense lodgepoles, more deadfall, and rocks. He'd have to do that in daylight. He'd wait for dark to cross the river and daylight for the other side.

JANUARY 1991

IT WAS NOT QUITE SUNDOWN when Ad hoisted his pack, snapped on his boards, and poled down the slick track he'd made coming up. His sense of violation was so absolute there was nothing to compare it to . . . rape? Nothing existed outside it. He couldn't feel. He stood straight up on his skis, arms hanging at his sides, as though he were waiting for a bus. Poles dragged. The meaningless hiss of his skis as he glided steadily down toward darkness was the correlative of his present thinking on the subject, as the red cliffs rose before him and fell upward into dark and the snow turned red.

. . .

Later he would not remember this drive back to Livermore. The reptilian part of his brain was still in motion trying to sort out the chaos he'd seen. It was like a microburst inside his soul, the heart's furniture splintered.

Making sense of it meant making it logical, the inevitable effect of some hellish cause. Making sense of it meant making the worst of it, making it personal.

He'd certainly made some enemies among the new arrivals, running them off for trespassing or poaching, closing the road that ran through his yard. Ad tried to keep to himself. He just did what he could to protect his own space, his peace, his memories of the other world, the world before this world, the way of life that promised never to end and then ended.

These new people couldn't understand him. *Alone* was not in their lexicon, not among their desires. They took it wrong.

So, generally speaking, he was aligned, both in his own mind and in the minds of others, with the ranchers and the old-timers who were here before that Snipes guy bought twenty thousand acres of cattle pasture and peddled it in forty-acre lots.

Most of the worst friction was about cattle. The new people seemed to bear a curious grudge against cattle, though they weren't, so far as Ad could tell, vegetarians or environmentalists. The new people wouldn't build fences or fix existing ones, and they hated the law that said they had to fence cattle *out*.

In the minds of the newcomers, cattle were simply not natural. Ad wondered if they'd rather have buffalo. Buffalo, which required monumental fences, also caused vastly more erosion than equal numbers of cows, being heavier and, by nature, fast movers as opposed to amblers. Plus, all that high fence cut off the migrations of other herds.

Would the new Re-Creationalists prefer buffalo nosing around their campers and shacks, occasionally goring their children?

Ad liked buffalo. He knew some folks who raised them. That's how he knew they were hell to manage, hell to fence, and a constant threat to humans.

Mostly, Ad speculated, the newcomers hated themselves for having been duped into buying forty acres of cow pasture, complete, as it turned out, with cows.

And that Snipes. A piece of work. The first time Ad ran into that monument to progress the man was up on the ridge, hidden by timber but not three hundred yards from Ad's house. Snipes had a tractor up there and some kind of high-tech drill rig punching a six-inch-in-diameter hole eighty feet deep. He was planning to lower some kind of sonic device into the hole and listen for uranium.

Ad ran Snipes's ass off, somewhat agog, and realized only later the dimensions of the offense taken.

Yet Snipes could not be imagined to be the vandal himself. Could he have hired it done? There was Snipes's son. What could the old man make him do? Then there was that Olson kid, son of one of the new landowners, in and out of trouble more often than socks in laundry.

Or could it have been impersonal? To Ad it seemed that the depth of devastation, the nature and placement of the rage, demanded it be personal. But wasn't that how earthquake, hurricane, and tornado victims felt, that it had, somehow, to be personal?

No. It was no one. It was two or three no ones. Two or three hurricanes on snowmobiles. Three hurricanes on snowmobiles and crystal meth.

It was dark when Adkisson passed Mike pulling a six-horse trailer a couple of miles from his ranch. Ad slowed to stop and wasn't surprised to see Mike's truck skid and the trailer jackknife some, since, as usual, Mike had a lot of get-along and the electric trailer brakes worked on only one side.

Ad rolled his window down as Mike backed up even in a cumulus of road dust. The simple fact of Ad's being there, then, meant something was wrong.

Ad said, "Somebody whacked my house. Whacked hell out of it."

Mike lowered his head and studied the floor mat. He blew a bubble and said, "I've got to put these horses into this pasture up here, then I'll meet you at the house."

That night Ad stayed at Black Thorn Ranch with Mike and Liv. He thought about calling his ex-wife with the ugly news but decided he wasn't ready to utter the necessary sentences. Though they were divorced, they got along, and he'd built the house when they were together. In some sense he'd built it for her and their daughter.

He could fix the windows and stovepipes. The house still stood. He could live with a few dings in the trim and the floor. Only the house's poetic space, its content, had been raped. The next day he would get the sheriff and, with Mike's help, start cleaning up. Actual repairs would have to wait for spring.

When Ad woke in the morning, Mike was out doing chores. Liv poured him some coffee as he phoned the sheriff's office and made arrangements to meet a deputy at the only café in Livermore.

Ad walked out to the barn to find Mike. Mike had a cow in the stanchion and his sleeves were rolled. He had one arm in her up to the elbow. "Calf's upside down. I can't go anywhere."

There was a stain of shame, a stain of sorrow in his voice. "I can't go," he said again and looked down, shaking his head.

Ad felt a wave of loneliness arcing through him at the thought of facing the wrecked house without his friend. He said, "Anything I can do for you before I go?"

Mike shook his head, feeling around thoughtfully inside the cow.

"You sure? I don't have to meet up with that Boy Scout until nine."

When Adkisson arrived at the Forks Café, he saw the deputy's miniature four-wheel drive with its self-important complement of lights and thought, Useless.

The deputy was inside, carrying his gun around. He was a young fellow Ad didn't know. He sure was enjoying his job, though.

Ad filled him in, pointing out they'd have to go up into Wyoming and loop back down by Camel Rock. The deputy intoned, "Can't we just go up Cherokee Park?"

Ad looked. He can't be that ignorant, he thought. More like he's afraid to go up into that country in winter, desperate not to. He wants to drive up the plowed county road as far as Devil's Canyon, look where the county doesn't plow, determine the road impassable, and go home. Maybe stop in here and take his sidearm for another walk.

Ad said, "That road won't be open past the turnoff. The county doesn't keep it open. I went in on skis yesterday, but I know an old winter road no one uses anymore. It's the road the old-timers used to get to Laramie. It's out on the prairie. It sticks to the ridges. We should be able to thread our way between drifts. There used to be a bridge across the ditch at Camel Rock. We'll have to ask the foreman to doze it out for us today. I can get us there."

"If you want me to go up there—up into Wyoming, I mean—I'll have to ask for special clearance."

Ad looked.

"OK. If you, as a citizen and victim of a crime, want me to go up there, it's my job to try." The deputy said this in a tone that suggested Ad didn't really want to go up there either, and his hesitation was a final invitation to postpone the investigation till spring.

Ad looked.

The deputy went out to his vehicle to ask for permission to go up into Albany County, Wyoming, in order to access his jurisdiction in Larimer County, Colorado. He came back and said, "They said don't take too long."

Ad looked.

He carried one-by-sixes from the barn and nailed them over the windows facing west and the windows facing north. Plastic alone would never make it through the winter. He didn't want to return in May and find the living room full to the rafters with snow.

In the dark he drove back to Black Thorn. He called Jean. She cried and they both decided not to tell Althea, not till the mess was cleaned up.

The next morning Adkisson and Mike took two pickups to the cabin. They tore down some plastic for light. From the inside, they took out all the window frames and loaded them in one truck. Sixteen double-hung wood frames with jagged shards.

They used scoop shovels to clean up the broken glass and rubble. They filled Mike's pickup bed with wreckage: the dining room table that had been Ad's mother's, all its splintered chairs.

There was also the sundered hutch, the debris of dishes, the framed photos, the bookshelves heaved over, and all the books covered with molasses.

There was one object Ad kept looking for. He found it outside in the snow. The small soapstone carving of an Eskimo man had been pitched through a window. The Eskimo's face had sheered off.

That carving Ad had considered the most beautiful object he owned—that and the fretless banjo that lay snapped and held together by the strings like a crippled marionette, equalized, in the back of the pickup.

The Eskimo man he held in his hand still wore the heavy, hooded sealskin parka, mukluks, and mittens. He was still bending roundly to begin dressing the beautiful goose he has killed. He holds one wing open in one hand to expose the breast to his knife. The goose's neck stretches down over his breast.

The expression on the man's face, Ad remembered as perfectly as he remembered the clear notes of the fretless on wine-soft summer nights, as perfectly as he could imagine the sound of its breaking.

The man's face had shown a certain matter-of-factness, a shyness in his joy. Now, where the face was sheered off, leaving rough stone broken along a single plane, was not no face but another face Ad could see in the stone-grain, gray against the polished black of the rest. Not unlike, Ad thought, the face of the man in the moon.

This was the Man in the Stone, and he looked mournful and angry by turns.

Clara's landscapes slashed. An Amish quilt slashed. An inlaid Hessian chest splintered. A little girl's collection of glass horses crushed to powder.

Ad rested his chin on his crossed arms on the mounded pickup bed. The junk was a landscape of things, flayed, emptied of difference. Shard from an heirloom vase nudging a tube of toothpaste axed in half. Lyle's jewelry box, the box he made for auger bits. Ripped photo of a three-year-old boy in a red cowboy hat, sitting his father's ornery, Roman-nosed horse, squinting into the too-bright sun.

In his hand Ad held the Man in the Stone.

A bird's-eye maple music box exploded. A can of Safeway peas with a pick hole in it. On the summit of the junkscape, bed frame, table frame, picture frame, framing square folded in two.

On the far horizon of the truck bed, details were harder to make out. It was colorful, painterly, this reduction to matter of things.

He still held the Man in the Stone in his hand.

MONDAY

AN HOUR BEFORE daybreak he was saddled and gone. When he heard himself admonish himself and his horse, "Let's not take any chances, now," he laughed. He rode out into the fecund darkness of the hay meadow. The new-cut three-inch stubble made a burning sound under the horse's hooves.

When he came to the riverbank he turned his horse's head to the right. There had to be a bridge for haying. He found it, and the horse's rubber boots on the gray two-by-twelves sounded like a deerskin drum. On the other side, more meadow, for half a mile in the not-quite dark.

Something—he never saw what—darted away and the horse doubled under. "Easy now, take it easy. You ain't seen nothin' to be afraid of yet." Mike did not feel afraid. He was elated with ease. Nothing like it ever before. He was, for the first time since childhood, entirely unworried as he crossed a series of big irrigation ditches and rode up the meadow skirt into the loden-dark lodgepole forest.

He came to a fence, rode one way, then the other, stitching through the thick saplings that grew between the big trees. Then he cut the fence, rode through, and took twenty minutes to stretch and splice the wires behind him. It was light. No use letting out stock and, worse, sending a telegram about his passage.

The horse pulled steadily upward toward the crest of the Medicine Bow. He followed game trails where he could, but they always, sooner or later, veered in the wrong direction. He followed logging trails unless the earth was soft, imprintable. The horse's boots would make no mark on rock, like iron shoes, no trail in short grass or shallow pine needles, but in loose dirt or mud they stamped a print so distinctive they couldn't be mistaken, once they found out whose horse was wearing the sneakers.

Two hours from the river, well inside the National Forest, the morning sun was soothing his shoulders and the pine smell was sharp. They were moving through a stand of older trees, loosely assembled, and Mike was mind-wandering and letting the horse choose his path, when, from above, out of air, a loud voice said, "Hi!"

Mike pulled up and froze.

The voice from the sky said, "Up here."

Done for, thought Mike, as he craned his neck back to look up. There, twenty feet off the ground in a tree, was a man in camouflage fatigues, blackened face, holding a bow in one hand, seated on a tiny platform of boards between two limbs. The man smiled. "Where ya goin'?"

"I didn't know it was bow season."

"Next week. I'm just getting ready."

"Right. So long."

The man said nothing more. Blood was pounding in Mike's head as he stepped his horse away, thinking, That could be it, right there.

Adrenaline waned as Mike and Potatoes picked their way through a stick forest. "Son of a bitch, Potatoes, why didn't you tell me there was a guy in the tree? You knew it or you would have spooked when he said hi. Jesus."

Mike smoothed the hair on the back of his neck. He had to think clearly now. First, there was no way to tell if the pickup ploy had worked as a diversion or, if it had, for how long. Now, if this bow hunter went home and turned on the nightly news, the sheriff would be up here with dogs, helicopters, the works.

Maybe the guy would never see a picture of Mike. If he did, Mike knew, he'd be hard not to recognize. If he lit out, he'd never know for sure if he was being followed till too late. If he stayed put, he'd know where he was, and he'd be in a zone safely behind their expectations.

Dark was coming down through the dusk. Mike kept rolling his eyes into the trees overhead and blowing bubbles. He was just inside the Wilderness Area, looking for a spring to camp by. He was telling himself to quit looking at trees—how many hunters could you ride under in one day, and wasn't one enough?—but looked up one more time.

There, lined out on the limb of a big pine, were four wood grouse, fool hens, watching him. He looked around for a way to get one. There were no stones on the needly forest floor. He dismounted and picked up a silvered limb eighteen inches long and three in diameter.

The grouse watched him. To say *intently* might be a stretch. Fool hens are one of those evolutionary puzzlers, like flying opossums. No explanation. So they were watching him, but being grouse they had no apparent idea. Mike reared back and sidearmed the stick at the little row of judges. Hoping to clobber two, he was satisfied when one plummeted. He was more satisfied still to see that the other grouse had not frighted but stood, as it were, their limb.

"How can something that dumb survive?" Mike picked up another throwing stick and whacked another bird. This one wasn't dead on impact. It struggled to its feet and wobbled toward him. He grabbed it by the neck and gave it a twirl, picked up the first grouse, his reins, and went looking for a campsite.

He dug a hole and built a fire in it, wrapped the dressed grouse in a leaf of foil he'd brought instead of a Dutch oven, and buried them. He was wondering if more good or bad fell from trees.

APRIL 1991

"DR. TRENT, your favorite customer is here to see you."

"Oscar? Oh, hell, what's he gone and done to himself now?"

"Not likely to be anything he hasn't done before."

"No, I guess not."

Oscar was propped on his elbows as they wheeled his gurney in, still wearing his black hat.

"How ya been, Doc? Stayin' even?"

"Fine. What'd you do now, Cowboyhead?"

"Horse fell down."

"What happened, you couldn't get something *new* to go wrong?"

"Guess not."

Oscar still wore a cowboy boot and spur on his left foot. His right boot had been scissored off and his jeans slit to the thigh. His leg was fishbelly white and his right foot was jutted to a sick angle. He looked down at his leg as though it were a mangled tractor. Matter-of-fact.

"You know what's stupid is I knew there was a frozen spot at that end of the arena. Even had Roger put special shoes on that nag's back end, cleats. My partner made a good head catch and my loop was good, too. We were building a pretty good time. We dallied and turned, and down we went. But that's not the stupid part."

"You're kidding."

"Nope, the stupid part is, as much as I was expecting what happened to happen, I still didn't kick out of the stirrup in time. How bad is it?" The question was oddly giddy and gleeful.

"You need X rays. It isn't good. But hell, Oscar, a little more hardware won't hurt you, one more appendage held together with alloys and screws. Pretty soon you won't be able to break bones. You'll be out of 'em."

"Do I get to stay in the hospital?"

"Do you *want* to stay in the hospital?"

"I love the hospital."

"Sorry?"

"You heard me. I love the hospital. This time of year, with A-I-ing and branding coming up, I can't afford to be stove up too long. It's just that I've noticed over the years the only time I get any rest is in the hospital."

Ad knew that, when his hay was up, Oscar took two weeks off every August. He took his wife and kids up to the northern part of the county and helped put up his father-in-law's hay crop. Oscar's vacation was a haying vacation. A haying-again vacation.

"What about the food?"

"Everybody's always crying about food in the hospital. But you know what I think? It's hot. And they bring it to you in bed. You got no idea what that can mean to someone like me. Besides, you never ate what my wife cooks. She can ride and rope and drive a tractor and fix fence. She might go as far as a ham sandwich, but she doesn't really heat anything up. That'd be her limit.

"Say, did that deputy fella ever catch the miscreants that busted up your place?"

"Oscar, that deputy couldn't find his ass in the bathtub if he used both hands. Did he ever find out how you had two cows break their legs in one day?"

Four days in the paradise of Ivinson Memorial, and Oscar was out in time for branding. He had a new plate in his leg, a heavy-duty zipper of a scar from ankle to knee, and a knee-length cast.

Oscar liked branding because it was a community event, a kind of work party, like haying used to be. If two or three ranch families and their hands and their kids and their friends pitched in, you could get each family's calves branded in a day instead of a week.

Mike had tried to convince Oscar that a community of small ranch families was a perfect Marxist society, where everyone had enough but not too much. Everyone worked together—loaning machinery, lending a hand—a Utopian idea, a way of life.

Funny, thought Oscar, I thought that was freedom. Marxism is like ants.

. . .

Also, Oscar liked branding because it was as much for the kids as it was for the adults. The new calves were unafraid of being roped and they were light enough for kids to handle.

So all the ten- and twelve-year-old fledgling buckaroos flailed in the pens with their ropes, eventually heeled a calf, dallied, and dragged it to branding.

Oscar liked to do his own branding. You want a clean, visible brand, not too deep. They had four hundred calves to brand that day. Afterward there was a potluck barn dance planned. Oscar was trying to figure out the best way he could dance with a cast on.

He worked the branding iron all morning, occasionally jumping in to help flank some of the wilder calves. The other men thought Oscar was crazy to be working on that leg, but then they'd thought Oscar was crazy all their lives.

Then someone pointed out the blood that had filled his cast and was slopping over, soaking his jeans. Oscar looked down in mild dismay. "Damn," he said, and handed the irons over to Mike.

"Wonder if he's finally gettin' some sense," someone said to no one.

TUESDAY

AT FIRST LIGHT he tied Potatoes under a tree whose canopy was wide enough to hide the horse from above and started back toward the bow hunter's blind.

Once within hearing distance—though there was nothing yet to hear and might not be for hours, if ever—he gathered some dead branches, lay down behind a silver-gray rotting log, covered himself, and fell asleep.

When morning was hale he woke to voices.

"If a guy rode by here horseback, how come there's no tracks?" It was Jim Thomas.

Nobody said anything as Jim circled outward from the tree with the blind in it. Then, on a stretch of bare ground blown clear of pine needles, he found one clear print.

"OK. I get it."

"Can you track him?"

"Sure. But I ain't gonna do it afoot. I need some horses. I'll start tomorrow."

1990

ON SLOW NIGHTS in the emergency room, Ad watched the weather channel. The lady said the highest concentration of lightning strikes in the world is along the Front Range of the Rockies. In dry timbered terrain, this statistic makes people nervous. Still, the lightning and the forest fires they engender don't exactly count as weather. You can predict the weather, sort of, and suit up accordingly.

California is nice if you don't like weather. The urban rip from Fort Collins to Colorado Springs is nice if you like plenty of sun and dry air punctuated by powdery snows. Those geographies are predictably writhing with human lives and human consequences.

No one recommends Wyoming for its climate. They recommend its lack of human consequence. Up here it's scenery that sells and winters that usually drive the newcomers out. Even on weathery days you get your sunset, and sun shines in the wind.

There is no spring, just that time of year after the ground thaws when the snow won't stick. It's snow, thaw, snow, thaw, and the flowers come up in the snow. The winter wind goes to gumming but keeps blowing long after it should have quit. Even natives to prairie life get desperate from years made of wind.

Summer isn't hot. You can work up a sweat in the hayfield, but just open your shirt and turn to the breeze, accept the gift.

They always sell real estate in June, when the creeks are high and the land is briefly green between white and brown.

Ad thought about weather. For instance, from another planet, weather on earth would look pretty constant. Day on one side, night on the other, not much in between.

But no two snowstorms in a man's life were alike. Ad had been snowed on in every month there was. Four feet in a night sometimes.

Snow went sideways as often as it fell. Sometimes it went straight up. Ten above in a good gale was colder than forty below. Once he ran out of supplies and skied thirty miles to Laramie.

Worse than the wind were those rainless weeks on end in summer, maybe a tease of virga in the afternoon. You knew when it did rain its overture would be lightning, like a match on a spill of gasoline. Ad lost three horses to one bolt of lightning. Lyle lost five cows to one. Haystacks apotheosed in fury. Everybody knew somebody who'd been smoked out of the saddle.

About fall Ad had no complaints, unless it was a few drunk and trigger-happy hunters sending high-velocity loads whizzing over his roof. Beginning in August, caravans of Jeeps crept up the road, full of bow hunters, camouflaged and face-blacked like they were sorry they'd missed Vietnam. Three months of successive hunting seasons. But that wasn't weather either.

Fall mornings were cold and clear. The peaks took a giant step forward and the sky went two or three notches more blue. Afternoons were warm with aimless breezes. The yellow aspen leaves shushed against the green timber and purple mountains. They looked like they were lit from within.

At night there were so many stars, so sharp and clear, it was as if you could smell them burning up there. They'd give you a pretty good idea of where you were.

TUESDAY

MIKE RODE ALL AFTERNOON, following the sun. Then clouds lit up and he kept riding. He rode under pinball stars. He rode through sparse open timber on pine needles and short grass, leaving a spare track, careful of the little shoots of broken branches and twigs. He made good time, often trotting through parks and on stretches of logging road, steadily westering as the land inclined to the top of the Medicine Bow.

When the ground softened or opened to dust, he backed and went around it. Helplessly he tracked up every spring creek he crossed. He circled a lot of wet earth and rode on all the bare rock he could find. He changed direction like an ant.

As he was doing all this, he knew exactly how he would be tracked. It was just a matter of how long the tracking took. Partly a matter of luck. Every evasive move he made was time spent in order to gain time. Eventually he would be cornered, but since he was the one deciding where to go, he started trying to think of corners he could get out of.

JANUARY 1991

MIKE ARANS GOES OUT to the mud porch and grabs his black felt hat, or what's left of his black hat. The truth is, so little is left of its ability to hold itself into the shape of a hat, he can't pick it up. He has to grab it. He grabs it and puts it on.

Once it was a nice hat, custom-made ten-X beaver with a wide brim, tall crown, and a thirty-dollar horsehair hatband. Now it's a serious drooper: brim corrugated into a collapsed lampshade, crown worn through all around except in back, making the top of the hat a flap that blows open so that, especially riding fast or in a good breeze, Mike looks like a big cowboy Pez dispenser. The hat is sweat-stained and manure-caked from brim to crown. Children decline to touch Mike's hat unless it's on a bet or a dare.

As an afterthought he snaps up his Brazilian rainstick and goes out. The pickup motor sounds like liquid on high boil when he starts it. Typical ranch beater. He idles out across the thawing mud of the driveway, over the frosted bridge, and up to the pasture gate, the last old-fashioned pole gate left on the place, rails silvered from fifty years of weather.

It isn't fitted by hand with drawknife or spokeshave either. The ends of the gate upright and the uprights on the heavy timber gate frame are turned, machined, as if on a giant lathe. Every time Mike lifts and slides the pole latch and swings the gate back he thinks, How in the hell they done that I'd like to know.

Now he's idling the pickup, enjoying the dusty-smelling heat starting to blow from the defroster, chewing his bubble gum, studying the gate.

This little spread he is renting has changed hands every couple of years for the last twenty. A gloomy litany of good intentions and hard tries. Now it was his turn: ex-hippie kid from New Jersey, Swarthmore dropout, busted radical, and longtime ranch hand. Now it was his turn.

This was the life he had determined to lead. Hell or high water, he'd see this out. He'd made himself some promises twenty years ago, even before he'd got done with saving the world from capitalism and corporate rapacity. He would himself become a Utopian figure, an honest laborer in the fields, skilled torchbearer of horse culture in the western mountains and plains. In other words he wanted to be a cowboy when he grew up.

Busted by the FBI was what he got, on vague trumped-up charges, principally conspiring to blow up the Liberty Bell. He was not conspiring to blow up the Liberty Bell. He was doing social work in the black community in Philadelphia. He was coordinating self-help and political awareness programs with the Panthers. On the other hand, there were people in his SDS cell who, had they thought of it, would have loved to conspire to blow up the Liberty Bell.

Once they stole a philosophy class at Columbia. Two minutes before the scheduled first meeting, a girl from the cell accosted the professor in his office and, by dint of feigned hysteria, good looks, and pressing personal problems, managed to make him fifteen minutes late for class.

Meanwhile, the cell leader, himself a dissertationless philosophy PhD, entered the classroom and announced a room change. The students gathered their texts and notebooks and innocently filed—like prisoners of war, which they were—down the hallway to another, unoccupied classroom.

Cell members replaced legitimate students in the original class, and the "real" professor began the first of his scheduled lectures. Down the hall, the guerrilla professor started in on Marx, Marcuse, and Huey Newton.

Each week one of the fake students stopped coming to class until, much to the dismay of the tenured dignitary, like the fourth little pig he had none. He never suspected anything but his own loss of touch until he realized that, though all the students had dropped, none of them had asked him to sign the requisite slips. He went to the dean and presented the mystery one week before midterms.

Meanwhile, down the hall, the class went swimmingly. Many of the students acclaimed it the best class ever. Many were ready to enlist in the Revolution. By midterm the SDSers knew the jig was up and they got away clean. That was fun.

Jail was not fun. When Mike got out he knew he had to make himself scarce. He had to go somewhere and do something. His phone was tapped. He was under surveillance. They were waiting to hit him again. He swore he'd never go into the slammer another time. He'd die first.

Back then he'd thought it was still America, even with J. Edgar Hoover running the country, even with shameless quislings in high places, like Rizzo. It was still America, and you could be a cowboy. You could work hard and get by. You could trade a conventional notion of success for an unconventional way of life that involved freedom, morality, pursuit of happiness.

You could keep to yourself and not hurt anybody. You'd have to be poor, but you wouldn't have to worry. As long as you could work you wouldn't have to worry.

As he sits staring at the old pole gate, he thinks what he bargained for was a long way from what he got. He had the work part right, and the poverty part. But he hadn't counted on sleepless nights fretting about foreclosures and pink slips and unpaid debts. Sickness, accidents, the rain that falls equally on the honest man and the thief.

The way things were going—beef prices, hay prices, machinery costs, enclosure, development—he didn't see how anyone could hang on in this life.

Well, I guess I'll keep dreaming until the dream is over, he thinks, even if I have to wake up working for someone else. Even some rich, ruling-class guy whose ranch is a hobby. I'll ride the hobby horses and punch the hobby cows. I'll hang on till there's nothing left to hang from.

He gets out and lifts the slide on the gate, shoots it back, and swings the gate away. He chuckles at the far cry the gate makes and, addressing the gate, says, "Smart-ass." He drives into the pasture, considers closing the gate, decides he won't be long, and doesn't. He approaches the scattered herd and begins to loop through them, looking them over.

Some are standing in small groups staring, others are far-flung. He clunks the truck into compound low, takes his foot off the gas pedal, and slowly cruises the herd of pregnant cows like a submarine spying on a bunker-pocked coast. He drives close enough to each animal to make it stand and walk. He studies every one, scanning for a thousand signs: lameness, labor, prolapse, glassy eyes, cancers, swellings, infections, drooping ears.

Missing the slightest thing could cost an animal. Losing a good cow was a heavy hit. Some things you couldn't help, but if you missed something you could have helped you'd kick yourself all the way to the bank. One bad year calving, weaning less than ninety percent, he'd be shut down. He was already in debt up to his droopy hat.

He burbles slowly past the black and black-and-white cows, who follow him with their eyes till their eyes hit the sides of their sockets, then they jerk their heads over for another scan. He is scanning them for infirmity, they are just scanning. He stops, backs up, looks closer at one, looks again, blows a bubble, drives on.

Having looked them all over, he turns the truck to face the mountains and cuts the motor. He blows two bubbles.

For the last month things have been pretty sane. After October's gathering, cattle drive, pregnancy testing, shipping, and before the three long months of calving ahead, there is that blessed little window of time in which to repair the trucks and tractors, break a couple of colts, nail new poles on the corral, patch the roof of the house, maybe even see a movie.

He picks up the rainstick from the truck seat, steps out to face the sunset. He wouldn't want most of his neighbors to see him doing this. A rainstick is a long, hollow, bamboolike baton stuck full of dowels like Saint Sebastian. It is sealed at both ends and loosely filled with seeds of various sizes. When you tip it over and tip it back, it sounds like rain in the Amazon Basin. Mike turns the stick and begins to chant, "Rain, rain, come my way; now's as good a time as any. Rain, rain, come my way; now's as good a time as any." He turns the stick over and over and hears the rain inside.

Mike has brought the rainstick out to the sunset because his cows are getting close to calving. The high country has had a dearth of snow so far. Another year like last year of no snowpack, poor pasture, bad hay, and forest fires would not be welcome.

But the real reason is that when it snows it isn't too cold. Cloudy weather is better for calving, and low atmospheric pressure brings the calves on. So Mike chants his chant and rotates the rainstick over his head as he strides to the top of a rise and faces the bruised and bloody sunset, letting exotic seeds rush their only song, which is the of sound of tropical downpour on grass roofs and ten-gallon leaves.

The colors were draining into darkness as he jounced the pickup home over the pasture. He wasn't looking at the herd anymore, he was just looking, blowing bubbles, letting his mind wander.

It's true what they say about big sky. It was streaked with pink all the way to the eastern horizon. Big as the end of the world. The line of cottonwoods along the creek eased from green to black.

The irrigation ditch was easy to cross, so he wasn't thinking about it. He was watching a redtail pyrne down to hunch on a dead limb when the front end of the pickup rose up over the lip of the dry ditch and mushed to a halt, killing the engine.

Mike said, "What the . . . ?" Then he remembered the dead cow. Number 439. She had died in the ditch two weeks ago. She was old, scruff and bones. She'd produced good calves in her life, but he was expecting her to go so he didn't think much of it. He had, however, meant to drag her out of the ditch.

So Mike is remembering "dead cow" as the crucifying odor of advanced putrefaction takes the cab of the truck. Holding his breath and blinking hard, he rolls down the window and leans out. The left front wheel is furrowed deep into the loins of the partly liquid carcass.

He starts the motor, throws the gearshift into reverse, stomps on the gas, and dumps the clutch. Blue smoke furls out of the tailpipe, and the rear wheels spin uselessly on the lip of the ditch. Mike exhales a thimbleful of air and sips it back. He is strangling from the smell. He doesn't even have to breathe to smell it, to be awash in it.

He needs four-wheel drive to get out of this cow, and the hubs are out. He fairly falls from the cab and leaps into the cow. He turns one hub and, gagging, staggers around to the other and turns it, turning blue. He crawls into the truck from the off side, slides behind the wheel, and tries again.

This time the truck churns back, and both doors fly open like ailerons. The snow tires howl and fling cow guts into the sunset. The transmission shrieks as he floors it and the truck rushes backward, a released party balloon. He slams on the brakes and the doors slam shut. Then he grinds back another hundred yards, still not breathing. Finally, he rolls to a stop, but by then he is hanging out the window sucking down the sky.

As he drives back out the gate and idles, Mike is thinking his wife, Liv, is sure going to like this one. Liv is a Finn, the daughter of a famous World War II Finnish general. Mike knows damned well she's the prettiest girl in the county, but at moments like this it strikes him that Finns don't have much of a sense of humor. Stalin found that out. And now, as much as he loved her and felt deeply blessed to be sharing his ranch life on the skids with her, he felt guilty for having gotten her into this. He knew she wouldn't joy, as he was already beginning to, in the makings of a great getting-stuck-in-a-cow ranch anecdote.

She hadn't wanted a ranch life to begin with. He'd talked her into it. He'd talked up pictures of a peaceful bucolic life and she'd gone along. Now she was just plain scared. And it takes a lot to scare a Finnish girl.

He leans his head on the steering wheel and chuckles. That's OK, he thinks, I can be cheerful enough for everyone. He gets out and closes the gate, trying to think of someplace he can drive the truck into the creek, deep enough to wash it off but not deep enough to get it stuck or douse the distributor. There isn't any. He looks at the gate in the rearview mirror and blows a bubble.

When he dropped out of Swarthmore, everyone he knew was a Marxist / Leninist / feminist / radical. They believed the people could handle the power. He wore geeky black plastic glasses and had zits. He carried a briefcase full of leftist propaganda wherever he went. He had never actually read Marx. So what? He knew what equality was. They were all so sure of everything back then.

SEPTEMBER 1971

HE REMEMBERED with the clarity of trees seen in lightning, though he'd been drunk and a little stoned on pot, returning to the apartment, the hideout, on Pine Street in Philadelphia. He turned the key and opened the door. Everything was white light. He could sense that there were a lot of people in the room, but he was blinded and no one spoke.

He raised his hands to shade his eyes and made out floodlights on tripods, a TV camera. Two suits grabbed his arms from behind and told him to lie face down on the floor. He was too stunned, fortunately, to resist. He said, "Why for?"

They said shut up. He lay face down and they cuffed his hands behind him. One held a sheaf of *Zap Comix* under his nose. "Are these yours?"

"Yeah. Why?"

"Agent, add pornography to the explosives charge and the conspiracy charge."

Mike, who had been clinging to the idea that this was a farce, a scare tactic, or even one of his friend Gleason's stupid theatrical jokes, especially the part about being busted for comic books, gave up on all that when a bright badge slid into view and they read him his "rights."

The FBI was busting them. The FB-fucking-I was busting the hell out of them. Conspiring to blow up the Liberty Bell, mainly. Six days in jail. National news for six months before the hotshot lefty lawyers demanded the Bureau's purported evidence, which was not forthcoming due to nonexistence—outside of the comic books, that is—so they threw the case out.

It had been a pretty major deal at the time, of course, but he remembered with some astonishment that he had never been afraid. He had just wanted to prove those twisted mothers wrong. Noam Chomsky wrote a deposition on their behalf, which helped.

Still, Mike's father, a professor of engineering, was not happy with the way his only son's life was tending. Well, west was where it was tending now. His father loaned Mike some cash and sent him to his sister, who had married a rancher in Colorado. Put him to work on the cowboy gulag.

JUNE 1970

"YOUR PROBLEM IS, people, you don't know who the enemy is. That's your problem. The age-old historical enemy of civilization and knowledge."

Something struck the dean's shoulder. Something not quite solid, not quite limp. He could not identify it by feel, but it touched him again as he was saying "Black studies." This time whatever it was fell onto the outdoor stage at his feet.

He looked down in time to see that it was a rope with a loop on the end, like a lasso. It was a length of clothesline.

The loop cartoonishly slipped (was tugged) off the stage and into the belligerent mob. That was when he was saying "Radical Studies Institute" or maybe it was "divestment of government contracts." Distracted by the clothesline, he couldn't quite remember.

Whatever he was saying, he was thinking, Who in creation do these surly brats think they are?

The rope struck his knee, and this time, by watching it off the stage into the crowd of hirsute barbarians, he could see who was on the other end of it.

It was a big bearded guy in a cowboy hat and black plastic glasses. He had shoulder-length hair and high-heeled cowboy boots with fancy stitching. Actually, the dean admitted to himself, it was a really big guy—maybe six-four, two-forty. His patched blue jeans were tucked inside his high-topped fancy boots. Actually, it was a really inebriated really big guy dressed up like a cowboy with a length of clothesline that he was trying, unsteadily, to coil. He was trying to make another loop to throw at the dean.

The clothesline slipped off his shoulder again. He raised his arm to slap it away as though it were a hornet. The big guy was definitely out to rope the dean. The dean said "solidarity of knowledge." He tried hard to concentrate, to keep his voice from quavering.

The big cowboy was making another loop with an empty bottle of tequila in one hand. The depleted bottle both comforted the dean as he said "freedom of speech" and discomforted him as he said "responsibility," because that was when he began to speculate, as his soft hands clutched the podium, on what might be his fate if the big, drunk, ugly, hippie cowboy managed, by chance, to drop the loop over his head.

Would he be dragged, kicking and bawling, from the stage like a dogie to branding? Would he be trampled to death or viciously rent by the radical horde of baby-boomers? The dean was immeasurably relieved when, as he was saying, "higher principles," the big guy dropped both rope and bottle and tipped over backward, smiling beatifically.

He lay on his back in the grass beneath the stage and began to sing, with eyes closed and in no relation to any known key, *"Avanti popolo, a la riscossa, bandiera rossa, che vincera."*

WEDNESDAY

THE SUMMIT OF THE MEDICINE BOW is no summit. Where Mike crossed, it's a long level of snow-fat timber. He rode through a patch of bright yellow flowers. Brown-eyed Susans. Susan, his mother's name.

Potatoes swooped his neck down and ate some. He knew he wouldn't get hit in the mouth with the bit for it. "You're right, bud. Too late for discipline now."

After a long time in the smell of dry pine needles, the pitch began to slope off to the west. Some clouds lumbered in and looked like rain, and Mike prayed for it, but it never did. His tracks would stay his signature.

Down, down, sky flowing through the pine boughs overhead. He turned his horse northward and rode till he came to a ravine. He followed it down till it showed water. Thick willows and saber grass. He dismounted and kissed the surface of the inch-deep spring creek, drinking deeply but right off the surface, careful not to suck up any silt.

Then he sat in the grass and held his horse by the reins while the horse drank. The horse drank a long time. He lifted his head, chin dripping, to look around, bent back to the water, and blew into it from his nostrils. Then he went back to drinking.

They went on. At the top of a rise was a clearing, and Mike could see a far line of blue patched with white that wasn't sky. He decided to stop for the night at the next water he came to. The grade descended gradually. They kept going down. The sun went down too, but faster, before they reached the water, which was the confluence of two spring creeks full of beaver ponds and gallied willows.

He couldn't cross without foundering his horse, so he turned back, not retracing his trail but following the right-hand creek as low as he could. "I'm going to make that Indian follow me every inch."

Then it was too dark to ride anymore and he still hadn't found a crossing. He wished he'd retraced the other drainage. He gave up and lay down. He tied the horse's reins to his ankle and went to sleep.

When he woke the sun was hot and pine smell bit the air. He could hear the seethings of trucks on the highway four miles west. He opened a tin of ham and ate chunks off the end of his knife. There was no hurry. He didn't want to cross the highway in daylight. He'd have to cut the fence on both sides of the road. He saddled up and went north along the creek until he found a beaver dam big enough to cross on.

Potatoes slipped and struggled three times in the bitten sticks and black mud. When they were across, Mike stroked the horse's mane and said, "I wouldn't do that with just any horse."

They pushed north, contouring through the lodgepole stands and occasional clearings deep in rabbitbrush. They crossed a clear-cut. The peaks of the Continental Divide floated on their left. They crossed a granite-studded ridge. The lichen in the boulders was a blaring orange, and for the first time he could see the lush meadows of North Park below, like a blue-green dream of ocean or the cast-off dress of summer itself. With the Never-summer Mountains hovering beyond it, Mike thought it was the most beautiful place he had ever seen. He envied the men whose work it was to put up all that hay.

He waited for dark, then rode down an open sagebrush slope to the highway department fence. He looped the reins over a post and walked two posts away to cut the wire. The four strands were tied by vertical twists, so he started at the bottom, and when he cut the top wire the fence rolled open like a wave.

He led Potatoes through and tied him to the other side of the same post. He took a coil of smooth wire from his saddlebags and spliced the wires behind him. No one drove by. He led the horse across the asphalt, silent in its rubber boots. He went through the fence on the other side the same way. He couldn't make it look perfect, lacking a wire stretcher, but he did the best he could with what he had. Then he crossed a big irrigation ditch and entered the dark belly-deep grass, like a ship launching into a green whispering sea.

Riding through the deep grass in the dark, hearing the seed tops brush the horse's belly and flanks, wetting his own boot toes, Mike was happy.

He knew the furrow he made would show his passage as clear as an arrow, but he didn't much care. Riding was like swimming in this dark hayfield. Then he came to the river, the upper reach of the North Platte. He said, "Maybe they'll think we're an elk."

Potatoes drank, then stomped through the shallow water on a gravel bar. On the far side, the sea of hay resumed. He turned north and rode through it all night.

1970

AVERAGE HEIGHT BUT BUILT like a wrestler, thick in the neck and upper body, infinitely black eyes and hair, Jim Thomas was confident in his Apache good looks. Slowly, head down, studying the trail, he watched each combat boot swing forward to step— toe, then heel—trying to stay light and even.

He was in a dead man's trance of concentration, eyes scanning for the slightest irregularity in the chaos of dirt or leaves, a glint of catgut or piano wire. Irregularity came disguised as regularity—usually too much. He watched for forms, anything inorganic on the organic page of the jungle. He was reading.

"Just like hunting arrowheads when I was a kid in Arizona." A reptilian radar, peripherally tuned for the made in the context of the unmade, the tidy out of context. "Here the stakes are more interesting."

Of all the soldiers in the platoon, Jim spent the most time walking point. He liked it. He was good at it. He was still alive, and the others were perfectly OK with letting him take more than his share of the risk.

But today he walked second. Scarier than first, in a way, because he didn't trust anything about the first guy except his inattention and dumb luck. Just dumb-lucky enough to accidentally step over something that a second guy could trip.

So Jim kept concentrating just as hard, scanning with maximum intensity—a dreamlike adrenaline-borne attention to infinite jungle complexities and possibilities, when another one of those little fuckers just stood up from behind a bush in his Cong pj's and, apparently unarmed, smiled at them.

Every grunt in the platoon watched him as they moved past, like he was the Grand Canyon or something. No one freaked and fired. They'd all seen this trick before. They'd seen the cheery willingness of an individual gook to sacrifice his whole gook life just to get a dozen Americans to give away their position and, if not, shame them.

It amounted to a kind of counting coup. Maybe there weren't any NVA in the area. Maybe it was all a bluff and a boast. Whatever it was, was frustrating and unnerving as hell.

"Let's go to a faraway war with strict orders not to shoot the enemy," Jim seethed. He was dying to kill. Knock the bastard down. But he walked away with the rest, leaving the smiling enemy smiling.

That night he approached his CO. He requested permission

to carry a crossbow. "I'd get those little bastards to sit down again, sir. I'd flat-line every one. You'd never hear a thing."

"There are no government-issue crossbows, soldier. And, no, you can't have your mother send you one. We are the best-armed fighting force in the world. It wouldn't look good, chief. Request denied."

Jim Thomas was fourteen-sixteenths Mescalero Apache. The odd sixteenths were a Spanish conquistador and a Welsh rail-roader. Jim's Mescalero mother had always told him he was a great warrior in a long line of great warriors, the great red hope of future war culture.

Back in the States, after it was over, people who didn't know Jim were generally, to say the least, horrified to hear him talk about how much fun he'd had in Vietnam.

"Fun?"

"Sure, bro, you know: rape, pillage, and murder, in that order. The smell of hot blood. I'm an Apache, remember?"

In fact, Jim had returned from the jungle after all that terror and boredom on a very even keel. He was hired at a state university in northern California to run the veterans' Upward Bound program.

After two tours, Jim was helping to rehabilitate the more Judeo-Christian American soldiers who had been messed up— by fear, for instance, or for instance the guilt of having to blow away grenade-toting women and children pretending to beg for chocolate.

"It never bothered me," Jim remarked. "Someone with a hand grenade is not cute, not complicated. You just shoot them. It's your duty to life to go on living.

"I scrounged around for a while trying to find a crossbow. Charlie used them all the time, but I never found a captured one.

I started to make one out of an old M-1 stock and trigger mechanism, and a leaf spring out of an ancient Renault. Cable for the string. I fletched lengths of bamboo for bolts with feathers I found in the jungle.

"I was working on the sights one afternoon, sitting with my back against a cinder-block wall. The cinder block was cool through my drab T-shirt.

"With his mouth wide open to scream, but with no scream coming out, an underfed boy about ten ran across the street toward me, holding in his outstretched hand, like a snake he'd caught, a live unpinned U.S. Army–issue grenade.

"My forty-five was resting by my knee. When the slug hit him he flew backward a good six feet, skinny little kid getting hit by that caliber. He probably weighed about fifty pounds, but I didn't think he was so cute. I felt zero remorse. The remarkable thing about violence is how unremarkable it is. A mist of blood hovered over his child's body.

"The grenade never went off, little son of a bitch. I just kept working on my crossbow while some GIs cleaned him up and consoled his high-pitched mother. Bitch probably told him to do it. I'm a soldier, bro. I got a no-fault policy.

"I knew that to survive you had to be just as ruthless as the enemy, which, for me, culturally speaking, was easy.

"Not so easy for most American soldiers because of all the guilt trips they were raised with. That's why they whipped us. They were tougher. They weren't poisoned with sentiment.

"I was even more savage than the Cong were. I liked it.

"I never asked if I could carry the weapon I'd made. I kept it hid. The first time one of those guys stood up in his pajamas I sunk a bolt into his Adam's apple, right up to the feathers. He sat back down quick. But the lieutenant was pissed. I'd disobeyed him. He confiscated the bow. That's when I knew we'd lose the war. Not that I cared, not that it mattered who won the thing, but that's when I decided not to re-up for a third tour."

1978

SIX YEARS IN HUMBOLDT COUNTY, going to school, then working for the university, marrying his pregnant girlfriend, living on the Hoopa Reservation, freelancing in a ski mask with a sawed-off shotgun guarding other people's sinsemilla. Once his son was born, he left him and the girl and came to Laramie. He set up as a range detective. The sheriff's departments of two counties used him as a tracker.

A range detective is somewhere between a private investigator and a hired assassin. They work for ranches when large-scale rustling flares up, usually big ranches, ranches so big you could drive a semitrailer onto one and not be noticed.

A couple of cowboys on horses using portable corrals gather up a bunch of cows, load them into the semi, and drive away. County sheriffs are uselessly undermanned to deal with rustling, so when the problem becomes intolerable the rancher can hire a range detective, who camps out, stalks, and lays for the rustlers. Upon catching them in the act, he shoots them from long range with a high-velocity rifle and leaves them there, dead in the evidence.

It isn't legal but it's allowed.

Jim also worked for the county sheriff's department that had—another vestige of Old West necessity—a mounted posse.

They mostly found lost children in mountainous terrain, wayward hikers, and small plane crashes. Once every ten years or so, a real manhunt.

Mike saw Jim in the convenience store, nodded. Waved when they passed on the county road. Jim picked up loose ends for the department if he was handy. Like the time lightning struck one of Mike's haystacks.

Mike was on top of the flaming stack, tearing out bales and heaving them away from the flames when the local volunteer pump truck showed up and, right behind, Jim Thomas. Jim climbed onto the stack and fell to throwing bales beside Mike. They worked, sweating in the smoke, for two hours. The fire was out, half the hay saved.

Jim's hands were shredded from handling bales by the wires without gloves.

"You should have those looked at."

"Got any bag balm?"

"Sure. Come to the house."

So they began, a little, to recognize each other.

OCTOBER 1985

MIKE'S PHONE RANG at midnight. Jim Thomas.

"Where're you calling from?"

"The country club. I need a favor."

Mike knew Jim played golf but not, so far as he knew, at night.

"I need a lift. Drive your truck down the county road that borders the golf course on the north. Meet me at the eighteenth hole."

Mike pulled over and dowsed the lights. He got out and climbed over the cyclone fence and crossed through a scrim of aspen trees. He found Jim gutting out a mule deer right on the green, a pile of steaming innards four feet from the flag. Jim's compound bow and brace of arrows lay off to the side.

"Help me get him in the truck?" Jim said, smiling, his arms bloody to the elbows.

"Are you nuts? On the eighteenth hole?"

"Don't worry, bro. They won't catch me. And if they do, they won't do anything to me. I'm an Indian, remember?"

They loaded the carcass into Mike's pickup and drove to Jim's house. They skinned and butchered the deer in the garage. Then, in the living room with beers, Jim pulled out a redwood box and some cigarette papers. He said, "Humboldt County. Straight from the Hoopa Reservation."

JULY 1991

MIKE RAISED HIS HAND to knock on Jim's door. He heard strange noises from inside, so did not knock but leaned to listen. There was a periodic hissing thump, like someone hitting a rug with a broom, but slow, and what sounded like occult chanting. Mike listened closer, holding his breath.

Someone was reciting Dylan Thomas in a thick Welsh accent, and the thump fell at the end of every other line. Mike listened till he heard "Time held me green and dying though I sang in my chains like the sea." *Thunk.* Then he knocked.

"Open."

Mike opened the door and an aluminum hunting arrow

flashed across the room and slammed into the padded target in the corner. Mike peeked around the door and watched Jim nock another arrow to his compound bow, draw it, and let it go. *Thunk.* Silence and power, the target twenty-five feet away. *Thunk.*

"Target practice. Helps me unwind."

"Who was reciting poetry?"

"I was."

"In a Welsh accent?"

Jim recited the opening lines and slammed another arrow into the target.

"A Welsh Mescalero. Where'd you learn that?"

"College, man. Didn't teach me nothin' I could use except for this one professor who made us recite poetry by heart. We never talked about it, just listened to tapes of poetry, and poetry being read aloud, and poetry memorized and recited by the students. Only good class I had in college."

Mike looked around at the mostly bare living room and kitchen: folding table, folding chairs, TV, dishes in the sink, rifles in the corner, shoes and boots in a pile by the door, and, of course—*thunk*—an archery target.

There was a low bookshelf with paperbacks loosely stacked and, on the top shelf, an *Encyclopedia Americana*. There was a bullet hole in the cover of the first volume. "How'd ya do that?" Mike asked, pointing.

"What do you mean how did I do it? With a pistol."

Mike just stared at the bullet hole in the encyclopedia and waited. Jim hung his bow on the wall.

"See, after 'Nam I got the GI Bill. But I was afraid of college because I didn't know anything. So I bought the encyclopedia at a yard sale and gave myself a year to read it. Just stayed home, smoked pot, and read the encyclopedia."

Mike stared and waited.

"When I got done reading the son of a bitch I shot it. Partly just to see where the bullet ended up."

"Where did it end up?"

"M."

Mike reached toward the M volume. Jim covered Mike's hand with his own. "You always want to know where things end. Let's look at something the bullet went through."

He pulled out H and opened it seemingly at random. The bullet hole was in the middle margin right next to the heading Homestead Act. In his Welsh accent, Jim read aloud.

" 'The secession of the South enabled the Republicans to pass the Homestead Act in 1862. Under the act, a free quarter section (160 acres, or 65 hectares) of land in the West was offered to any citizen or intended citizen 21 years of age who would settle the land, beginning Jan. 1, 1863. The act did not limit the amount of land that could be sold to individuals, and an area eight times the size of Kansas was made available because of grants to railroads and states, the allotment of Indian land, and subsequent sales to settlers and others, and the continued sale of public land to speculators.

" 'Before they secured title, homesteaders were required to live on the land for five years, during which improvements were to be made and modest fees paid. If they wanted to gain mortgageable title on which to borrow for additional improvements, they could acquire their land by cash purchase after six months of residence. This clause was extensively abused in later years by speculators seeking to acquire great acreages through the use of dummy entrymen—' "

"No kidding," Mike interrupted. He had taken Jim's bow down from the wall. First he studied the little colored balls on the sights; then he drew it back, testing the weight of its pull.

Mildly annoyed, Jim read on. " 'Extensively advertised by the land-grant railroads, the states, and real estate groups, and by letters from earlier immigrants, the free homesteads drew immigrants to the West in great numbers. Land offices in the Great Plains and Pacific Coast states and later in the Interior Basin were besieged with heterogeneous crowds of people clamoring to file declaratory statements that would hold their claims against latecomers. Not again until the Social Security Act was adopted in 1935 did the government do so much to create hope for a better life for so many.' "

Mike thought about the Indians. He thought about abuse by speculators and dummy entrymen. It reminded him of Snipes. He thought about claims to hold land against latecomers. He thought about a better life for so many.

"The problem with you, man, is that you think things change," Jim said. "You think things disappear. Bro, the American cowboy has been disappearing since before there were cowboys."

FRIDAY

WHEN MIKE CAME TO A FENCE he turned one way or the other, it didn't matter, until he found a gate. If he turned one way one time, he turned the other way the next. He went through seven gates before the sky brightened to an eggshell hue.

He could see the cover of the timber brooding just ahead. The last gate had a sign nailed to it: THIS IS NOT YOUR ROAD. KEEP OUT. It was hand-painted badly in blood-red paint on a slab of plywood. He had to get into the timber, and trespassing wouldn't be the worst thing he'd done lately. He went through the gate and rode up into the trees. Pine branches fingered the rising sun.

He passed a washing machine tipped on its side next to a heap of sheet metal. He passed a pile of tin cans and glass bottles in a shallow hole. Plastic milk bottles, scraps of cardboard, sodden mercenary-soldier magazines were strewn about. He passed the front half of a pickup resting on its axle next to an ancient collapsed Ditch Witch abandoned in its own gravel trench. There was a shelter like a steel lunch box.

He was nearing the fence he knew was the National Forest boundary when a shot cracked the still morning air and Potatoes spooked. Mike twisted in his saddle to see a man in coveralls standing amid the garbage with a rifle pointed at the sky. He had long sandy hair, a dreadlocked beard, and grease stains down his front. He squinted into the world as if the sun was hurting him.

Mike said, "It's OK, I'm leaving. Didn't mean to bother you."

The man glared and said nothing. He leveled the rifle at Mike. Mike turned his back and rode to the fence. Going through the gate, he remembered to breathe. Once through he let out a low whistle and pushed into a trot. Thinking hard, he blew two bubbles in a row.

DECEMBER 1990

THE INSIDE OF the hunting shack was unfinished Sheetrock, three army-surplus cots, a card table with four folding aluminum

lawn chairs. There was a Coleman space heater next to the table.
There were two small windows out of which nothing could be
seen but white air and twisting snow, like being inside a hive of
white bees.

Wayne sat in one of the aluminum chairs, rolling a spliff. He
had long hair, dark, and dark eyes, almost Hollywood good
looks. Jordan lay propped on one elbow on one of the cots, as if
in imitation of a Syrian bas-relief, his short curly hair like a
young bull's. You could feel the rage coming off him like heat.

The two had met at the Juvenile Detention Center, both
busted for accumulations of drunk driving, possession with
intent, and a complete disregard for court appointments. In
detention they'd been amused to find that, though the boys had
never met on the outside, their fathers were friends.

Both were from "broken homes," though all the parents and
stepparents were assiduously decent and law-abiding. Jordan had
been adopted by his first set of parents. When his adoptive
mother remarried he was eleven.

Jordan's mother had married a rancher, and suddenly Jordan
was compelled to do chores, ride horses, work cows, fix trucks,
mend fence, and do all this 4H Ag stuff, which he made no secret
of hating. High school, while it lasted, had been a gold mine of
ways to express his rage and hatred of his adoptive stepfather.

Dave was not as good-looking as the other two boys. He was
short and puffy-faced. Peach fuzz grew under the flaps of the cap
he never took off. He was standing by one of the two windows,
watching it snow. His father was a real estate salesman, recently
fired from his company and drawing unemployment.

They were waiting for the latest round of pills to kick in.
They'd been cranked for three days.

Wayne licked the joint shut and said, "So I still don't understand how you got your old man to let us use his snowmobiles and his cabin. What, does he trust you now that you're out of the justice system?"

"Easy," Dave said. "The dumb fuck thinks snowmobiling is a healthy activity for troubled youth. He thinks solitude and wilderness are healthy."

"Far out."

Wayne studied the joint. "What does he think about meth, pot, beer, and guns?" A giggle escaped him like boiling mud.

"We haven't got any guns." They all laughed and looked at each other.

Wayne could feel the drugs start a new surge through him. It was like being afraid when there was nothing to be afraid of. He loved it. He said, "I can't sit around here anymore. I've got to *do* something."

"Oh, yeah? What have you got to do?"

"I've got to fuck something up. Something or someone or both. It doesn't matter. I've just got to fuck something up."

Jordan said, "I'm with you, man. Something or someone. Any ideas? The trouble is, up here there isn't any someone. And there isn't any something, either, unless you mean rocks and trees. It's no fun to fuck up rocks and trees. It's a blizzard."

Wayne said, "Yeah, Dave, maybe your old man is smarter than you think. Maybe we're pretty harmless up here. Three pussies."

Jordan said, "Let's burn this fucking shack down. Let's torch it."

Wayne said, "Too obvious. And too cold. Where would we spend the night? The old man took the truck, remember, shit-head?"

Dave stared out the window. "It's like being on an island."

By now they were all beginning to feel the pull and swell of the chemicals.

"Well, I've got to get out of here."

"I'm with you man. Let's shred some trails."

"Let's blow this reefer first," Wayne said, and lit it.

They stepped out of the shack into a dizzy wildness of weather that seemed part of their own wildness. "Far out," they said. "Far out." "Far out."

Wayne felt the harried snow stinging his cheeks. He liked it. It was like needles going all the way through him. He felt invincible. He laughed maniacally for no reason, zipped up his black snowmobile suit, and said, "Who's got the beer?"

Dave said, "I've got the beer, fuckhead, be nice." He giggled.

Wayne straddled one snowmobile and the other two rode double on the second. Wayne pushed the starter and smiled when he felt the machine come alive. This was no lady's snowmobile. This one had power. Yesterday he'd had it doing eighty on the county road. It was like the horsepower of the machine was coming out of his own body, or like, riding it, he had no body, just machine. He could control it with his will. He didn't have to *do* anything, just will the power and it was there.

The pot had taken the edge off the pills and the snow seemed profoundly soft, silent, willing. He twisted the throttle, sending a two-stroke scream into the timber. He felt the joyful surge of velocity.

Snow sprayed up behind him and he thought he knew what God was.

It wasn't love. That's just what they told you. It was him. And if it was him it was hate. It was snow and horsepower and control and wildness and the search for violence. He heard the shriek of the other machine behind him and thought, I'll take those fuckers for a ride.

More throttle. He leaned his body and the machine swirled a glorious rooster tailed sweep around the shack. When he came full circle he tottered upright, straightened out, and accelerated more down the two-track road deep in snow, pine trees beginning to blur in his peripheral vision. He whooped a war cry, a cry of joy and defiance, like a howl he thought God would understand, a violent prayer.

Behind him, Jordan returned his cry. They made gentle esses in the road and felt the machines undulate beneath them, cresting drifts, becoming one with contours, like speedboats through swells.

Wayne gave it more throttle. There was a hard turn coming up in the road but he didn't ease off, just leaned way into it, willing himself through it, spraying up a curved wall of powder. When he made it through the turn he whooped again. His buddies both returned the call and drove hard through the turn, and the meth plunged through their veins. They could feel everything there was to feel all at once, and it felt good.

They flew for several miles in satanic joy, free of all they hated and possessed by all they loved. Wayne stayed in the lead. He still knew where they were, but then the road ahead, recumbent in snow, began to look unfamiliar. His mind, his confidence, began to lose its grip and he wasn't sure anymore. He decided he didn't care and his confidence rushed back. He didn't want to know. His allegiance was to not knowing. He could handle it. He accelerated into it with all his heart, all his hate.

They were howling along the top of a ridge when Wayne saw a NO TRESPASSING sign nailed to a dead tree. It was like an invitation. There was a narrow logging trail that turned steeply down through the woods.

He looked over his shoulder at the clenched grins of his

friends, speeding to catch up. He whistled and pointed at the sign and curved cleanly onto the steeply pitched trail. Jordan and Dave barely made the turn and laughed when they righted without dumping their snow machine.

Going down the hill felt like floating, and they cut back on their throttles to accommodate the sweet gravity. After a quarter mile they sailed into a flat clearing and slid to a halt, idling.

There was a log cabin. Wayne knew where they were. He revved his beast and combed out another hard spool of circles. Barely taking notice of the house, his compatriots followed.

They crossed a small draw and rose up the side of a mesa where they were in full view of the plains. Another quarter mile and they came to another log house, this one much bigger and new.

Wayne cut his engine. Dave said, "What are we doing now?"
Wayne said, "Picnic."

Dave killed his motor too, and down off the ridge, out of the wind, the silence rushed in so hard it was like an explosion.

Jordan recognized the house. It belonged to a friend of his father's. He'd been to supper there a few times. He remembered Dr. Trent. He had liked him. He remembered the way Dr. Trent had of talking straight across to a kid, no condescension, no secret parental motive.

Dave said, "Where the fuck are we?"
Jordan shook out a cigarette. "Doc Trent's."

"I've heard of him. My dad and Mr. Snipes were talking about him. Said he was an asshole."

Jordan looked at Wayne, and a wave of amphetamine chill keened through him. He realized his teeth were clenched from riding the snowmobile. He still felt the vibration in his body and he felt like he'd been chewing steel springs. He lit his cigarette and said, "Yeah. Asshole."

Wayne lit a smoke too and asked where the beer was. They sat on the snow machines in front of the house and drank beer and smoked cigarettes. They laughed crazy, giddy laughs at stupid, druggy jokes, and the cold started sinking into the high like dampblack in a mine shaft.

Dave said, "I wonder if there's any whiskey in there."

Wayne said, "Or guns."

Jordan said, "I'm getting cold. Let's book."

Dave swung a leg off the snowmobile and said, "Just one second." He walked up to the window by the front door. Wayne followed. Jordan sat on his machine.

Dave took out a pocketknife and tried to pry the window open. Suddenly Wayne jabbed the window with his gloved hand and shattered the glass. Wayne looked back at Jordan. The sound of glass breaking speared through them like blue electric light. They burst into hysterical giggles. Then they stopped laughing and stared at each other again, childishly.

Jordan said, "What are you doing, you fucks?"

"Don't worry, asshole. There's nobody in miles to catch us."

Wayne reached through the window, unlatched the sash, raised the empty window, and jumped through like a fish. The front door opened and Wayne came out. He called to Jordan, "Come on, faggot, it's show time."

Dave went in and came out grinning with a half bottle of rum he held up for Jordan to see.

They all went inside. They passed the bottle around. The alcohol seared going down. Wayne took a swig and passed the bottle back to Dave. Then he whooped, picked up a chair, and heaved it through a closed window. The sound of the glass

shattering went through them like ice cubes tumbling through
their guts.

It was great. Dave picked up a bronze statuette of a rearing
winged horse, and heaved it through another window. All three
raised the war cry and passed around the bottle.

Wayne walked into the kitchen and came back with a bag of
flour and a bottle of molasses. He ripped open the bag and scattered flour on the sofa, then dribbled molasses all over it. From
the hoots and giggles of the others he knew it was the funniest
thing he'd ever done.

Dave picked up a fire extinguisher from behind the cast-iron
wood heater and sprayed the room. Now *that* was the funniest
thing.

Wayne picked up a footstool and took out another window.
The sound of glass breaking through the meth was the best feeling of his life. Dave took out his pocketknife and slashed the
sofa. He made a rip in the canvas of a painting on the wall. It was
a painting of two deer in a snowy meadow, one just raising its
head and looking in the direction of the viewer.

Jordan drank the last slurp of rum and threw the bottle
through a window. They were all teary with laughter.

Wayne went out to the back porch and came back with a
double-bitted splitting axe. He swung the axe over his head and
down into the mahogany dining room table, splintering it. He
kept swinging it.

Not to be outdone, Jordan took an alpinist's ice axe down off
the wall. With the deliberation of a botanist, he walked to a
framed photograph. A woman and a little blond girl smiled out
of the picture. They were making bread together, kneading big
loaves, smiling. With the ice axe Jordan carefully broke the glass,
making a single pick hole in the child's face.

Again, the sound of glass breaking was electric heaven. He proceeded methodically around the room, delicately punching out the glass of every framed photo, of which there were many.

Meanwhile, Wayne was in the bedroom with the axe, splintering the bed frame and slashing the mattress. He came out with a double handful of mattress ticking and threw it in Dave's face. Dave turned over the glass coffee table. Pure shattered joy.

He toppled a tall bookshelf. He went to the kitchen and got more molasses and a bottle of maple syrup, with which he anointed the books. He pulled down the oak and glass dish cabinet, which crashed magnificently before Wayne went at it with the axe.

Dave used the pick end of the ice axe to rend the black-on-black Amish quilt that hung on the wall. Then he used it to punch holes in the stovepipes in the kitchen and living room.

Everything that would splinter, Wayne splintered with the axe. Everything that would break, they broke. Everything they could pick up, they threw out the broken windows into the snow. They broke every window and the snow started to blow inside.

Dave and Jordan went out to the garage and popped the lock off with a steel bar they'd found on the back porch. Inside the shed they found a pair of bolt cutters with which they set about cutting all the wires, belts, gas, and hydraulic lines on the old tractor. Then they took a sledgehammer to the headlights and windshield of an old pickup.

They knew Wayne had found a twenty-two rifle in the closet when they heard him empty fifteen rounds into the ceiling, all the while screaming with joy.

They were still high as thunderheads when they looked around for more to wreck and couldn't find a thing.

They started the snow machines and rode back through the blizzard like gods.

1990

OSCAR RIDING BEHIND his three bulls. After sky the thing we have most of here is grass, he thought. Sweet flag, cattail, timothy—it pulls the horizon away with it—bottlebrush, tickle grass, panic grass. Oceans of it, waves of wind spelling themselves out onto the prairie.

To be grazed or burned. Grass has two fates, both of which it survives.

He thought about the Wyoming grass dinosaurs ate, in a Wyoming we wouldn't recognize. How after the last ice age, woolly mammoths turned these prairies into themselves. Then the bison; now a commensurate number of cattle, sharing grasses with elk, deer, antelope, rabbits, chipmunks, blind moles, and sundry insects, transforming the blades into flesh, grooming it green.

For ten thousand years, people torched vast prairies to attract the herds when the grass came back anew.

If there's nothing to eat it and no Indians around to burn the big beige lawn, lightning is waiting in the wings.

Before the Europeans, perhaps before the indigenous peoples, between grass fires and forest fires burning themselves out, especially in drought years, the sky was gone, the air tawny and bitter, and the flaming prairie came over the horizon more terrifying than sky had ever been.

There are oceans of grasses at the bottoms of oceans and on the bottoms of oceans that are gone.

Grass is a long time and a big space. Your own life in it? A match going out.

Also, Oscar didn't think you could name the flowers. And why do you want to refer to them? What are they to us? All pleasures. All bruise colors on the side hill. The pastures and meadows throb with successions of flowers. The woods pant with flowers. Lucent in their occupations, refulgent in their sleep. Whether crimson or claret, cerulean or sapphire, we are nothing to them, not even danger.

So why do we want to give them to our sweethearts?

ONCE

FIXING FENCE BEGINS as soon as the snowdrifts let go. When Oscar was a kid his dad ran a ninety-thousand-acre cattle operation. Oscar and his father and his sisters had close to two hundred miles of fence to fix before the herds could be driven to summer pastures.

Someone had to build all that fence in order for it to break and get fixed. That would have been the summer project of a crew who dug postholes by hand and set pitch or Texas cedar posts and tamped them with a spud bar and strung wire, from first light to last, for three months. In good ground, setting a post takes less than half an hour. Up around where Ad lived it could take half a day. One post.

Out on the prairie the fence didn't need much attention, but on some of the higher timbered permits elk tore the fence to shreds on a regular basis in their migrations, and there were always those spots in the lees of ravines that drifted deep and chopped the wire into useless scraps and pushed posts over or snapped them under the cetacean weight of snow. Steel posts were even worse, bending to 90 degrees and snapping off at the ground if you tried to straighten them.

Two hundred miles of fence. On the upper permits, fixing a mile of fence took half a day. They drove along what was in the open, but in heavy timber or through the canyons, Frank turned a kid loose with a handful of smooth wire, a pocketful of staples, and a pair of fencing pliers. He'd pick them up on the other side of whatever topography it was, and if new posts were needed, he carried them in, however far, with spud bar and shovel, and set them himself. How good a fence post is is all in how you tamp it.

A month of fixing fence and it was time to drive the different herds to their summer homes, sometimes camping out a night or two on the way.

WEDNESDAY

JIM TIGHTENED THE CINCH and swung up onto his chestnut mare. The sheriff handed him a two-way radio.

"What do you want me to do with this, call him up and tell him to come back?"

"I need to know where you are in case you need backup. I want you to call in every two hours or if you spot him."

Jim swung his horse's head toward the timber where the bow

hunter had seen Mike. As soon as he was inside the treeline out of sight, he tossed the radio into a juniper bush.

He picked up the almost imaginary track and followed it. Where it disappeared he looked for broken branches, matted grass, anything. Where it crossed rocks he followed his intuition. He went where he'd go if it were him. When he lost the trail for more than a short while, he spiraled out until he picked it up again. He could see disturbances on the ground anyone else would miss. It was a slow, painstaking process, but his patience was limitless, which meant, in a way, he'd already caught his fugitive.

After two hours of tracking, finding, losing, finding, now and then a clear print, as in the mud of a creek bank, he had enough of a sense of direction to go by. He returned to his trailer. When he emerged from the timber, the second horse, tethered to the side of the trailer, nickered.

Highway 14 and Highway 127 make a half circle around what he now knew was the search area. Unless Mike doubled back and headed east, toward home, he'd have to cross one of those highways. Probably somewhere in North Park.

August 1965

THOSE TWO KIDS were mostly hats as they rode through the ranch gate and down the red road before dawn. It wasn't till years later they figured out that when Frank sent them to rope and doctor calves with hoof rot, he was just trying to get rid of them. But what could be better for a couple of incipient cowpokes than to spend a fine summer's day riding and roping in the high pastures?

The dark shapes of the sand rocks were like boats at anchor. They threaded their horses through them. Oscar said, "Sorry you had to wait for me to milk that blamed cow."

Ernie said, "We ain't burned no daylight yet."

They plashed across Sand Creek and loped up the far bank. They talked as they rode, about horses and rodeo and cows and basketball and their respective parents. Ernie was two years older than Oscar, a dark good-looking kid, hired on at fourteen as a rock-bottom-wage ranch hand who wanted to be a real cowboy someday.

Oscar hadn't, but had sometimes wanted to ask his older friend about sex. Not how you do it—every ranch kid knows that—but more, how do you work things around so that you can get it done? Finally, riding through the sharp-smelling sage, he mustered the gumption to ask, but it turned out that Ernie didn't know either, though he allowed as how he'd about considered it to death.

They rode up the watershed between two creeks. Oscar was playing with his lariat—swinging it over his head like idle thoughts since there wasn't a cow in sight, roping yucca and larkspur, roping his horse's front feet and letting him step out of the loop like the dead-broke cow horse he was.

By midmorning it was scorching. "Hotter than young love," as Frank used to say, and they still hadn't seen a cow. The Camel Rock Ranch was big enough to support several thousand cow-calf pairs, which meant it was also big enough to ride over all day and not see any of them, just because you didn't happen to ride in the right place.

At noon they saw some cows on the far side of Sand Creek, which, that far up, spooled at the bottom of a huge canyon. The cows weren't far off in a straight line, but the two boys had to ride for an hour to negotiate the downside of the canyon and find a place to cross that was anything less than breakneck. Then they rode another half hour, picking their way up the steep far side. Both kept their toes barely in the stirrups in case a horse should fall in the scree. It was like swimming a horse through loose gravel.

When they came up on the other side, the cows were gone. By picking up tracks they found them—twenty pair or so—all pretty healthy looking. Ernie said, rubbing his neck, "I don't know but what that little brockle-face isn't looking somewhat peaked." Oscar was building a heel loop before Ernie finished his sentence.

They cut out the calf and started following it, first at a trot, Ernie off to the left, Oscar back a length and to the right. When he had his loop ready, Ernie spurred his horse into a gallop. The calf zigzagged, but the good horse bore down on him like a heat-seeking missile. Ernie swung his rope and laid down a perfect throw. He took his time making a dally, keeping his horse running along behind the calf.

When Ernie dallied and turned his horse, the calf swung around like a rowboat into a river on a long painter. Oscar's horse quartered across and made the corner behind the calf. He threw his loop downward so that it folded over the calf's loins.

The calf made the rest happen, made the loop stand, stepped into it with both hind legs. Standing in his stirrups, Oscar took up slack like a fly fisherman setting the hook. He stopped his horse and dallied, lifting the calf into the air, stretched between the two horses. Ernie said, under his breath, "Too bad the kid can't rope."

There was nothing really wrong with the calf, but they shoved some sulfa pills down his throat anyway, unwilling to admit that they were just having fun.

They turned the bawling brockle-face calf loose, running for its mother. They tied their horses to a wizened cedar tree that sang a dry song in the wind. They sat in its shade. Neither kid had brought any lunch, or even any water. As for food, they could tough it out. As for water, two kids who knew the country as well as these should be able to find some. But for a long while they just sat in the shade and listened to the light summer breeze in the cedar needles.

Ernie said, "You need to tighten the curb chain on your bridle."

Oscar said, "Ernie, what in the hell are you going to do?"

"I don't know. Look for work. A ranch to work on. Maybe I'll be the foreman on a big ol' ranch like your dad is."

"There ain't no big old ranches anymore. Rich people just buy them to hide their money in. That's what Dad says. And the job you're wanting is already taken."

"Maybe I'll do something else."

"What?"

"Something."

They mounted up and rode back across the canyon and up toward the timber. "You thirsty?"

"You?"

"The spring at the Running Water is dried up along with nearly every other spring this year."

"I didn't notice you getting a drink when we crossed the crick and watered the horses."

"I ain't desperate enough yet to drink out of a lukewarm crick that's had cows in it."

"Where's the nearest spring?"

"Trent's spring is the best. We could ride up there. I bet they'd give us a drink."

"Right now I could drink a couple of gallons of that spring water."

"I guess the reason you don't shut up about it is you're afraid your mouth will stick closed."

"Damned if I ain't."

They touched their horses up into a smart walk and turned their heads toward Trent's.

That was another three scorched-out miles and they were sure thirsty by then, as much from dwelling on it as anything else. They thought they'd never been so thirsty nor would be again. They felt like they were dust all the way through.

When they rode up through the leopard-spotted aspen shade to the old homestead cabin, they could see no vehicle of any kind and thought no one was home. Suddenly Ernie's eyes flared like a scared colt's. Oscar looked too. It was Old Man Trent's daughter, Ad's sister, a girl just a year or two older than Ernie. She was on the front porch sunbathing in a minuscule bikini.

Ernie whoaed up, said "Jesus," then moved his rein hand and walked forward.

Kathy had seen them coming, had heard talking as they crossed the draw, but she didn't look up from her book until they were sitting their horses by the front gate. She was a striking red-head with green Irish eyes and the cheekbones to match. Her waist-length red hair was piled on top of her head. Her skin was like white chocolate.

Oscar and Ernie held their dusty hats by the crowns, not meaning to, over their hearts. She eyed them over the top of her novel. "Hi, Ernie. Hi, Oscar."

Ernie made a froggish noise in his throat and then managed, "Howdy."

Oscar was pretty much lacking oxygen and a funny feeling was ranging from his burning ears, which had suddenly started ringing, to his toes, which at that moment were strangely beyond consideration. Oscar opened his mouth but nothing came out so he closed it again.

Ernie tried another, more confident "Howdy."

"What are you boys doing up here? Didn't you run into Daddy and Ad? They went to town with Mom. I'm here alone. Reading. Do you boys read?"

Ernie said, "Cows. Looking for cows."

"Can't you find any?"

"Very damned few."

"You boys look thirsty to the bone. Can I get you some water?"

Oscar was staring slack-jawed at the girl's breasts. Her nipples were pushing hard against her halter top. She had to bend forward to get out of the lounge chair. It was unsurvivable. He watched her tiny waist, how it swept out into ample hips. He watched her as she turned and entered the house.

Ernie said, "You could stop talking now, Oscar."

Oscar clopped his mouth shut.

When Kathy came out onto the porch again they were both scrunching their faces oddly, attempting to memorize her ass and her sublimely round breasts, barely cupped in the halter top. Then they fixed their gazes on the ground.

Kathy had a Dixie cup in each hand, about the size of a shot glass. She stretched catlike as she handed them up. God, they were thirsty. They tossed back the thimble-sized servings and handed back the green paper cups.

"Want some more?"

"No, thanks. That was sure good. I guess we'd better be getting along."

Speechless, thirstier than ever, they jigged over the hill at a trot.

FRIDAY

SO AS NOT TO ENCOUNTER any more forty-acre militia heads, Mike stayed inside the National Forest border. He wasn't worried about hikers, they herd up in parks and wilderness areas. And it wasn't hunting season. Yet.

A yellow plume of pine pollen off the lodgepoles lifted on a breath of wind, and Mike sneezed. Potatoes stepped daintily through the sparse timothy and sedge.

The green serenity of North Park fell away behind him, as did the Snowy Range and the dreaming Neversummers. The terrain began to drift into high desert: cactus, sandstone, heavy scrub, sand lilies, and stands of dwarf cedars. The land tilted toward the salt-white Sierra Madres, which bobbed in and out of sight behind the low hills and conifers. He came to a government fence and went through the gate. He was in Wyoming now.

The pasture was planted in western wheatgrass, and where a spring gave rise to a flare of willows on the sidehill, he saw a small herd of brood mares and foals grazing the tall brome. He said, "Well, well."

He didn't know how big the pasture was, at least a square mile, probably more in this country. He dismounted and pulled a big screwdriver out of his ruck and used it to pop the rubber boots off his horse's feet. The mares paid him no mind. He was surrounded by shoeless hoofprints, old and new.

He rode into the midst of the horse nursery. The mares kept grazing while their foals peeked at Mike from behind their mothers' flanks and shoulders. They were torn between timidity and curiosity.

One stepped up on stiltlike legs, frizzy tail, goofy forelock, and sniffed, then nibbled the stirrup.

"Hey, little guy, you're pretty bold. I bet you got some kind of future ahead of you." He reached down to touch the colt, but the colt retreated behind his mother and craned his neck around to gawk at the stranger. "Haven't been handled much, I guess." A second foal stepped up for a sniff and likewise retreated.

A huge, nameless sadness fell inexplicably over Mike, a sadness equal in depth to the sense of well-being he'd felt since lighting out. He didn't know what brought it on. He sat on his horse, surrounded by mares and foals, and he sobbed. Then, like clouds giving back the sun, the feeling passed.

"How do you explain that, bud?"

ONCE

ONE HUNDRED YEARS AGO when Bill Lund built the Sabot Ranch it was perfect. Now, though the ranch had not changed—indeed, had improved as far as irrigation, hay production, and the species diversity that attends riparian wetlands—it was subperfect.

One hundred years ago five sections and a two-hundred-ton hay crop could feed enough cows to support a family in style, leaving enough time over for rodeo games and plenty of visiting. Bill Lund spent all the time he wanted managing cattle horseback. They calved in May or June. Two hundred tons of hay to mow, rake, and stack with a team of horses didn't seem like much out of your year. Today, that same land would support the same number of animals, and, given capital investment, taxes, production costs, and beef prices, wouldn't support an ant. In fact the ant would be in debt. Then he'd be evicted.

Bill Lund remains to this day a mystery. He'd learned how to handle a broadaxe, how to build with logs, from his Norwegian ancestors. The whole ranch—two-story house, two big barns, sheds, some five or six bunkhouses and outbuildings, even the schoolhouse—was all built by one man in his spare time from ranching.

His axe strokes are like a signature you can still read today—flat-hewn logs that had been cut, skidded, and hauled from lodgepole stands ten miles away—all with dovetail corners so perfect they'd put you in mind of factory-made drawers.

Not that that kind of logwork was unheard of, just that there was so much of it. To have butchered that much wood and also built fences, put up hay, and taken care of cows in all weathers through all the years. . . . It doesn't add up.

No way one mortal could have built that much, even if he *was* an all-night workaholic, which apparently he was. Unless, as Lyle conjectured, he knew something about hewing we no longer know.

For instance, did he hew logs green and have some method to keep them from twisting as they cured? Did he have some way of choosing logs that wouldn't twist when hewed green? Was he an alien?

The Sabot is a local Machu Picchu. However he did it—and it's there to prove he did—he built that ranch and lived there till he died. The hay meadow wired with ditches, sandstone rock sculptures laced about, the Medicine Bow with its snowy crest just outside the window. I don't know how Lund died, but he did.

Oscar Fields, after whom Oscar Rose was named, sold his ranch near Cody and bought the Sabot. He trailed his cows and all his horses the distance to Laramie. He and his son worked the place through the sixties. Then they had to start looking for summer pasture to rent, more cows to put on it, and started having to buy hay to make things work. They could feel the spin and pull of going down the drain.

They started running dudes. Now a lot of ranchers run dudes, but they call them *guests*. Oscar Fields retired as soon as he could, which meant he just went back to cows, but he had Social Security and his army pension—he'd been in the artillery in the First War and he was deaf as a snowdrift. You could tell when you were really boring him when he reached up to his hearing aid and turned you off. Oscar had hated running humans, but they did support the cows.

Oscar Rose grew up around Oscar Fields, since Oscar Rose's father was foreman of the Camel Rock Ranch next door. Young Oscar went to school in the schoolhouse Lund built. He saw Oscar Fields as just what he was, a real old-time cowboy, and he learned.

Not that young Oscar didn't learn from his father, but Frank did a lot of ranching with a pickup and old Oscar did everything with horses. Young Oscar watched old Oscar rope a steer when old Oscar was ninety. He was always well-mounted. As for heavy ranch lifting, he always had a horseback solution.

Oscar's wife, who was barely tolerable as a human being, was having Lyle Van Waning put a new sink in her kitchen. She told Oscar to go out to the barn where the sink was waiting and bring it to the house. She knew about sinks but she had never lifted a cast-iron one before.

Oscar didn't say anything. He went out to the barn and

saddled up his rope horse. He dropped a loop over the sink and dragged it behind his horse across the barnyard to the front door, scratching it all to hell and making him irrevocably unpopular in the kitchen for days.

Oscar died and his wife stayed on at the ranch. Frank died and the family scattered. But since Frank died from asbestos he'd been exposed to in the navy, the government awarded him half a million dollars. It tickled Frank to be half a millionaire before he checked out.

The Roses were set to buy the Sabot when old Oscar's wife was done with it. Young Oscar's veterinary practice could take up the slack left by the dudes. They had leases on several nearby forest permits and school sections. They were going to have a ranch of their own.

Being a full-time rancher and a full-time large-animal vet suited Oscar just fine. Until the time came to buy the ranch, they leased the pasture and hayfield, did all the fencing and irrigating, rebuilt pens and corrals that had fallen apart. They put up the hay. They used the old Lund barns for calving.

It was a done deal. Oscar had married and was starting a family of his own. They had a future they could imagine.

They didn't know that a certain Snipes individual had contacted old Oscar's widow and offered her twice what the Roses could pay, figuring he would still come out way ahead by selling the place off as forty-acre ranchette developments. The old lady took him up on it and, out of sheer meanness, kept mum. That was the real done deal.

To see Oscar at work in the hayfield was almost funny unless you were one of several unfortunates who were trying to keep up with him. He worked like he was behind even if he was ahead and the weather fine. He did have a beeper that occasionally sent him ripping off to stitch up some four-legged emergency, but the pace was the pace he liked.

He had a big flatbed trailer hitched to his three-quarter-ton pickup. He'd drive out into the bales, put the truck in compound low, set it on a course, and leap soulfully from the flopping door, and, hayhooks flashing, sprint to retrieve the seventy-pound bales, sometimes two at a time, run dragging his burden, and throw the bales onto the flatbed. Then he'd jump into the cab and adjust the course of the driverless rig, leap out, and run for more bales. He could do that for sixteen hours.

His friend Ad, the alpine athlete, was beginning to regret agreeing to help in the field in exchange for some horse hay. He was a doctor. He could buy horse hay. He thought on some level it was silly for someone with his training—and, well, income—to be running around a meadow as if pursued by lurid angels. That's not how Lyle had done it. Yet something made him try to keep up with Oscar's pace. The doc was in good shape for a doc, but he was beginning to realize that two or three days of this were going to be his limit.

AUGUST 1990

THEY WERE UP ON THE STACK. They were stacking. Mike had showed up and was throwing bales up to them from the flatbed.

Corners tied, cracks covered, the last stack was up. They'd been loading and stacking since noon and it was getting dark. Oscar said, "I noticed you holding yourself kinda longways and crooked as if there was something wrong with your back."

Ad said, "I'm just trying to gain your sympathy so you'll slow down. Your mom told me you don't realize how old you are. I told her you don't realize how old *I* am."

"Listen, Doc, you don't need to come down here and tear yourself up. I'd give you all the horse hay you want. You know that."

"Sure. It's just that I got used to haying somehow, all those summers with Lyle. Now if I miss haying time I feel like I've missed something."

"I know what you mean but I wouldn't admit it to anybody. So what's wrong with your back?"

"Oh, it isn't just my back, Oscar." They sat on top of the huge haystack. Ad touched the shiny points of his hay hooks together like prosthetic hands. He looked sidelong at his friend. "You know, Oscar, I melted my brain with too much education and alcohol. I wrecked my shoulders, elbows, and knees with thirty years of rock climbing. I ruined my back working construction to get through school. My stomach is bad. My ears ring. About the only thing that still works on me is my dick."

Oscar turned his head and stared a long moment at the snowy peaks in the alpenglow, then turned back to Ad. "It's sure gonna be a sad day when your dick gives out."

FRIDAY

HIS BAREFOOT HORSE now blending tracks with the mares, he circled behind them at a walk and said, "Let's take the kids for a stroll, ladies." He wondered if Thomas could read the rider's extra weight in the prints. He guessed maybe.

Driving the bunch before him, he rode down through spotty grass and sandy soil. The pasture was bigger than he'd hoped. More like five sections than one. The wheatgrass patch had been somebody's experiment. There were still fence posts around it but the wire had been rolled up.

He drove the mares and foals back over their tracks. For once the lack of rain was in his favor.

He drove them along the fence, looking for a good place to get out, headed east. He passed two rocky spots where the fence had been patched, where he could take it apart and put it back without much trace. He came to a third possible exit, turned the herd around, and rode back to the second one.

Pulling up, he let the mares trail off. He opened the fence and led Potatoes through. The ground was a tongue of sandstone. He fixed the fence and replaced the rubber boots. Sticking to rocky ground, he curved back to the north.

JANUARY 1990

FORMER RESIDENCE OF FRONTIER swashbuckler Butch Cassidy, the territorial prison is a theme park. Pony rides, shoot-outs, women in bustles tatting, a man with a handlebar mustache braiding rope, tying some with hangman's knots (he'll let you make your own length of rope), and, of course, the cells.

After Wyoming became a state and the prison moved away, the university used the grand old stonework blockade for a dairy barn. The jail cells were stalls. Then the town restored it to a replica of its former self to attract tourists off the interstate. It wasn't working.

Fair enough, thought Marty. Same thing we do with nature, make a museum of it, a replica of itself. The National Theme Parks System.

The territorial prison dining hall seemed an interesting place for a lecture. Marty was about to speak to a group of local ranchers and environmentalists. The title of the lecture was "Losing It All." The talk would be followed by an open discussion, during which Marty hoped no one, especially himself, would get shot.

Outside it was snowing hard. The blind night was rasping flakes like wood shavings.

Across from each cell, hung on the wall, was a portrait of a prisoner and a written history of his crimes and punishments.

Marty studied the blown-up mug shots as the crowd gathered in the dining hall. Some stopped and closed themselves quite briefly in a cell and laughed and said, "Sure is small."

With his silly cowlick and vacant gaze, Butch Cassidy seemed less interesting than many of the others. For instance the portrait next to that of Butch. A nineteen-year-old boy, infantile blue eyes, gibbous head, stared as if he didn't know what a camera was, or jail. His gaze zoomed as though, in his confusion, he saw right through the camera, the cells, the prison walls, out into the territorial emptiness, more disconcerting than cameras or jails.

Mostly Marty was getting a sense of deprivation and the innocent acceptance of a brutal fate. The boy, his history said, spent three years in prison for stealing a sheep.

Most of the other prisoners had similar fates, similar faces, similar auras. They looked uncomfortable in clothes. They looked innocent, beaten down, confused.

Marty joined the crowd in the dining hall. He was introduced by a professor from the Environmental Sciences Department. He rose to the podium, took a long drink from the glass of water, eyed the crowd.

The front row looked like a comic cowboy tableau of the Last Supper, though some of the disciples were cast in shadow. Front and center was a blond ranchwoman, maybe forty, colored ribbons braided into her hair and a long skirt. She wore a flat-brimmed cowboy hat, a no-nonsense expression.

Sitting on her right was an Indian in a baseball cap. He looked fierce and unlikely to contribute to the discussion afterward. To her left was an enormous long-haired cowboy in a hot pink shirt and black silk neckerchief, ultra-fancy high-topped boots with the pants legs tucked inside. He was wearing a black hat that looked as if it had been torn from the teeth of a Disposall. He looked vaguely Indian too, with a hawk nose and dark eyes. Or he could have been Jewish, but who ever heard of a Jewish cowboy? He chewed bubble gum and blew bubbles at even intervals.

On the big guy's left was a knotted little guy with laser-blue eyes. He was older, maybe eighty. He looked as though he had broken every bone in his body at one time or another. He had plain boots and tiny feet. His white Stetson hung on his knee.

Sitting next to the old cowboy was a blond clean-cut guy who looked a little too refined for Laramie, like a doctor or something. Next to him was a cowboy with a square jaw and squinted eyes. He wore glasses. The set of his mouth was hard. He looked ready to laugh or ready to fight, whichever was called for first. He looked tough but not mean, shoulders tight. Enough years and he'd be the old guy all over again.

The other disciples of the front row were hard to make out, but Marty could recognize the wire-rimmed glasses, ponytails, beards, and pithy T-shirts of the environmentalists in the second and third rows.

Back in the corner of the hall was a middle-aged white-haired man with a massive jaw and close-set eyes. He wore a pale blue polyester leisure suit. Marty thought, Who's he?

He began his talk.

"From nature's point of view, if nature had a point of view (maybe nature is nothing but points of view?), the opposable thumb wired to a clever and curious neural center has got to be the most catastrophic development in the history of evolution. For at least ten thousand years, human presence on earth has been characterized in great measure by heedless rapacity and destruction, except when the human presence is of insufficient density to matter.

"It is difficult to think of human activities that have not proved destructive to the earth whose earth we are, other than art, maybe, which we do for ourselves or our gods.

"Can the opposable thumb and the mind in opposition be used to enable, enhance, revere life on earth, rather than to grasp, control, destroy?

"There are examples of beneficial human stewardship of land. You all know your local history. Old-timers like App Worster started irrigating around here a hundred years ago. Some had the whole Laramie River to work with. Others, like App, worked the higher drainages. They took natural wetlands and creek valleys and made them wetter and greener.

"They slipped out ditches behind horses, built wooden flumes to lift water out of the creeks and spread it over drier ground. They managed to enhance what they had. Inadvertently—I stress *inadvertently*—they increased the diversity and health of the flora and fauna. Most of the water that grew the tall grasses ended up back in the creek and was used by ranchers farther downstream.

"They cut the hay to feed their livestock in winter. Once the hay was cut they put cows on the meadows to eat the short grass and fertilize the field for the next go-round. They dragged the fields to spread the manure evenly. All work with horses, mules, or oxen.

"The result was Edenic. More species of grass and wildlife, healthier populations, more feed for stock, a way of life. Make hay while the sun shines, the saying goes, and at that time of year the sun shines sixteen hours. So that's how long you work— mowing, raking, baling, or loose-stacking—long, hard, epiphanic days."

Marty looked up. The leisure-suit guy was glaring at him. Marty thought, I wonder what his deal is? The Indian was asleep.

"But as often happens in the human dialogue with nature, things started going wrong. Twenty years ago a pickup cost four steers. Now it costs forty. That forced ranchers to run more live-stock and put up more hay. Some ranchers were flat-out greedy. That meant more land, bigger tractors, sprinkler systems that can evaporate millions of gallons of water and deplete aquifers. Some ranchers drained swamps to get more acreage into production. Haying started to last three months instead of three weeks.

"Technology of any kind, from flint knapping to strip-mining, rocketeering, or particle busting, is a conversation we sustain with nature. For example, the conversation of strip-mining, or industry in general, historically might be likened to the conversation a rapist has with his victim. Environmentalism is, or should be, mostly listening for the subtleties and catastrophes that are nature's fluencies, trying to learn that language and learn from it, report it honestly. It's the intercourse of disciple and mentor.

"But of all the conversations man has and has had with nature, agriculture is arguably the most intimate, lively, and potentially loving one, since it is ancient, necessary, and since the answers of our interlocutor are comparatively clear and direct, like that of a long-married, long-loving couple."

The old cowboy in the front row leaned toward the clean-cut

blond guy and whispered loudly, the way people who are hard of hearing do, "What's interlocutor?"

"It's who you're talking to, Mac."

"Why don't he say that?"

"Shh."

Marty smiled and forged ahead.

"You know what happened to Lyle Van Waning's meadow? It got too small. The amount of hay it produced was not worth what it cost to cut it. The new owners let the ditches go and the flumes rot. The wetland ecosystem that had taken a hundred years to nurture dried up and died.

"The fertile peat soil wouldn't grow dry-land grasses, so not only did the wetlands vanish, the soil itself blew away, right down to the gravel. No more hay. No more ducks, geese, pelicans, killdeer, blue herons, sandhill cranes, western phalaropes. No more timothy up to your belly.

"Now you can say that land should never have been husbanded. Saying that doesn't help.

"Who speaks for the land? Or, more properly, who interprets the language of subtlety and catastrophe? Farmers? Ranchers? Environmentalists? What do you lose, from an environmental point of view, when you lose a family farm or ranch?

"Besides losing a way of life, a culture opposed to the dominant First World values of expansion and greed, you lose species diversity, care, and the thread of the conversation concerning a particular place. Generally speaking, one finds more wildlife diversity on a large, well-managed ranch than one finds in a national park. The dominant species in a national park, as in a zoo, is people. What you get in return is a housing development, a vacation spot, forty-acre ranchettes, or a corporate entity whose only allegiance, however they might protest, is to a quarterly bottom line."

Marty went on at length about how the American West had two things to lose, its distinctive, horse-based, non-progress-oriented culture, and its natural environment.

"In my mind they aren't two things but one. You lose either, you lose it all. What we want is the land and the wildlife itself, and a culture based on stewardship and care.

"Stockmen and environmentalists have long been at odds. They demonize each other out of fear. Both groups are afraid of losing what they value most. They burn up bushels of rhetoric over issues like grazing fees and wolves. But really, both embattled camps have more in common than they have to disagree about.

"In the first place, they both love the land. In the second place, they are both idealists. Nobody gets rich ranching, and nobody gets rich being an eco-warrior. No environmentalist ever put a ranch out of business. And if you can face up to the present and stop clinging to obsolete stereotypes, no rancher worth his salt is going to destroy the land that is his livelihood.

"There are slightly fewer cows on the high plains today than there were buffalo before the European presence. The modern rancher has learned that it is better for the grass, and better for himself, to manage cattle in imitation of wild mega-fauna herds."

The knotty cowboy leaned over to the blond guy and asked, "Mega what?"

"Shh. I'll tell you later."

Marty picked up. "Are buffalo capable of overgrazing? You bet. Can they cause erosion? At a high rate of speed.

"This is not a new idea. As the president of the National Stock Growers Association recently remarked, 'Ranchers are not environmental activists, they are active environmentalists.'

"Now I think I've raised enough issues to start a general discussion. I want to hear your stories, your views, what you see as solutions to our predicament. We are watching the West slip through our hopes for it. Can we find some common ground to stand on? Can we find a way to work together to save what we love and are losing?"

There fell the requisite silence. Marty waited it out. Then a mousy woman in the third row stood. She had long nesty hair and a red floor-length Navajo velvet dress. She also had what appeared to be a dead hummingbird on a leather thong around her neck. She began to tear up before she said, "I saw a fox once. It was dusk. The fox looked at me. Our eyes met. Meaning passed between us." She sat down and sobbed.

The old cowboy leaned over and whispered loudly, "She don't get out much."

Marty tried to smooth it over. That's what he was here for. He'd been an environmentalist all his adult life, but he'd come to hate environmentalists. They could be like Tammy Wynette and Savonarola trapped in one body. Marty had belonged to every green group there was from the Sierra Club to Earth First! until, one by one, they all made him gag. Now he worked alone. He wrote books.

He said, "Where did you see this fox, on public or on private land?"

"I don't know, by the side of the road."

"So it wasn't in a national forest or a wilderness area? What is that around your neck, if you don't mind my asking?"

"It's a ruby-throated hummingbird I hit in my car. I didn't even know it. I peeled it from the grille. I wear it in atonement."

The old guy stood up. He wasn't much taller than when he'd been sitting. Marty could see how stiff his joints were, like the

Tin Woodsman after a gullywasher. "They want to reintroduce these wolves. We spent a hundred years gettin' rid of them sons-abitches and now they're bringin' 'em back." He sat down.

Here we go, thought Marty. "I'd prefer a hands-off approach," he said. "The wildlife biologists aren't doing a very good job of reintroducing wolves. Wildlife management has never been our strong suit as a species. It remains ever beyond us. But left to their own devices, wolves do a good job of reintroducing themselves.

"I mean, a wolf is a lot like a human. He doesn't know who he is if he doesn't know where he is. If you take a wolf from the Yukon and airlift him to Wyoming, he's going to be scared and disoriented and he's going to get into trouble. And if you think wolves aren't smart enough to know what causes trouble, you don't know wolves. Wolves have reintroduced themselves as far south as Laramie, and most of the ranchers don't even know they're here."

A redheaded middle-aged woman in a tweed jacket stood. She said, "I'm an environmental lawyer. I live on forty acres. My taxes are ten times the rate for agriculture. You talk about the economic plight of ranchers, how hard they work. Well, I work as hard as anybody. I resent the subsidies for people who own thousands of acres. If they can't make a living ranching they should do something else."

She was pissed.

Marty felt his grip loosening. He didn't want a brawl. "I'm sure you work as hard as anyone," he said. "The difference is you probably are not living below the poverty line despite millions of dollars in investment. You wouldn't, probably, be willing to. Also, no one is going to tell you that, no matter how good you are at your job, you are not allowed to do it anymore."

The cowboy with the glasses stood, holding his hat over his heart as though he were about to recite the Pledge of Allegiance.

"Oscar Rose, Laramie, Wyoming.

"Time was, cows calved out with the rest of God's creatures in the spring. I just mention calving because that's what time of year it is and some of us have to get home.

"I just wanted to say, last time I checked cattle were sold by the pound, and neither the producers nor the consumers affect the prices. The bosses of the three major packing houses get together to determine that. There are laws that are supposed to prevent that but they don't. On a twenty-dollar steak in a restaurant in New York, the producer gets twenty cents.

"As a matter of survival then, ranchers breed their cows to drop the calves as early in the year as possible. But it's a hell of a thing for the calves and the people too, this birthing into a sub-zero world.

"Right now we are in the middle of up to three months of calving. Somebody has to check the cows every four hours and be ready to pull calves fixing to get born upside down, or backwards, or with one leg stuck back. That's a lot of waking up. Midnight, four, eight, in all weathers. In a cold snap you don't want the newborns to freeze to the ground before they get their legs under them.

"Time was ranchers let cows take care of themselves. They could afford a few losses. No more.

"Anyway, I just want to tell the people here that we don't want subsidies and we don't want to be rich. We just want a fair market for our product. We want to live on the land and take good care of it.

"So I'm not complaining. I don't mind the work. Just let me do it. I don't mind being invisible. I just don't want to disappear."

THURSDAY

ADKISSON SAT ON HIS ROCK. Down on the county road he saw a plume of dust sizzling across the parched flats like some kind of hunger. "Here comes Oscar."

Oscar lurched to a dusty halt and got out. "What are we gonna do, Doc?"

"What are we gonna do about what?"

"Mike."

"What about him?"

"He roped Merriweather Snipes to death and rode out. They're after him. I bet they get Jim Thomas to trail him."

Ad just stared, trying to take it in. Surprising as such news was, its inevitability, its fatality, was what was really stunning. Oscar waited for him to catch up.

Ad said, "What in the hell can we do?"

"I don't know, but we've got to do something."

"We don't even know where he'll go."

"Yes, we do."

"And how do we know?"

"Because of something he told me three years ago."

JANUARY 1972

SO MIKE WENT OUT to stay with his sister and her husband, who asked around for work for him.

"Guy's name is McLeod. Ranches up the Laramie River."

"How far up?"

"All the way up."

"How far is that from here?"

"In a straight line?"

"Yeah, in a straight line."

"It isn't in a straight line from here. Especially in winter now."

Mike had to drive his rusted-out truck with the orange fender and two blue doors twenty miles to Livermore, then forty to Laramie, then twenty over to Woods Landing, and then back down into Colorado, another thirty miles. In summer it would have been half that far, but it still wasn't in a straight line.

After he turned off at Woods Landing and followed the river south, things started looking pretty lonesome. The white, misted winter air, still, slumped into the valley bottom. Hoarfrost grew like white kudzu on the fence posts, fence wires, and willows. The hay meadows were comatose in deep snow and the hay-stacks sported cornices.

After two and a half hours of driving he was about twenty crow miles from his sister's house. He turned down a fresh-tracked lane and rumbled over a cattle guard. The ranch house was an old one, a two-story stockade of a building, logs quarter-notched and chinked. On the west side of the house was a rock chimney made from local gritstone. Handmade shakes.

When he stepped out of the truck the cold was like a mild electric shock. The air was dull with damp. A vague sense of dread fell over him. He'd never felt so isolated in his life.

The miniature woman who answered the door directed him out to the barn, where he found a bandy-legged little guy in coveralls chipping ice with a spud bar from under a sliding door. Mike introduced himself and the guy handed him the spud bar.

"Now that you're here I can go look after them cows. When you get done with this door, there's three more froze up just like it. And before it gets dark you need to break the ice on the water troughs. Use the axe for that. There's a trough in every one of them pens."

He quit after a week. He never rode a horse. He chipped ice. The isolation was over the top, a distant howl. The day he decided to toss it in it started to snow, and no one went to town for four more days. When it finally came, he left behind the county snowplow.

JUNE 1990

MIKE AND LIV INVENTED Nude Irrigating as a way of being more natural in nature. Liv was Nude Irrigating one afternoon when two old-timers came down to look at a stallion and instead saw Liv out in the hayfield in nothing but her hip boots and they nearly had strokes. Old-timers belong to a different culture. They haven't all the way adjusted. And seeing a beautiful woman Nude Irrigating could really kill one. So Mike and Liv had to stop it.

Back before Nude Irrigating came to a stop, though, sometimes irrigation would lead to other things. Mike and Liv lay on their backs, hidden in tall, shushing grasses, and watched the sky. Mike saw a cloud he thought looked like a horse with wings. He said, "What does that cloud look like to you?"

"Like it's going away with noplace to go."

. . .

Then they played a game called Tell Me a Story from Your Life. Liv said, "When I first started high school in America there was this bully in the class. He wasn't a regular bully who bullied everyone, he just bullied this one Jewish kid, like the Jewish kid was some kind of project. The bully never actually beat the kid up, just called names, insulted him, humiliated him relentlessly. The teachers never saw a thing. He had a gang of followers who laughed when they were supposed to and urged the bully on. I'd never seen anything like it. There was nothing I could do.

One day I walked into the library during lunch. There was no one in there but me and this bully. He looked up at me from his magazine, then went back to reading. I had to do something. It just came over me.

I took a fire extinguisher from the wall, pulled the pin on it, aimed it at him, and squeezed the handle. It knocked him over backward in his chair and covered him with foam. I hung the thing back on the wall and left."

Mike blew a bubble. "He never reported you or tried to get you back?"

"Nope. He was too ashamed to bring it up."

"I'll be damned." He kissed her forehead. "You're something. Did the bully stop harassing the Jewish kid?"

"No. He did it even more."

On the edge of the irrigation ditch, Liv sat with her jeans rolled, lolling her bare feet in the chilly water. She held her camera in her lap. She thought of all the colors locked in the absolute black of the camera waiting to be released back into life in another light.

Sitting alone in the middle of the hayfield like that, she felt like a rowboat lost at sea. She wanted to take a picture of the ripe hay, capture something of its infinitude. She listened to the seed tops brushing together in the slight wind. The sound reminded her of another sound, something else exactly, but she couldn't place it.

Then it came to her: her first dance as a young girl in Finland. She wasn't allowed to wear nylon stockings, but all the girls did. They wore woolen leggings over them until they got to the dance, not just to hide them but because the nylons would have stuck frozen to their legs.

The sound of the seed tops was the same as the sound of her nylons as she walked out, that first time, onto the floor to dance, the musty woolen smell of the cloakroom fading behind her.

WEDNESDAY

JIM TRAILED HIS HORSES up the Laramie River, south into Colorado, camped at Chambers Lake. He liked the idea of beginning this hunt by driving a hundred miles in the opposite direction from where he knew the fugitive was. It seemed right.

What would he do when he caught up with Mike? He hadn't decided. He had decided not to decide. He'd told the sheriff he'd find the man, and he would.

He tethered his horses on some good grass and slept on the ground under hard stars.

He had coffee before it was light and loaded up. He drove to the highway and over Cameron Pass. When the road hit its downgrade off the pass he began driving on the shoulder in second gear and reading the fence wires that lined the road like a difficult musical score. Many times he stopped, got out, and studied the wires. The few trucks and cars that passed him suspected lunacy or dissipation.

All morning he crept along the wire. He knew what he was looking for, knew he would find it. He had no more hurry on than the puffy dry clouds that floated overhead.

At the town of Walden he stopped in two gas stations and a grocery store to ask. Out on the highway again he drove the shoulder, stopping, getting out, studying, getting back in, driving.

It was three o'clock and four miles north of Cowdrey where he saw Mike's splices and the clear incision of the horse's passage through the deep uncut hay, clear as a road sign or a suicide note.

He unloaded one horse, went through the wire just as Mike had, and fixed the fence behind him. The horse he left, he left tethered on a long cotton rope to a post, where he could graze. The other horse he hauled eighty miles to Rawlins and put up in a friend's corral. He left his rig and got a ride back to the tethered horse with nearly three hours of daylight left.

Jim set out through North Park at a smart trot, having gained two days on Mike. He rode right up the groove, the furrow he could see in the hay, easily, even after it was dark.

AUGUST 1990

OSCAR HAD QUIT his vet practice to ranch full-time. He rented a place on the Laramie River for four years.

The day the tractor blew, Ad was helping him. Oscar had been haying sixty days, dawn to dark. The tractor was a used one. It had cost six thousand dollars. When the engine blew, Oscar knew it wasn't just the life of the tractor that was over. It was his current life as a rancher. He was too far in debt to recover. That tractor was the straw.

Ad and Oscar just looked at each other over that last, lost cause. Over Oscar's shoulder, Ad could see the kids playing. They were climbing up on the loader and leaping into a loose haystack. They shrieked and yowled and slid down the side of the stack. Ad thought their laughter at that moment was the saddest sound he'd ever heard, the way the distance devoured it. Oscar moved his family to an apartment in Laramie and started vetting again.

THURSDAY

NOON THE NEXT DAY, Jim rode into the pasture with the brood mares and foals. He studied the Babel of tracks, contradictory constellations, signs with no meaning. He admired the tactic. He rode straight across the pasture to determine its dimension. Then, no sense trying to sort out the tracks, he rode through a gate and circumnavigated the perimeter.

He was losing a lot of time, he knew, but it wasn't really time to him, it was just what he was doing. On some deep level of affection, he knew he wanted Mike to escape. He also knew there wasn't anywhere for Mike to escape to. That made Mike the same as everyone.

He'd almost completed a circuit of the fence, ten miles, almost half a day, what with having to follow out every tongue of rock and check every hoofprint (there turned out to be a band of mares and geldings on the outside, which was distracting), when he ran out on a long finger of sandstone, and where it gave itself back to the sandy soil, there they were—the rubber-booted prints he was seeking.

It hadn't rained in three weeks. That was in Jim's favor. But he still didn't know if Mike was running west into the desert or north to lose himself in the Wind Rivers, the Absarokas, and then the big timber country of west Montana. What Jim didn't know was that Mike would run out of horse long before Montana.

The track led back into the National Forest. It labored over every ridge and plunged into every drainage, headed northwest. Jim was about ready for another horse himself. He thought if you could stretch the wrinkles out of this country, it would be as big as it seems.

1973

MIKE WASN'T DISCOURAGED by his first ranch job any more than he was discouraged by the bust. All his life he had been possessed by a kind of preternatural buoyancy—whether due to the presence of some extraordinary resilience of spirit or to the abnormal absence of some normal neural faculty, it was hard to say.

Just because he had to try again from scratch, it never crossed his mind that he wouldn't be suited to ranch life. Not once. He just wasn't suited to life on Mac McLeod's ranch.

He landed a job on the Mesa Mountain Ranch near Virginia Dale, where the murderous Jack Slade had once been station master/cum masked bandit of the coaches he was hired to protect.

Compared to the upper end of the Laramie River valley, winters at Mesa Mountain were mild, and there wasn't that screaming isolation to deal with. You could almost always drive to town for a beer.

Mike remembered how at first his appearance had confused people. In 1973, shoulder-length hair and an earring could get a man into trouble in the Mountain West. America was torn apart by the war, and by losing the war—dress codes were red flags to some. Long hair scared rural people and they reacted.

But this particular example of pinko anarchy was wearing a beautiful full-brimmed Stetson and boots with his pants legs tucked inside his boot tops to show off the fancy stitching.

Basically, it was a good thing he was so big. No one wanted to mess with him physically, and he had no trouble ignoring things he was meant to overhear.

In ranch country, the long and small is, eccentricity is accepted, even when it takes the form of low-level meanness. If you are a good worker, eventually you will be accepted by the community. A good, hard worker. It's just that the standards for what hard work is are probably higher on a ranch than any other place—outside of diamond mines in South Africa and general slavery.

Lucky for Mike he believed in work as much as they did, though they wouldn't have explained its importance in equal terms. Mike was strong. He dove right in. He kept going until whatever it was was done.

Most of the jobs he got at first required no skill whatever: cleaning stalls, scoop-shoveling corncobs, digging holes and ditches. But Mike fell to in a way that got attention.

He was easygoing and he loved to laugh. His laugh was like a school bus, big, capricious, bright. Mike's laughter made others happy, too.

All the time he was doing swamp work around the ranch, he was watching the guys with the horses, the way they moved through the cows, slow and easy. He studied hard, asked every question. He remembered the answers. He paid attention.

He got to ride a ranch horse when they moved the herds around. He bought himself a rope and started throwing it at a chopping block. There were plenty of experts around to teach him, loving, as they did, their own expertise.

He made it through a year. Then he bought a horse of his own.

Standing at Mesa Mountain was a quarter horse stallion renowned throughout the state for his bloodlines, size, speed, and temperament. The ranch had a band of brood mares that threw five or six foals each spring.

He picked out a zebra dun colt and made a deal with the boss to work the price off over six months. A zebra dun looks like a buckskin but has zebra stripes on his legs and a stripe down the middle of his back. On the colt's papers Mike wrote *Potatoes Browning*, one of R. Crumb's cartoon freaks. He loved the blank stares he got when people asked him what he'd named his horse. No one ever asked him why.

He got books out of the library and studied at night like a PhD student: horse handling, training, riding, care. He devoted his life to that colt, at first just handling him next to his mother, talking to him, petting him, giving him his hand to smell. Then the halter and leading.

From the get-go Potatoes was a dream. A horse you have once in a lifetime of horses.

1974

THE DAM WAS a dark blood bay. Mike dandled the lead rope in one hand and scratched the star on her forehead. The colt was fuzzy-headed and leggy, springy as a deer. His haunches made a perfect peach.

He lowered his head to make his neck longer and peered around his mother. Abstractedly he sniffed some flowers. Mike hunkered down in front of the mare. Curiosity got the best of the colt and he stepped forward. He smelled Mike's hair and tried chewing on it. He nosed the hat off.

Mike reached out and let Potatoes breathe against his hand. When the colt put his nose close to Mike's face, Mike blew gently into his nostrils. The colt stood back and thought about it. It wasn't long before Potatoes Browning was halter broke and broke to lead.

Mike rode a ranch horse. He joined the roping club in Livermore and devoted himself to roping like it was a religion. Every Thursday night, and the whole first year he never caught a steer.

But he kept coming back and trying. That's what got their respect. He asked too many questions and they chided him for his hopeless ignorance. "You don't know what a rawhide bosal is? Jesus, you're worse than I thought."

They'd answer. And he never asked the same question twice. They could tell he wasn't trying to fake anyone.

He took to wearing loud flowery shirts, and his long hair flailed out behind him when he rode. They called him the Flyin' Hawaiian.

The arena was right off the highway, and tourists and travelers sometimes stopped to watch. One night a boozy buckaroo from Texas with silver toe caps on his boots and silver collar tips stopped to swagger around and look down his nose at the way things were being done.

When he saw Mike he fairly swooned with mockery. He pointed, terminally amazed. In a loud voice and acid tone he said, "Who's the hippie?"

No one said anything for a good three beats. Then Oscar stepped up and squared with the Texan, put his nose in the guy's face. He looked like he was eager to remove the Texan's eyeballs and put them in his shirt pocket for him. He said, softly, "I reckon he's *our* hippie."

1977

MIKE LEARNED TO ROPE. He followed with abandon, threw with concentration. He was head-turningly athletic for his size, though he never did make much time between a set-up horse and a struggling calf.

By all accounts Oscar was still the handiest, especially as a team roper, but he was often too busy with his vet practice to make the rodeos.

You don't have to rope to be a rancher. Many ranchers, especially the older guys, rope little to zero. There's always someone around who *can* rope if there are no pens nearby and an animal needs to be doctored or loaded into a trailer.

But to the younger generation the art of ranch roping—chasing dodging calves over rocks and brush, catching, dallying, all the time praying your horse doesn't step in a badger hole and go down, the breakneck possibility—and the sport of rodeo roping are part of the tradition they wish to exalt and perpetuate.

Most of the time Mike was learning about pickup transmissions and postholes, hay bales and frostbite. But he was also learning about horses and cows.

Every evening he finished work before dark he worked Potatoes in the round corral, clucking at him and pitching the end of a lariat at his heels, getting him to change gaits, directions, respond to words, and to stand and face his trainer.

As soon as Potatoes was two and used to the saddle, Mike got on him, not even a halter on his head, just the round corral for control. He stepped into the stirrup and paused. The horse froze. He swung his leg over. Potatoes turned his ears back and waited. Mike gripped the horn and cantle. He was ready. Nothing happened.

Mike said walk and Potatoes walked. Mike said trot and asked with his hips. Potatoes trotted. They even loped around a few times and the horse never bucked.

A year later they were roping together.

Mike put in ten years at Mesa Mountain. He was a valuable ranch hand.

The next time Mike ran across Mac McLeod it was to pick up six heifer calves that were out in a pasture with some other cows. Mesa Mountain was buying them. It was a clear day below zero.

Mac decided not to bring a horse. Whoever the ranch sent could do the roping. It was too damned cold. Mac sat in the cab of his pickup with the motor running and the heat on.

He watched as Mike and Potatoes went after them one after one. They never missed a loop and had them loaded inside an hour. Mac was impressed. He thought Mike looked familiar but he never made the connection. Mike didn't want him to. Mac said, "Nice horse."

1990

IT WAS RENT TO BUY. When Mike started trying to make it at Black Thorn, he hired someone to put up his hay for him. He wanted to ride the horses. He didn't want to drive the tractors.

The first summer Ad and Mike rode together often, moving cows that were someplace they weren't supposed to be and looking them over for signs of weakness.

They would ride up to fifty miles a day through country so rocky and boggy and thick with wind-fallen timber, even the horses were occasionally stymied. You could break your neck without even trying.

But just as often it was a pleasure riding under soft sun through chiseled country, not seeing much to do, talking, not talking. If they found a calf or cow with hoof rot or pneumonia, Mike would head, Ad would heel.

The more dangerous exploits tended to occur when rogue animals, usually dry cows, got into bad places and kept diving at a run into timber, rocks, or willows so thick a cow could actually burrow in and stand and elude her pursuers.

The only new thing happening was complaints from Merriweather Snipes. The cows, he said, were grazing on private property where they didn't belong. They were bothering the Proprietors. Mike just loved that word.

FRIDAY

HE COULD HAVE MADE BETTER TIME down off the mountain, on the flats, in the open, but to stay out of sight he had to stay inside the mountain's tree line. The range ran north–south, so he rode north, going up and down every ridge and every canyon that emptied itself onto the prairie. It was like he was stitching the mountain to fasten it down. It was taking a lot out of his horse.

Just inside the forest he couldn't be seen, but he could see out over the sea of sage whose shore was the edge of the timber— timberline, but not as in the altitude above which trees can't grow; this is the lower limit, the razor-cut agreement of trees not to venture into the wind-scrubbed plain.

At night he stopped inside a small enclosure of rocks overlooking the town of Encampment. He watched as pickups gathered in the lot of the dance hall and bar on the edge of town. The trucks, Mike thought, were like a school of trout, as dusk deepened, gathering in the ripple of a rock in midstream. The lights came on and he could hear the drunken laughter float up to him. He thought a beer or two would taste pretty good right now, after a week of riding.

He watched the now brightly lit parking lot below as a cowboy with an almost unwavering gait came out and unloaded a
horse from his trailer. Less unsteadily he swung into the saddle,
rode toward the dance hall, up onto the covered porch, then,
leaning forward, he opened the door, ducked under the lintel,
and rode into the bar.

Mike thought, That's a well-broke horse. He could hear the
cheers and laughter of the assembly. Probably a bet was at hand.
Five minutes later, perhaps after shooting a game of pool from
horseback, the cowboy rode out of the bar, loaded up his horse,
and went back inside for another round.

1989

MERRIWEATHER SNIPES thought about how confidence had
gotten him a long way in life. It was his self-fulfilling prophecy,
like a credit line: if you have it they give it to you. People place
their own confidence in those who already possess it. Not to
mention the thrusting jaw and smoky, resonant voice.

Jet fighters had made him the man he was. He'd never gotten
over it. When he got out he didn't want to fly commercially, that
was for wimps. After firebombing jungles, where could you go
for excitement? He'd had a flair for incinerating people too small
to see.

Snipes had no qualms. What he had was confidence. Confidence, to Snipes, was power. He knew about ends and means. He
was fond of the bottom line. It takes a man to look reality in the
eye, take it by the horns, and not blink—ever. Darwin told him

all he needed to know about right and wrong: survival was right, extinction was wrong.

What good was all the sentimental self-righteousness of an extinct species? he'd like to know. Morality, in the scientific sense, was really just weakness, and pity for weakness. Does a lion apologize to his lunch?

In winter when the snow was soft he'd chain up his Jeep and go drift charging, just for the fun of it, "opening the road," driving fast right down the middle, hitting drifts wherever they crossed the road, relying on momentum to take him through, feeling the horsepower, the churning. It was almost like flying, bucking through snowdrifts at thirty or forty miles per hour. He said, "God, I love this country."

After a couple of years designing RV interiors, he got a job in real estate and rocketed through the ranks. He versed himself in techniques of making money off the land, techniques that didn't involve farming, just farms.

He'd seen the governor of Colorado get rich enough to be a politician by acquiring timberland west of Denver before the Front Range boomed. It was all timing, bucking, surfing, catching the perfect wave.

The governor had bought thousands of acres at agricultural prices, bulldozed a snake's nest of roads in there, and turned it over in forty-acre "parcels" for luxury mountain homes thirty minutes from the city. He made millions. Never lifted anything heavier than a telephone.

All Snipes had to do was pay attention and wait for his own wave. He was thinking a killing and early retirement. Anybody who said you can't buy happiness hadn't tried. Snipes had bought lots of it and planned to buy more, all there was. It was like a philosophy.

The inviability of ranching these days just happened to coincide with the urbanization and industrialization and touristification of the Front Range of the Rockies. *Just happened.* He knew his history. It was just like the eradication of aboriginals *just happened* to coincide with the disappearance of the buffalo, which *just happened* to coincide with the building of the railroads, which *just happened* to coincide with the discovery of gold in the Black Hills, the sacred homeland of the Lakotas.

He couldn't believe how easy it was. All you had to do was be there. With confidence.

It was easy to buy a ranch with a bank or a backer's help if your stated intention was subdivision. You could relieve some poor moron of a goat-roper of his insolvency, turn around, and be a flat-out pilgrim of progress. Take the old homeplace, the old Poverty Flats, the old Starvation Corners, chop it up into forty-acre "parcels" so that sixteen times per square mile more people could enjoy the hunting, fishing, and scenery. Wasn't that democracy? *And* you got rid of those stupid, reeking cows.

Merry hated cows. He had a right to hate them, having grown up on a farm in Nebraska. "Plus they cause erosion," he added to himself piously. The profits to be had were enormous. Snipes knew. He had them. Him and his backer, O'Fallon.

Then there was uranium, titanium, molybdenum, and diamonds. He'd never sell mineral rights along with a parcel. So far he hadn't struck what he was looking for, but he was close. A matter of time. For instance, take uranium. Uranium travels. You can tell where it's been even if it's gone, and you can track it down. Uranium is elusive prey, which just made it more of a challenge to a natural-born hunter like Snipes.

He knew that uranium *had* been on the ranch he and O'Fallon had just bought. He was hot on its trail. Where had it snuck off to? Where was it cowering now? Merry's best guess at the moment was that it had slinked north into Wyoming.

He imagined a rip-roaring strip mine. He imagined nuclear reactors like leviathans of the plains. Toxic waste? No problem. Reservations were dying to get it. Failing that, shoot it into space.

So his wave was now and he was all over it. Getting major backing for the project was as hard as ordering a pizza. Denver was full of like-minded real estate cowboys who were helping each other help themselves to the millions being invented.

Most of the Front Range was gone and going upscale. But what about the common man, his modest dreams of arrival? The common man wanted his own piece of paradise. Forty acres from which to view the view.

Now was the time. With the state selling itself at such a reeling pace, a sense of wilderness, rather than proximity to the city, had become an attraction. People wanted something farther away and wilder. The hunting, the fishing, the swooning sunsets.

He bought twenty thousand acres on the Colorado side of the line from a ranch based in Wyoming. Merry got backing and bought it for what it was, montane cattle pasture. He'd carve a mess of roads in there and turn the land over at five times its cost in forty-acre ranchettes. Peddle the scenery, the wilderness, the ecstasy of ownership.

Snipes was counting on an old American imperative, that of dominion. Never mind that none of this country was accessible by road in winter. They'd find out. When they wanted to sell it he'd be there to help them. A great realtor has return customers, meaning you had to sell them something they *thought* they wanted but, after a year or two, thought better. Up there you could sell the same piece of property twelve times.

You tell them it's an investment in the future. You don't tell them it's an investment in wind and snow. You never mention mineral or water rights.

From Paradise Valley to Telluride, from Aspen to Santa Fe, the abjectly wealthy had already been culled. Now it was time for the low-rent operation: working-class people willing to sacrifice their hard-earned savings for a brief idea of arrival. A tradition if there ever was one.

The ranchland had come with water rights: eight cubic feet per second picked up out of Sand Creek for riparian irrigation of a thousand acres of hay, ditches designed and incised over a hundred years.

You sell the meadows to ranchetteers while the grass is tall and green. Then you sell the water rights, for a fortune, back down the Wilson Ditch into Colorado. The hay meadows turn back to scrub prairie, and the ranchers down Sand Creek in Wyoming aren't even in the right state to complain.

Then minerals. He'd find that uranium, track it down. He'd sell the icing to these idiots and keep the cake for himself. And if the uranium got away? Diamonds.

There was a diamond fashion tumescing in the world of investors in nonexistent objects. And indeed people had found small low-grade industrial diamonds lying right on the ground near Tie Siding.

So any fool could figure it out: you scatter a few diamonds on the ground and then find them. You get big backing and big machinery and set to stripping. You pay yourself magnificently from handsome stock sales for two or three years before filing chapter eleven. Then, Bermuda and a yacht. Nothing left behind but a big old harmless hole in the ground.

So far the plan was working like a French train.

He'd build himself a house up on the ridge, somewhere with

plenty of view so he could keep an eye on people's comings and goings. He'd be a booster, a good Samaritan.

He knew how to play King of the Hill.

SATURDAY

IN THE MORNING, after downing a tin of fruit cocktail, Mike rode on. Topographical features of every kind were giving out; mountains, rivers, valleys, outcrops, bluffs all diminished as he rode north, as if they were gradually being defeated, worn out by the expanding sky with its omniscient sun.

On the side of a final uplifted mesa, in the thick sagebrush, was a wooden buck fence, probably four miles of it—the kind of fence the first sheepmen built a hundred years ago, all of wood, buck posts and poles, so much of it in the incinerated brush it made Mike tired just to look at it. There was no limit, he thought, to the amount of work those old guys would take on.

It was noon before he came to water, and he let Potatoes Browning drink for a long time. Down on the brushy flat sprawled the town of Saratoga, like someone spilled it there. He was running out of timber to ride in, the pinstripe lodgepoles giving way to scrub limber pine and juniper, the grasses and bright blue and yellow flowers giving over to blood-red earth and colored pebbles brightening in the sun.

He came to the National Forest boundary fence and wondered why there was so much plastic hung from it and ghosting in the wind, why there was metal roofing and scraps of plywood strewn on the ground. There was no dump or landfill as far as he could tell. Then he saw the sign: DIVIDE PEAK RANCH—35 ACRE LOTS. Just like home, he thought.

Looking over the sun-washed brush country, he made out several nondescript heaps of human leavings—plywood, tin, a pickup camper without the pickup but propped on poles. He could see no vehicles that had any chance of moving, nor any movement on the slopes. He crossed the fence and rode on carefully, remembering he'd been surprised before in a place like this.

He came to a long trench gouged in the earth by a Caterpillar and four twenty-foot lengths of cement sewer pipe stacked up. Funny. There was no water in miles. He blew a bubble and rode on.

Over a rise, on the downhill side, was a small camper trailer lying on its side, tumbled by the winter wind. Nearby, in the lee of some rocks, a similar model, still upright, and with a fiberglass San-O-Let next to it and a weathered picnic table. Nice.

Every property offered its apparition of ruin. Poles collapsed and abandoned mid-construction, some already so weathered they might have been the remains of homesteads, but most were recognizable as recent efforts, sporting melted Sheetrock, torn Strongbarn, pressure-treated pilings, particleboard.

There were fifty-five-gallon drums, auto parts, cast-iron objects Mike could not identify sown over the land like Satan's idea of flora.

He passed a collapsed shack with a moribund Jeep beside it, and beside that a barrel in which someone had tried to cremate four or five small animals—goats, Mike guessed—without much success.

Bedsprings, pots and pans, broken dishes, flatware, stoves, refrigerators, TV sets, scattered as if by a tornado. It reminded him of the inside of Ad's house after the vandals got it. He passed an old frame line shack that someone had quartered with a chain saw in order to transport, presumably intending to tie it back together somehow, someday, but they must have got distracted, for there it lay, a roofless, flayed hovel, sawn in four and tumbled on the ground.

Mike blew a bubble and said, "Bud, I thought Wyoming had more sense than to allow this type of progress. I knew Colorado would, but somehow I gave Wyoming more credit."

He rode on. When he crossed into BLM land, where fences ceased, he still saw a lot of junk that had blown in.

The geology was characterized by bluffs and mesas with little cover besides deep dry brush. The earth was turning red. Sandstone slabs flashed bright green, blue, and orange lichens. Some of the hills looked soft, like melting cheese. Others were hard and linear, showing the strata of eons like meaty scars. The red and yellow and ocher hues blended blue with distance. The sunset flushed the reddish shades. It was beautiful and barren and empty, and the sky took everything away.

"Potatoes," Mike said, "this is the kind of country where a cow needs a mouth ten feet wide and has to run sixty miles an hour just to stay alive. But ain't it something?"

1993

THE BULL MOUNTAIN Proprietors Association had a book of bylaws called "The Covenants," like you could go to hell for crossing them. Mike loved that. Under the rules of the

Covenants, none of the Bull Mountain faithful could fence out cows because fences tended to ruin the wilderness effect.

So the Proprietors became angry and frustrated. Mike went to one of their meetings and offered to maintain the old ranch fences, put his cows on the old pasture, and pay the people for it. By putting the land back into production they could cut their taxes to one tenth.

Nothing doing. They wouldn't have fence and they wouldn't have cows. Snipes spoke for them all.

Legally Mike didn't have to do anything. The only reason he ended up riding over and rounding up cows and sweeping them into the National Forest like dust under a rug was because the Proprietors, egged on by Snipes, were scattering livestock all over the country on ATVs, often injuring the animals.

One especially perceptive fellow saw a bull standing in the middle of a cattle guard, slowly crossing it. Bulls are dedicated professionals. The man rammed the bull in frustration and impatience, breaking the animal's hind leg above the hock and leaving it there.

Mike couldn't afford to lose livestock like that, so he and Ad kept riding.

The grass on the old ranch meadows was good, even while it was dying, so the cows kept returning and Mike and Ad kept shooing them back.

By the third year Mike realized he would have to do his own haying, two cuts, three months, and leave most of the riding to Ad, who lived up where the cattle were. Mike would come up every two weeks or so, or after a rainy day had stopped the haying.

Ad did the riding and Mike drove around in circles on a tractor, which was not his chosen life.

Ad was spending all his off-time horseback, which was all right, but if he had a wreck out there and got crippled (killed would be less of a problem) no one would know about it, and once they found out they would have no clue as to where to start looking—bogs behind the reservoir, Deadman Mountain, sections six, fourteen, sixteen, thirty-six, Bull Mountain, Sand Creek Pass, Sand Creek, Sheep Creek, Cow Creek, George Creek, Trail Creek, Trout Creek, the old Van Waning place—basically anywhere in an area the size of Connecticut.

As time went on, Ad found that most of his riding was needed on the part of the Association that the old ranch used to hay, where he and Althea used to irrigate horseback for Oscar when he rented it during the transition period. It was good grass, and Ad didn't blame the cows for returning to it out of the government pasture. He just felt like the Sisyphus of cattle, stuffing them up the hill and letting them roll back, again and again, like oiled marbles.

He had gathered a small bunch and was headed for the National Forest. He rode past a school bus that someone had backed into an aspen grove and blocked up for a—well, a house.

Adkisson had the cows lined out beyond the bus when a tiny, irate, scraggle-bearded, fierce-eyed man came striding toward him from the incongruous yellow bus. "These your cows?"

"I work for the guy who owns them."

"Whose cows are the S brand. Yellow tags?"

"I know whose they are. They're not my responsibility. Why, are they out?"

"Out? Look. I bought this parcel and hid the school bus on it to hunt elk from. I chose a spot with deep grass. I woke up this morning and there was about fifty of them sonsabitches eating all my elk bait."

"Your what?"

"Elk bait."

Ad looked at the school bus and back at the livid man. "Gonna shoot 'em right from the school bus?"

The man boiled. "Course."

Ad said, "Those cows are supposed to be on a section up on the side of the mountain. They are well fenced. The only way they'd get out is if somebody left a gate open. I'm sure they've already been put back where they belong. Meanwhile, my charges are getting a little ahead of me. So long."

Trotting his horse, Ad caught up with the herd, which had just stalled out at the top of a rise. He had another couple of miles to push them. They had to cross a deep aspen draw, but there was a break in the trees, a passage through which he could drive them.

When Ad crested the rise he pulled up short. Down in the draw, choking the pass where he had to punch the cows through, was Roger's entire S herd, grazing peacefully.

He had to get the cows across that draw without mixing the two herds, not a great difficulty for two or three riders, but it would be a test for one, even if he was well mounted, which, that day, he wasn't.

He galloped his chargey black mare in a circle around the bunch he was moving so they stopped and stared, confused, and started milling. Then he raced down the hill whistling and whooping and flapping his coiled lariat.

He got Roger's cows moving on a trot and chased them up into the nappy aspen grove. Some of them were already splitting off to join up with Mike's cows, and he kept having to gallop after them. Then some of Mike's cows started following Roger's.

By the time he got the right cows through the pass and had turned back the wrong cows straggling, he was just about out of horse.

"Sure hope that school-bus guy goes back to town before Roger's cows come for more elk bait."

1989–1993

WHEN THE CAMEL ROCK RANCH broke up and sold its Colorado holdings to developers, it wasn't hard for anyone to imagine how the once limitless pastureland full of wildlife would look with forty-acre ranchettes in the foreground of the Snowy Range. In fact, though it never quite got to the point of a trailer-and-shack density of sixteen per square mile, it came out of the chute pretty fast and headed in exactly that direction.

The old ranch had bordered the Trent place on two sides. Since most of the land wasn't worth much as development property, lacking trees, water, and winter access, it sold for little to people who didn't have much.

Realtors punched the idea of individual ownership, peddled the idea of wilderness, and it caught on like a rash. Many people who had worked hard all their lives gave everything they had for a piece of the sullied dream, even if it didn't have trees or water and in winter it was a wind tunnel.

The developers came out fine. New owners became quickly disillusioned, bored, and angry. After all, they had nothing to *do* there. They fished out the streams in a year, and the large game animals wasted no time relocating. Many angry, poverty-eaten, ripped-off dreamers got loosed on Ad, destroying simultaneously the landscape and the culture it had spawned. Again.

Several of the first Proprietors set up right against Ad's fence so they could at least be *near* some trees and water. Furthermore, it was closer to the top of the ridge and the view was better up there. Campers and trailers and flyaway shacks began to close in.

It was common for these folk to park a camper or an RV on a site and begin cobbling up some kind of collage of a shelter—usually the cheapest materials available. Some edifices fell down in a year. One guy built his house out of PVC pipe and covered it with Visqueen. A plastic house! Soon it was a pile of plastic, and not long after that it was plastic strewn for miles over the prairie. Some made do with the trailer, some with the camper off-loaded and propped against the wind, some with a canvas tepee.

There was another strange thing they did. Often, before they built anything, they brought in piles of junk—Kentucky bank accounts. Like a Switzerland of safe-kept junk, all the junk they'd hoarded in their yards in town, or maybe just the overflow, the junk capital gains. And besides, you never know when, if you are building something especially, you might need a good piece of junk—angle iron or sheet metal from a shower stall.

One guy brought up an ancient Airstream and a flatbed trailer loaded with scrap. He parked them on his forty, left them there, and never came back.

Another guy brought up all this salvaged equipment—paleo backhoes, bulldozers—and dug up everything; like a kid in a big sandbox with real toys. He dug trenches and holes. He dammed a dry ravine. He peeled back every inch of topsoil.

Then there was the Ferris animal cruelty case, which is documented elsewhere.

During those early days of development Ad woke each day with a little cold stone of nausea in his gut, a sliver of dread at the base of his skull.

Ad tried to act civil, for his own sake, when people tried to sneak through his road. He treated them like children. "Are you lost?"

If they sneered at him or smart-mouthed he would explode. But he was trying to be better about it.

Up in the timber with the Power Wagon, he was cutting dead logs for firewood. It was midafternoon. He'd had a couple of beers with lunch, and then a nap. He was logy and irritable. The army surplus Wagon was backed up to a stand of beetle-killed limber pines and obscured from the road by living trees.

He cut the motor on the chain saw, and the silence heaved back with a little wind in it. Going to the truck to get the axe, he heard them—two high-pitched motors coming up the Boulder Ridge Road, revving and changing gears, ripping the air with their screams.

Well, thought Ad, that's the road they're supposed to use. He opened the door of the truck as they came into sight. First, a man on a dirt bike, beard, shades, shaved head. Then a woman on an ATV, long-haired, blond, with a baseball cap.

Then they did it. Right at the NO TRESPASSING sign, where a faint trail turned off, and then a fainter trail dropped into the south draw, right there at the NO TRESPASSING sign, the guy whistled back to her and motioned for a turn. He turned. She turned. They sputtered down into the big timber of the south draw.

In a heartbeat Ad was into the big truck and starting it and hurtling down the trail after them, popping branches on both sides.

It was a narrow logging trail down in the bottom of a ravine full of old lodgepoles. The road was overgrown with pine boughs so it didn't seem as though a truck could get down it. But it was just new saplings and small branches the truck exploded through. Indeed it exploded into view just as the unsuspecting couple turned their own engines off. Suddenly there was this big army truck and this really angry man leaping out of it.

Something about the confidence, control, and proprietary nature of the whistle and hand motion right before the turn had made Ad lose it. "What the hell are you people doing here?"

The bald guy sputtered. "We got lost."

Ad would have none of it. "Right. Right there at the NO TRESPASSING sign, you suddenly got lost. Look. I've had enough of this. Who the hell do you think you are?"

That's when Ad noticed the guy he was dressing down in front of his wife or girl or whatever was packing a pistol with an enormously long barrel. Like some modern-day Buntline Special. He didn't let up, just kept yelling at the guy, thinking, If he goes for the pistol, it's so long, I'll rip his throat out with my teeth before he ever gets it out of the holster.

Finally he told them to get out and not come back. He got into the truck. It whined in reverse as he backed out, instantly flooded with remorse.

"Hell. They were probably just going down there to screw. It *is* pretty down there in all the big trees. I humiliated him in front of his woman. In another mood, maybe I wouldn't have minded. I gotta cool down. Give people a way out. Damn. It was something about the way he whistled and pointed and turned that really got me."

The next morning as Ad drove past the sign he saw it had nine bullet holes in it. Tracks showed where a dirt bike had spun out of there. He said aloud, "Takes a hell of a man to kill a sign like that."

Then there was the time he caught five guys hunting in the west draw. He rounded them up, politely explained that they were not to hunt on his section. They were cheeky. They said, "Just because it said NO TRESPASSING we didn't think it meant we couldn't hunt here." They got into their truck and prowled away.

Ad, who had Oscar in the truck with him, went to the corner to check, then turned back and fell in behind the hunters, who were driving very slowly.

Seven mule deer bounded across the road and down into the timber. The hunters, still on Ad's land, heedlessly piled out of their truck and ran after the deer, shooting as they ran.

Ad couldn't believe it. He was after them, yelling. He called them names. He insulted them, keeping up a steady stream of invective, which they ignored until they had loaded up and driven on again. The deer got away.

When Ad climbed into his truck, Oscar was laughing. Ad said, "What?"

"You were just screaming your head off at five guys with guns, and you don't have one. My dad used to do that."

"Yeah," Ad said. "I guess I got kind of a thing for yelling at guys with guns. I gotta quit that."

SUNDAY

HE HAD LOST TRACK of the days and nights he had been riding. The landscape was starting to resemble another planet. He rode over a hill round as a loaf of bread and tiger-striped with coal seams. From its top he saw a county road he would have to cross and a good-sized creek on the other side.

He could see twenty miles all around from the hill. No one traveled the road. There was no way to disguise his tracks. Was he still being followed on the ground? He hadn't seen any light planes or helicopters, which, by now, he had expected. He scanned the light-shot blue sky, listening for dronings.

He stepped his horse onto the road and noticed it was packed so hard he left no tracks, whereas the red soil all around minted perfectly identifiable prints. He thought about, and decided against, staying on the road. Even if he saw or heard a truck coming, he might not be able to get out of sight in time or, in this landscape, at all. There were fewer and fewer features to hide behind as he rode toward the Great Divide Basin.

He traversed the road and descended into the creek bed, which, for the otherwise desiccated and Martian landscape, had a surprising flow of water in it. He hid beside a cutbank and watered Potatoes Browning. The horse drank long, lifted his head, drank again.

It could be forty miles of sun and dry brush and mesas before they found more water. Mike filled his canteen, drank as much as he could hold, dunked his hat in the sulfur-tainted stream, and put it back on. He mounted and rode.

The horse was walking slowly, stumbling often, giving out. Mike hadn't eaten in two days. His beard was full and bushy and hot, the way he usually wore it in winter. In the desert it was an oppression. He considered hacking at it with his knife. He considered stealing food from a ranch if he came to one. He considered stealing a horse.

As the sun went down it seemed like the world was upside down, the red ground and red sandstone heaves going black and the all-day-empty sky taking on all the life in pastels and cobalt in the clouds. The sunset stretched all the way east and he kept riding, through purple thistles, mountain mahogany, creosote brush. One big rock loomed like an aircraft carrier.

He tended his horse to the east, looking for the road he had crossed. The road would work in the dark. He went trackless for five miles, all the time watching for headlights. None came.

He had no more horse left. He could see Rawlins blazing into the night sky, like a hole that let the earth's molten core shine through. He left the hardpan road and slipped up an arroyo. He unsaddled, hobbled, and hid under his tarp, just in case they started looking for him from the air before he was ready.

He was pretty sure he had blown it by now. The story wouldn't end with the right rhetoric or style. Still, it would be all right to give out in the Red Desert, die with his horse, and be scattered by coyotes—disappearance was what he was after. So long as Jim didn't catch up to him and ruin everything. Come to think of it, though, that ending had a certain charm as well.

Everything was continuing not to matter.

APRIL 1992

WINTER WAS SO OPEN it was scaring everyone until a late April snow came down in the dark. In the yard light, Mike and Liv watched flakes the size of miller moths flutter thick and fast, like an angel massacre.

When they woke in the morning the sky was so blue it was purple and the sunlight made the snow glint and sparkle like spun glass two feet deep over everything. The fence posts had hats; the rails, mantles.

They sat by the woodstove and planned the day. Mike drank a Pepsi with his pancakes and then popped a cube of bubble gum into his mouth. Outside, they clipped on their cross-country skis and broke trail out to the shed. They leaned their skis on a post and Mike started the tractor while Liv fed the stallion.

Then it was all around the corrals and pens, feeding the other horses and some heifers. They hitched the feeder to the tractor and loaded three round bales to haul through the deep feathery snow to where the cows stood in a bunch, up to their bellies, not a clue what to do next.

Mike started the feeder spinning and laid out a windrow for the cows. Driving the big tractor through deep snow made it seem like they were in a tugboat, chugging through a sea of white sugar.

Once the cows were all lined out and eating, they drove back along them, looking for animals that might be in trouble. The calves were still small so they were up to their necks in it. They had to follow in the wakes of their mothers just to move. All but two looked healthy.

Mike mentally noted their numbers and drove home. They spent an hour together scoop-shoveling dried ears of corn onto a flatbed trailer. Then Liv drove, and Mike shoveled corn out to the cattle.

Back at the house, Liv asked Mike if he needed help with the calves. He said no and blew a bubble. In that much snow he could probably rope them sitting his horse. "Besides"—he grinned—"I know what Finnish girls like to do in the snow." Innuendo included, she knew he meant skiing.

Well, there *was* something sexual about it—even strokes in

the deep quiet powder, maybe a little hiss of ski on each stride as the snow took the imprint of a clean, elegant track.

Mike put spurs on his shoepacs and stomped and waded out to the corral. He haltered the big buckskin gelding called Wood-pecker. Liv clipped on her three-pins again and glided smoothly through the sparkles toward the canyon at the head of the meadow where the cows were.

She carried a fanny pack with an extra pair of gloves, waxes, matches, and a *puukko*, her father's (very sharp) sheath knife.

Riding the big horse through deep snow in bright sun toward the cow pasture, Mike blew bubbles. He was basking in the winter sun's correlative: the mellow, joyful peace that had made him love being a cowboy. He felt part of all the things most people never feel part of. Snow. Sun. Sandstone. Sky. He was doing what he liked and knew. It was now. And this now had no pressure, just permission.

These days it was rarely like that. He was usually beset with the kind of vague dread that made him feel cheated.

It would have been one thing if it had just been him alone. But he'd gotten Liv into this deal, and he felt responsible for her happiness too. She wasn't a woman put on earth to work hard and stay poor. She deserved better.

Mike got his peace of mind in fits and starts. Moments like now, riding a furrow in deep sun-graced snow to doctor a couple of calves.

He rode up on the first one. The calf faced him and stood, ears drooping. Mike could have dropped a loop over her head without swinging it, but he flashed the rope over his head, rolling his wrist before throwing it, just to make it official.

The calf pulled back and started to fight, but it was small and Mike was strong. He didn't need the horn to hold her. He took his time, dallied and tied off, dismounted, and opened the saddlebags for the syringe. Woody faced the thrashing calf and kept the rope tight, looking almost bored.

Mike drew a double dose into the syringe, thinking to save reloading it for the second calf. He waded over and flanked the calf into the snow. He put his knee on her neck and pulled back the top foreleg so she couldn't struggle. He held the foreleg under his other knee, pulled up a pinch of hide, and administered the medicine. Then, syringe between his teeth, he called to Woody, who took a step forward. Mike removed the slack loop and turned the calf loose.

Liv had decided to ski along the top of the bluff above the pasture to get to the canyon. From there she could see the Mummy Mountains, incandescing in their winter finery. She watched Mike doctor the calf. She, too, was enjoying this day of well-being, the luck of loving one's life.

Mike looked up and saw her on the red rim against deep sky. He waved, and she lifted a ski pole into the air.

Syringe gripped in his teeth, he slogged back to Woody and coiled his rope. He left his loop built and hung the coils on the off side of the saddle, swung up, and went to look for the other calf. Liv paralleled his progress on the bluff.

Mike shifted his seat and felt that his saddle was loose. He thought he'd better cinch it up before roping again. When he swung his leg over the cantle, his spur picked up the loop in the rope. Before he touched the ground, the loop tightened around his ankle and pulled the rope under the saddle, which spooked the horse. The coils on the saddle horn tightened, and when the horse bolted Mike had himself roped by the heel.

Feeling the rope slide under the saddle was enough for Woodpecker to shy, but when he saw he was dragging his rider behind him, he panicked and began to gallop through the snow at an angle to the bluff. The faster he ran, the more frightened he became, Mike plowing behind him as if in pursuit.

Liv saw the whole thing happen. The horse was headed toward her, but at an angle. Daughter of the Finnish general, wife of the disaster at hand, she flashed out her *puukko* and held its handle against the pole grip so that it stuck straight up. She gauged the horse's speed and trajectory and poled off the bluff. She dropped off the six-foot sandrock rim and schussed toward the emergency.

She was accelerating at a scary clip for cross-country skis, and she had to make a half telemark to correct her course. Woody flashed past her. She raised the knife and slashed the rope. Mike slid to a stop and lay still, a drumstick rolled in flour.

As soon as Woody felt the line go slack and knew his rider wasn't chasing him anymore, good horse, he stopped and turned his head as if to say, What the hell was that?

Liv made a smart telemark stop, kick-turned, and skied over to where Mike lay in the snow. The knife blade winked in the sun. She thought he was badly hurt, would have to be. Then she thought he was wracked with death throes. Then she saw he was laughing into the sky, syringe still clenched, severed riata hooked around his ankle. Through the syringe, he pronounced, "Thanks, dear."

The complexity of emotions that heaved into her chest only allowed her to say, "Mike, you fuckhead." Then they both were laughing. But Liv's mirth was not pure. She was thinking, One scary thing after another.

Mike said, "I guess I need to go home and get another rope, bein' as you shortened this one."

"Whatever." She shook her head, smiling, and skied toward the canyon.

ONCE

JORDAN HUNG HIS SHOULDERS over the top rail of the corral and watched the foreman heel a bull calf out of the mill of calves and drag it behind the horse out of the holding pen. A stocky guy in coveralls pulled back a foreleg, and Jordan's mom sat down in the mud and pulled a hind leg, her boot in its crotch, and turned off the loop. Smoke billowed between flank and iron as if the heat came out of the calf, not out of the iron.

Jordan never helped at branding, claimed it was the smell he couldn't stand. He had a neat row of cigarette burns down his arm like buttons. He watched them drag another calf.

OCTOBER 1980

DESPITE HIS SUMO SIZE and un-good looks, Mike delighted in being a magnet for the affections of children. His laughter tumbled out from a true place, like spring water, or rolled like promising thunder after a dry spell. He'd cant his head back and flash his perfect teeth and laugh. Ad called him the Pied Piper.

Mike had a friend on the Mesa Mountain Ranch, Sissy, the boss's fourteen-year-old daughter. Every afternoon when the weather was fine she'd jump off the school bus and scamper down the lane. She'd throw a halter on her little bay mare and find out where Mike was working. Then, bareback, her hair furling behind her like blond freedom, she'd gallop out to find him. Fencing, haying, irrigating, it didn't matter.

That big, ugly, happy, hippie cowboy was the only person in the world she could be honest with. He made her laugh, and ordinarily she never laughed.

She liked to ask him questions about the world beyond the world she knew, about cities and college and jail and the ocean. He colored his answers with rosy dismissals, as if the world she didn't know was less magnificent than the world she knew, and that both worlds were forgiving and ultimately harmless.

Mike put special effort into making her laugh because he sensed a rooted and ineluctable sadness in her, a depression she covered up but never got clear of.

They joked and laughed and Mike kept working. She'd hand him the fence pliers or help him set a sack dam in the ditch. At dark the two went home together, the girl racing ahead on the bay and Mike trailing along behind in the ranch pickup. If Mike was horseback they sidekicked home at a walk or raced each other to a cottonwood tree, and Sissy always won. They were friends like that for four years.

Mike taught Sissy how to tickle trout out of the creek that ran through the hay meadow. He watched her willowy fingers ease under the rock she lay belly-down on. He said, "What you going to do if you catch one?"

"Just let him go."

In a sparkle of droplets she lifted a speckled brook trout into the air and grinned. She was about to release the fish when Mike said, "Hold on."

Sissy looked down and saw the reason. Six inches of fishing leader trailed from the trout's mouth.

Mike wetted his hand and took the fish. The hook was too deep to extract. He said, "Now what do you want to do?"

"Take him home and eat him, I guess."

Mike grasped the trout behind the gills and pushed the head back till he heard the snap.

She said, "I hate it that we have to kill things and eat them."

Mike said, "I always try to picture whatever it is I'm eating and imagine I'm taking something in—not just into my body, but into my heart. Like with trout I kind of pray I'm getting some of their quickness, not just their flesh."

"What do you get from deer?"

"Wariness, readiness."

"What if you ate a dog?"

"Depends on the dog."

"Horse."

"Wisdom and sadness—more than any human could bear."

"How about a cow. Stupidity?"

"No. Cows are accepting, and nurturing of their young."

"What if I ate a hummingbird? Would I fly somewhere far away, and would my heart thrum itself to death?"

They walked home holding hands. In his free hand Mike dangled the trout from the monofilament leader.

There happened to be a roping down at Livermore the day after Sissy shot herself with her father's .30-'06. By the time Dr. Trent saw her she was still breathing but as good as gone. The ER nurses had seen doctors punch holes in the wall before—nothing unusual. "One thing about a ranch," a nurse who knew was heard to whisper, "there's always a rifle around. It's just too damn easy . . . dear girl."

They went ahead with the roping because that's what these folks do, they go ahead. They grieve by knowing just to go ahead. Every next day is a living elegy.

The cowboys roped in turn, but there was no banter, no speech at all among them, no applause. It was like a ghost rodeo. They were steer roping—turning steers, they called it. Oscar had the time to beat.

The few people who had stopped in off the highway to watch, of course, didn't know anything. They thought they were watching a rodeo.

Now, even people who don't know much about rodeo know that whatever happens, whatever damage, however stove up by broncs or bulls, whatever broken bones or internal bleeding, the cowboy has to rise from the dust into an ocean of pain and make it on his own to the rail as if nothing at all has happened. They can always go to Doc Ad later but for now they've got to walk that shattered pelvis, or whatever, out of the arena without letting on.

There's a particular expression cowboys wear to get this done. It's the expression of someone who has accidentally swallowed turpentine.

Rodeo isn't really about roping and riding. Ranches are about roping and riding. Rodeo is about damage and vast quantities of physical pain. It's not about if you get hurt, it's about when.

Mike was trying to concentrate. He had a chance to win. But with the unphysical and therefore unmanageable pain he already freighted—before he backed his horse into the box—he felt, figuratively, like that archetypal broken bull rider making for the rail, but the rail never got any closer, and the pain was not something you could take, later, to the hospital. All he could see was Sissy, galloping across the new-mown hayfield toward him, nothing on her horse but a halter, waving her hat, blond hair aflame in the sun. We have to go on living.

The steer came out of the chute and Potatoes was right on top of him, head down, ears back, bearing down. But the steer did something unpredictable. He zigged to the left just as Mike was about to throw. Then he zagged right and Mike had to throw long. It was a good loop but Mike had yet to dally.

As big as he was, and as strong, he was often able to yank an animal back into line by main strength just where most guys would let go. But there was Mike, at a hard gallop, nothing but the knot in the end of the rope in his hand and no thought of turning loose.

He got pulled out of the saddle and he still didn't let go. He hit the ground on his chest and he was plowing up the arena with his chin.

He was covered with dust, humiliated, heartsick, as he rose and did what everyone was expecting him to do, tourists and locals alike: he rose out of the dust and limped, head down, over to the rail fence.

What they were not expecting was for the great big long-haired cowboy to drape his arms over the top rail, hang his head, and begin to sob uncontrollably.

No one said anything. They were stunned. The locals knew, but it was part of the deal that they say nothing, do nothing, let it alone.

Pain here is repudiated as a matter of survival. All kinds of pain.

Then Oscar did something none of them would ever forget. He didn't say anything. He crossed the arena, looking at the ground, over to where Mike was weeping on the fence, and he gently, slowly, deliberately, dusted off Mike's shirt and jeans.

1985

OSCAR RIBBED HIM. "So, uh, Mike, when Liv first laid eyes on you it must have been love at first sight?"

Mike looked hard at Oscar to make sure he was getting the tone right and said, "No. I had to wear her down." No irony. That's the way it had been.

Liv was a radiant, high-boned Scandinavian beauty. Her father had been among the soldiers who had proved that one of the rules of modern warfare is you just don't mess around with Finns.

When she was twelve, Liv's father had been imported to the states as an instructor in mountain warfare. The army was proud of its Tenth Mountain Division, but having repulsed the Soviet invasion more often using cross-country skis and silent knives than guns, it was more or less proven that the Finns were in a class by themselves.

Liv went to high school in America, and after college she became an interpreter for the United Nations. She soon married a man of means who wanted to move out West and do the out-West thing.

They came to Laramie and opened the town's first ever ski shop. For Laramie, then, a ski shop was a little ahead of its time and so, apparently, was marriage for Liv's husband. They divorced.

So there was Liv, alone in Laramie, Wyoming, running a ski shop where no one cared about skiing. Alone. Miraculously, beautifully, miserably alone.

Mike didn't know how to ski, but he used to go into Liv's shop, almost unable to breathe, to price the socks. He priced socks on a regular basis, too shy to speak. Then one day he bought a pair. Nice wool ones. Handmade by Lapps. But he still couldn't say anything and had trouble getting bills out of his wallet.

Then, as fate would have it, they ended up at a party together. They were introduced. After slamming several Cuervo Golds, Mike asked Liv, the beautiful, dour Finn, to dance.

He made her laugh and feel at ease. Her accent made him dizzy. He spoke to her in childish terms of his work in the land-scape, close to nature. When he talked of his love of horses, those mysterious, fragile bundles of willingness, wildness, and grace, her eyes shone with tears. She was beginning to think that appearances and conveniences were overrated.

He asked her to come out and see the ranch he worked on. He wanted her to experience the kind of conversation with nature that agriculture is: you ask a question and wait, maybe decades, for the answer. Maybe the answer is no. "You don't really have any say-so."

He wanted her to see how beautiful his horse was as he grazed the green pasture under snowy peaks and indigo skies, the purple ridges in the middle distance. He wanted her to meet his dog.

So Mike learned how to ski and Liv learned how to ride. They got married horseback and all the guests had to be horseback, too, no matter how hokey they thought it was. Mike hand-sewed himself a buckskin wedding shirt.

After the reception the newlyweds rode out into a big pasture, away from the crowd. Blue and yellow wild flowers were bending in deep grass. They rode through a field of sweet clover so yellow it was gold.

Mike didn't know about the stallion that had been turned out into that same pasture that morning, nor had he noticed that the mare Liv was riding was in heat.

They were loping through the wind-wanton grass when the stallion galloped up, his member swinging impressively between his legs, and started to bear down on Liv's mare.

Her first impulse on seeing the muscley, flaring stud was to stop, which was fine with the stallion, who reared to mount Liv's mount. For someone who has never seen horses breed, the violence of it can be unnerving.

Mike reined in and wheeled his horse to watch, arms crossed on the saddle horn. Liv never forgot the brilliance of his grin at that moment when she looked at him imploringly. He was laughing his famous laugh.

She said, "What do I do now?"

Mike stopped laughing and blew a bubble. "Well, I'm not sure, but if I was you right now I think I'd put the spurs to her."

She did, and Mike sprang his horse forward and turned the stallion. They put some distance between themselves and the steed, who was willing but unable to run very well with that much of a hard-on.

Mike jumped down and let Liv through the gate, then shooed the still straggling stallion. Mike was still fairly cramped up with laughing. Liv was yelling at him—their first spat—but it didn't matter because it was all in Finnish.

Mike lifted her down and kissed her.

MONDAY

DAWN FLOCKED THE FLAT LANDSCAPE with yellow splotches and fired the sky, but clouds soon dissolved in heat, and Mike and his horse were left under the pale empty shell of blue. He rode under the tarp, covering himself and his horse in it, partly for shade, partly for camouflage. If they see me from the air, he thought, they'll just think I'm a piece of junk blown in from Colorado.

He rode. He kept the red vein of the county road in sight but distant as it ran into Rawlins. Rawlins glittered but nothing moved there.

The land was flat with a few distant bluffs like atolls. The earth was red and splotched with gray sage and green brush, explosive little tufts of quack grass. He was riding up a gradual rise, keeping the county road a mile to his right.

Even from that distance he recognized it, the big blue gooseneck trailer pulled by the red-and-white pickup caved in on the right front quarter. It was Oscar's. He pulled up and stopped. He stared for a long time. He saw no movement. He thought about it.

Could be a setup, he thought, but Oscar would sooner die than be used in any way to betray him. He counted on that. Could Oscar have found him before the Indian did?

The truck was parked at the top of a long wave of ridge that overlooked the Great Divide Basin. Right on the county road.

Mike snugged the tarp down over himself and the horse. He approached the trailer, wary as a fish, from behind. When he was a hundred yards off and still saw no movement he stopped again.

He recognized the horse in back and began to feel this was no trick.

He circled the trailer to the left. If that wasn't Oscar in the driver's seat, his shoulders slightly hunched, then the sheriff had made a mannequin to look just like him and put it under his hat. Mike rode up, still under the tarp.

Oscar got out of the truck and said, "Jesus, Mike, are you pretending to be a hill, or what?" He took off his hat and rubbed the back of his neck. He looked around him at the huge, sky-singed desert. "If so, you could have fooled me."

"Too bad it's not you I'm trying to fool."

"Yes, that is a shame."

"What are you doing here?"

"Waiting for you."

"How'd you know where I'd go?"

"I know you."

"Who else knows?"

"Doc."

"You seen Jim?"

"No."

Mike came out from under the tarp. "So?"

"I brought you a fresh horse."

"I need Potatoes for this."

"Potatoes ain't gonna make it."

"I know."

"I'll give you back your horse when you need him."

Mike looked down at Potatoes. "All right."

They unloaded the six-year-old sorrel mare from the trailer and switched the saddle. They filled Mike's panniers with supplies, a canteen of water. They loaded Potatoes Browning into the trailer. Mike mounted up and Oscar handed him up a cold six-pack of beer. Oscar stood by the horse with his hand on Mike's thigh. He gave it a pat and said, "You better get out of here before that Apache shows up and spoils everything. So long."

"So long."

Holding the six-pack on his pommel, Mike pushed the mare into a lope—the first time in days he'd been out of a walk—down into the huge palm of the Great Divide Basin that was all pale red and blue and green and yellow. It was like riding into a tangible sky. He joyed in the young horse's power. He felt invincible as he loped her over the soft million-year-old seabed.

He pulled her up after about two miles and twisted around in the saddle. He watched his friend drive the blue rig up the county road toward Rawlins.

JUNE 1990

MERRIWEATHER FINISHED THE BOOK he was reading, declared it sentimental tripe. He put it down and picked up the phone. Merry read a lot. Couldn't get enough of history and the people who made it. Audacity made history. History taught him that idealism was the same as foolishness. Often it was the direct cause of violence and death.

Pragmatism was the only philosophy that justified itself with the natural order. If everyone were a pragmatist, no one could be deceived. Everyone would have to be honest because you couldn't fool anyone else.

The book he'd been reading had been a history of sorts, a book locally written (and the prose style showed it) about a small ranch and the colorful local figures who'd wasted their lives on it.

The book focused on the peripatetic intelligence of one character in particular, his corny notion of being *part* of a place. "Hell," Merry said into the phone before anyone had answered it. If that character had been so smart, how come when he died the sum of his life's work had been sold at auction for a grand total of $120,000?

Smart my ass, thought Merry. I'll show them smart. I'll show them how to live off the land.

Someone came on the line. "Pete? Merry. Listen, I want financing to buy some more land up here pronto. This is going to be an amazing deal." Figures were mentioned, names mentioned, Snipes hung up.

He looked out the porch windows of his geodesic dome, through his own reflection, into the darkness. He knew they were there before he saw their eyes melting out of the night. There were seven cows standing around his Jeep, staring at him, chewing.

It was Sunday afternoon, and Jack Jackson stood in the middle of his hayfield with a small irrigating spade in one hand and a beer in the other.

"Jack Jackson? Merriweather Snipes."

Jack had to hold his beer with two fingers of his shovel hand in order to shake. Jack was good-looking, with almost female blue eyes and the physique of an alcoholic golfer. His eyes were teary. He was just starting to get drunk.

Snipes said, "How you liking the life of a gentleman rancher?"

"It's all right."

"You putting up all this good hay this year?"

Jackson looked at him with a dart of hopelessness, as if he

might cry. "I thought it was just like grass, like a lawn, you know? It grows. You mow it, you bale it, just driving around, you know?

"Then this cowboy, I guess he was a cowboy—he looked kind of like a hippie with a really dirty cowboy hat: big fella, from down in Livermore—anyway, he took me around and showed me the ditches.

"You know how many miles of ditches this place has? This guy told me they were all out of shape, all needing attention. He showed me how they worked—picking up water here, spilling it there, picking it up again in a lower ditch: flumes, headgates, and all—he showed me where they needed to be re-ditched or just hand-cleaned.

"Pretty nice guy, really. Then there's the fences. Four miles. Jesus. I just bought this place for the hunting and fishing. My wife likes to keep a couple of horses.

"I'm no rancher, gentleman or otherwise. I own a doughnut shop. Golf. I like to golf, not dig. I didn't spend my money just so I could have all this fucking work to do.

"I asked that guy—Arans, I think he said his name was—if he'd do the work, if I could pay him. He said the ditches were too far gone to get enough water on the son of a bitch. He said he didn't have the time. He offered to put cows on it and pay me for the pasture."

Snipes said, "Cows," and spit.

"I'd have to irrigate it anyway to get much out of it, even for pasture; that's what the cowboy or the hippie or whatever he was said."

Merry said, "Word has it you're plenty affluent enough to hire whatever you need. After all, you bought the place outright, didn't you?"

"Sure we did. For a song. The old man's legacy got divided among several relatives. They wanted their money out of it as soon as possible. They auctioned off all the machinery and stuff and took the first offer on the land. We got it for a song.

"At first we couldn't believe how lucky we were. We had to pinch ourselves. But things that seem too good to be true are too good to be true. I found that out."

Snipes felt the predator in his soul awake. He asked, "How much did you give for it?"

"A hundred twenty thousand."

Snipes said, "You couldn't get your money out of it now."

Jack looked surprised. He tipped back and drained his beer and pinched the can. "What?"

"Well, you know, all the development around here locally. Kind of glutted the market. It's made the land prices fall," he lied. "A lot of these ranchette owners just bought a bunch of lies covered with sagebrush—you know, 'Land is a good investment. It always goes up. Year-round access.' When they found out they'd been cheated, a lot of them put their parcels back on the market. The prices fell and they still can't get rid of them. Nope. Your timing was off."

Jack looked sadly down at his spade. He said, "Well."

Then Merry said, "Of course, you could sell it to me. I have a kind of sentimental attachment to it. See, when I was growing up the old guy who lived here was kind of like a father to me. My mentor, you might say. Yep, I spent a lot of happy summers in this hayfield. I'd like to fix it up and make the hay again.

"Financially I know it sounds crazy, but money isn't everything now, is it? I wish they'd contacted me when they first sold it, but I was out of the country. Paraguay. I'll give you a hundred thousand for it. I'll write you a check right now. You know you can only get in here by car about seven months of the year."

"Yeah, I found that out. I should have known. You know we actually met that Van Waning guy once. It was years ago, just after we got married. We drove up here in May. We got stuck in a snowdrift just up the road there, no shovel, no jack, no chains. We walked back to the old guy's house and asked him if he had anything that would get us out of the drift. He said he thought he did. So he walked with us up to his shed, and slid the door back. There was this huge old army weapons carrier, heavy son of a bitch, chained up on all fours with chains as big around as your wrist. He reached behind the door and handed me a scoop shovel. He said, 'This should get you out.' I thought he was kind of mean."

Jack looked at the ground and thought deeply for about three seconds. He looked up bleary-eyed at Snipes.

"Let's talk. Come on up to the house."

When Merriweather got back to his dome he made straight for the cell phone. "Pete? I got that hot deal going. I'll need your support with the others, but it's going to make you really happy when I tell you. . . . Yeah, a whole ranch, three hundred and twenty acres, beautiful hay meadow, antique log buildings, heaven on earth. . . . Right. . . . No, don't list it in Colorado. I have a better idea. Just list it in Hollywood. . . . No, I'm not kidding. . . . No, I'm not crazy. Haven't you heard of Montana? One point five million. . . . That's what I said. Trust me."

MONDAY

THERE IS A HOLE in the middle of the Continental Divide, where the rain that falls finds no river, where the rain that falls finds nowhere to go but back. It's the Great Divide Basin, which welcomes passage through the backbone of the earth.

Favored by travelers since the beginning of human time in America, it's where people in cars get their impression (lucky for inhabitants of all species) that Wyoming is all horizon and wind, and in winter it's a world of blowing snow. A lot of jackrabbits, sagebrush, and ghostly antelope. In cars people fail to notice the cloud-haunted immensity above, and geologic time writ large and red in bluffs, mesas, overthrusts, absent oceans in blood-drenched sun.

The middle of nowhere. There's a hole in the middle of nowhere, a place: the Red Desert.

What is there—besides the hissing interstate with its huge snow fences like sutures in the earth, besides the jackrabbits and sketchy antelope grazing down the distance, the great preponderance of sky, the paradox of crossing the Divide twice to cross it once—is a lushness of small bright things: hardy, civil grasses; humble yellow and dove gray and blue mosslike plants; splashes of blue, orange, and yellow lichen on red, red rock; little fairy rings of blue pebbles that memorize where a willing flower thrived and died and prove there isn't enough rain to scramble them back from symmetry.

JUNE 1991

OUT IN THE SHOP Ad was pegging and gluing a shattered chair leg, salvaging what he could. His house was synecdoche for what they were doing to the land itself, but inverted, because they vandalized the land by building on it.

He looked idly out the shop door and saw a plume of dust burning up the road. From the clip he guessed it was Oscar. Ad pulled out his pocket watch: two-thirty. Oscar and his family were due up for a picnic supper. They were bringing a bucket of chicken. So Ad began to wonder as he tightened the C-clamp and stepped into the sun glare.

It was Oscar, all right. Ad heard the ranch junk clanking in the pickup bed before he heard the motor. Oscar killed the engine and hit the driver's door with his shoulder to unstick it, stepped down, and limped over. "Howdy."

"Howdy yourself. Looks like that leg is still gimpy."

"Yeah, I just don't bounce back like I used to could."

"Maybe you got so much hardware in it by now you can't hardly lift it."

"Could be."

"What's up?"

"Well, I just came to tell you we can't make it up for supper tonight. I have to meet a sick horse down at CSU for surgery. I was wondering if tomorrow would be OK."

"Sure. You could have left a message on the radio. You didn't have to drive all the way up here to tell me in person."

"Oh, you know me. I can go to Collins through Cherokee Park. Any excuse to get up here and take a look at this country, the old ranch."

"Looks like hell, doesn't it?"

"Well, all the improvement didn't improve it any. Still, from up here the view kinda swallows all them shacks and trash heaps, puts things in perspective."

"That's how come they can keep selling it."

"I guess."

"Want some coffee?"

"No, I gotta go."

. . .

The next evening the Rose family came up for supper. Oscar's four kids flushed out of the cab like quail. Ad remembered Oscar saying he and Mary were going to stop having kids as soon as they found out what was causing them.

Ad hugged Mary, and as they walked toward the house he noticed Oscar was limping on *both* sides. "What did you do now, Oscar?"

"Don't ask."

"I'm asking."

"Well, you know Red's pony?"

Red was Oscar's oldest son, seven. All Oscar's kids were redheads, but the oldest kid got the traditional appellation. Ad wondered if one of Oscar's daughters had been born first, would they have called her Red? Ad guessed yes.

"You mean the black one, about ten hands high?"

"That's the one. Well, the little sucker wasn't acting right this morning with the kid, so I thought I'd get on him and give him a lesson."

"Don't your heels make furrows in the dirt when you ride that thing?"

"Yeah, but he can carry me. Anyway, I wanted to teach that ornery little bugger some manners, and I also had a bull I needed to drive into a pen."

Ad sensed the beginning of a classic. "Yeah?"

"I went out there and started chousing that bull on the pony. Bull got fighty on us and kind of charged. Caught me right below the knee. Picked me and the pony right up off the ground and threw us about twenty feet."

Ad grinned. "So what did you end up teaching that pony?"

Oscar tilted his head, as if listening for the answer. Then he said, "Humility."

Behind the two men, the four kids were swirling shrilly around Althea's old sandbox. Except for Red, who sat in the middle of it. It was starting to get dark. Red had a tin cup full of sand and a spoon. He was eating the sand with the spoon. One mouthful after another, serenely chewing. Crunch, crunch, crunch.

Ad said, "That's one hell of a tough little kid."

Oscar said, "Damned if he ain't."

SUNDAY

AD SAT ON HIS ROCK. It was an ordinary, crumbly granite boulder a hundred yards from the house. From his bedroom window—indeed, from his bed—he could see the whole Lara mie Basin, pulling its hugeness into its vacuum, blending from beige to powder blue, and, levitating above it, the Medicine Bow and Snowy Range. The Snowies make the Medicine Bow a laureate.

All this Ad could see from his house, but a small expeditionary force of limber pines had sprung from the main body of the timber and obscured the foreground. They made a perfect windbreak, made the house quiet in winter when all around it screamed.

In order to see the whole thing—his own house and the stand of timber he built it from; Deadman; Bull Mountain; Red Mountain; Jelm; Sheep Mountain and the Snowies; the stretch of the Basin; Laramie Peak; and Boulder Ridge reclining into the vanishing point, an odalisque to the northeast—he had to go out to the rock.

He liked seeing his house from a distance, in the distance. He took a pull from a bottle of single malt. He tried to let the distances sink in and simplify him.

SEPTEMBER 1989

HUNCHED OVER on the tall kitchen stool with his head lowered, Mike listened to the telephone. He covered his eyes with his free hand and shook his head. "OK," he said, and "OK." It was Oscar on the phone, and he wanted to go over to the desert mesas and run wild horses.

Mike had mixed feelings about getting involved in Oscar's day. First there was Oscar's absolute lack of any instinct for self-preservation. He set a scary standard. And when it came to hours, he was out of the house by six and rarely home by ten. He lived on peanut butter sandwiches and Instant Breakfast. But Mike wanted to ride after wild horses, too.

The morning they'd agreed on dawned crisp and fine. Mike loaded Potatoes Browning into the trailer and drove up to Oscar's. Mike was surprised when he pulled into Oscar's yard. He was expecting to see Oscar's rope horse saddled and ready to load. It could be a long day. Instead it was just Oscar, who threw his saddle into the back of the pickup and said, "Let's go."

Mike almost said, Aren't you forgetting something? but didn't.

Oscar had a plan to catch the wave of fashion for paint horses without any cash outlay. Instead of buying a stud, he planned to capture a wild stallion and pasture-breed him to some good quarter horse brood mares.

The mares would be tame, so, once foaled out, he'd be able to bring the colts in and gentle them with the rest of his young horses. People who liked the idea of a paint, he figured, would love the idea of a wild sire for their pets.

Plus, it would give everyone something to talk about. "That Oscar." He never meant to break the stud horse—that is, probably not.

Finally Mike said, as he shifted into third, "You figure on just walking up to one of those mustangs and throw your saddle on him? Maybe you should have worn your sneakers."

"No, I'll just ride one of old Ronnie's ranch horses they aren't using."

Mike pushed back his sorry black hat and rubbed his forehead. He knew there was more.

"Yeah, there's this one horse hasn't been ridden for a while. Got some real good speed on him."

"How long has it been since anybody rode him?"

"Oh, couple of years."

Mike stared. "How come they don't ride him?"

"Oh, he bucks a little when you first get on him. But, man, is he fast. By now I reckon he's about half wild. Get two jobs done at once. And besides"—he looked at Mike—"what better way to catch a wild horse than with one that's half wild?" He grinned.

Mike sighed. "I guess."

They pulled into a big open pasture. Oscar held the gate. There were seven horses in the middle of a three-hundred-acre field, watching them tensely. There was no corral to run them into. The ground was boggy in places.

"It's that big gray gelding."

"Can you catch him with grain?"

"It'd be worth a try."

"Did you bring any grain?"

"Nope. Drive over there and pull your rig in next to the corner of the fence and make sort of a pen. Then unload your horse."

Mike pulled in and cut the motor. He got out.

Oscar took the lariat off his saddle and said, "OK. You got the horse. I'll wait here."

Mike thought he was getting set up. He just wasn't quite sure how yet. He said under his breath, "We all spend the day somehow."

He rode out in a big circle around the horses, then diagonaled toward them to ease them near the trailer. They stood their ground until he was close. The gray gelding snorted, and they all bolted and ran curving away.

Putting the steel to his horse, Mike took a line to cut them off at the fence. The seven horses blasted down the fence line and Potatoes raced to cut them off, which he managed, with a sliding stop to the fence. His chest was pushing against the wires when he stopped, and the rasty bunch reversed to the right direction, but way too fast.

Mike spun and quartered across the corner of the fence. Sure enough, they swerved away from the trailer, gray in the lead, and when they did, Mike turned them on the other fence.

Winded, they trotted toward the corner. When Mike saw Oscar's big grin—he was leaning against the trailer with the rope—he knew the game wasn't over.

He was bringing them down the fence line nicely, nearing the trailer, when the gray rolled back on his haunches, causing all the others to do the same. They came right over him, parting around him like a wave. He made a move on the gray but it was late.

The only thing to do with broomtails like these was wear them down, which he proceeded to do. After half an hour of running them up and down the fence line they quit. Mike walked them into the three-sided trap the horse trailer made in the corner. Oscar walked in behind them to hold them there, and they began to prance and mill nervously.

Then the gray ran right at Oscar and never shied when Oscar raised his arms to shoo him. The gray ran over him, knocking Oscar to the ground. Mike wasn't there to turn him, but they held the other horses till they calmed.

Mike went back after the gray. This time he came in easily because the others were there, and horses hate to be alone. As he passed Oscar to join his buddies, and before he could think up more mischief, Oscar threw a loop over his head and he froze.

Oscar started talking to him and easing up to him along the riata. The horse was a statue wired to explode. Oscar talked and scratched the horse's forehead. He kept talking as he eased his arm over the horse's neck and haltered him. He led him to the other side of the trailer and tied him to it. He ran his hand down the gray's neck and scratched behind his ears. They turned the other horses back into the pasture.

It could have been any horse any day of the year, the way Oscar threw the saddle on him. Oscar said, "We'd just as well ride from here," and gave the cinch an extra pull since he knew the horse was going to buck.

Mike sat Potatoes Browning and watched as Oscar bridled the gray horse and dropped the halter, leaving it hanging by the lead from the trailer. Holding the horse by the reins, he stepped over to the cab of the pickup and emptied his pockets of several small note pads and pens. He took his wallet out and slid it under the seat.

He flipped the off rein over the horse's neck, swung up, and quickly found the stirrup. He stayed ready. He knew what was coming. He nudged the horse, and both riders stepped smartly into the pasture. Mike was waiting for the explosion too.

Something passed between the two horses, an invisible communication, a threat, and Potatoes Browning shied and doubled under. Mike hadn't been expecting anything from his horse. He hit the ground hard and stood up, astonished.

Oscar started to chuckle, then laugh, then howl uncontrollably. He folded over in his saddle. The gray hadn't done anything. Then he did something so unusual, if it hadn't been witnessed it would never be believed.

As Mike described it, the horse kind of sucked himself in and kicked into something like a backward buck. Then Oscar was sitting on the ground, but he was still in the saddle. Stranger, he was still holding the reins in his hand and the bridle lay on the ground in front of him, like he was still riding but lacked the horse.

At first he thought the cinch had broken, but when he picked up the saddle and looked, the cinch was still cinched. And he was holding the reins. The horse had sucked himself out of the saddle, and the saddle going over his head had raked the bridle off.

The gray horse was running across the pasture to join the others where they grazed. They looked up, unimpressed.

Both men sat down where they were. Mike said, "At least my reins are attached to a horse."

Oscar said, "That would have made a good story, only no one would believe it."

"Isn't there some other way we could have done this?"

"Oh, yeah," Oscar replied. "There's lots of things we could have done, but compared to what we did, all of them are boring."

TUESDAY

JIM GOT OFF HIS HORSE and looked at the tracks where the rubber-booted horse was loaded into the trailer, and where the shod horse took off at a lope across the desert. He knelt and drew a picture of the sun in the red dust, considering the possibilities. Would you call this aiding or abetting? What was abetting, anyway?

Anyone who would give Mike his truck and trailer and ride decoy into the desert would be in a hell of a lot of trouble, same as he would be if he got caught with Mike's horse. Could Mike have hijacked some rancher's rig and taken to the highway? What, and leave the guy with a horse he would then not ride back to town but lead into the maw of emptiness? No. Mike had a fresh mount and was now bound to cross the desert. And he had help.

Jim turned his horse's head toward town. He had a fresh horse, too. Things were getting interesting. He'd make a couple of calls.

JUNE 1989

AD PULLED THE DRAWKNIFE BACK toward him and the tree bark curled into a gyre. Steady as a faucet leak, sweat dripped from the brim of his straw hat. He was building a new barn. He pulled like an oarsman, at a steady pace, straddling the tree trunk, scooting down as he went.

It was mindlessly pleasing work, the way the bark peeled easily when the drawknife found the sweet spot between bark and
wood, the steady ache in his forearms. But it was slow. One hour
to peel one log. Then lifting and fitting with handsaw and axe.

A man working alone, by hand, can strip, lay up, and peg three
logs in a day. Maybe four if the logs are straight, which they
aren't.

Once peeled, the butt end of the log can be lifted and the log
dragged under the wall. Each log was twenty-four feet long and,
once cured, weighed about four hundred pounds. Ad felt the
stab in his lower back and breathed, "Just what the doctor
ordered."

Then he wrapped a log chain around it and, with block and
tackle rigged on a spar, he hoisted the next log onto the last log
and dogged it so it wouldn't roll off and kill him.

He had one end dogged, had climbed down the ladder,
chained and hoisted the other end, climbed up the other ladder
to dog the other end. That's the problem with working alone:
you spend most of your time going up and down ladders.

He was setting the second dog when he heard a motor. He
remembered that, as a child, it was more common to hear air-
planes than cars. The whole family would come out on the
porch to watch an airplane. Not anymore.

All the same, no one Ad didn't know ever came down the
road that ran through the yard. Whoever it was would stop and
say hello. So he kept working as the vehicle climbed the grade
below the house.

He was standing on the ladder, marking the log end with a
level, when he heard the car not stop. He turned his head, holding the level and pencil still, to see who was driving through. It
was a Jeep he didn't recognize, which accelerated as it passed.

OK. Sometimes tourists got lost. He decided not to worry about a minor annoyance. So when the Jeep came down the other way he would have stopped the driver and explained the situation: NO TRESPASSING signs mean something along the lines of NO TRESPASSING.

Only at that moment he couldn't because he had a log hanging from the blocks that wasn't dogged or even tied off. He couldn't let go of the rope. Worse, this time it wasn't just a Jeep, it was six Jeeps, a convoy, going like hell, raising a thunderhead of dust, like they owned the place.

All Ad could do was to hang on to the rope and read the license plate on the lead Jeep. It was a Colorado plate personalized to read: SELLIT. The number of vehicles and their velocity ripped open a headgate of rage, anger compounded by his present inability to do anything about it.

Once he had the log secured he climbed down and walked out to the road. He looked down across the prairie and saw them turn on the new-bladed road the developers had carved across the creek. "OK, assholes, I'll be here for you when you come back."

And come back they did, only this time without the one licensed SELLIT. Ad was fitting a quarter-notched corner—rolling the log out, cutting and fitting, rolling it back, looking, rolling it out, first one side, then the other, hewing high spots off the middle that kept the log from settling—when he heard them coming up the hill.

With the double-bitted axe like a baby in his arms, he climbed down and walked out and stood in the middle of the road. He hadn't meant to be holding the axe, he'd just forgotten to put it down.

The axe might have been why the caravan stopped a hundred

yards off, as if to think things over, and then approached at a cautious pace. He imagined five guys digging out pistols, but he didn't care. When he thought about it later he thought, That's what scares me about me.

They came up and stopped, and Ad stepped around to the window of the first guy in line. The guy behind the wheel was pinched and dirty-looking. He was wadded up behind the wheel like old Kleenex. He mustered a shit-eating grin and said, "Howdy."

Ad struggled to suppress the threat in his tone. "You lost?"

"No," the man said. "We know where we are. We're landowners. We're buying land up here. Each one of us here's got forty acres."

"Forty acres." Ad whistled. "Well, right now you're in my front yard. Either you are lost or you are trespassing. Take your pick."

"Our real estate agent up here told us this was part of the Proprietors Association. Said you liked it so much up here you bought a whole section from him. As an Association member, it says in the Covenants, you have to let us use this road. It's our main access."

Ad thumbed the edge of his axe. He took a deep breath and whistled it out in one long falling note. "My father bought this section forty years ago. I don't belong to anything you belong to except the miserable, lying, ham-fisted human race. If that land pimp told you what you say he did, he lied. Maybe you should ask him what other lies he told you."

The man's pinched face became vague, confused, a little frightened. A couple of guys from other Jeeps were getting out and coming up to see what was going on. Ad glanced at them as if they were shrubs and turned back to the first. "Did that real estate agent tell you you could access your ranchette in winter? Did he sell you your plots in June when the grass is green and tell you the creeks run high all summer? Did he tell you you could drill a well and find water less than five hundred feet down through solid granite? Did he sell you your mineral rights? Did he tell you you were lost, trespassing, sorry?"

The man just stared. He licked his thin lips. One of the troop sidled up and asked, "What's going on, Mel?"

"Guy says we can't use this road."

"The hell we can't. It says so in the Covenants."

Ad spat. "I'm not *in* the fucking Association. Do the Covenants say I am? You'll have to go around."

"How far is it to go around?"

"You have to go back down to the crossroads and go right. That's *your* road. It runs right through a seep, but you have four-wheel drive, winches, right? It'll give you something to do with these Jeeps. It's about four miles to the Forest Service road."

The third man barked, "What? We have to drive four extra miles? That ain't very neighborly, friend."

Ad didn't look at him. "I'm not your friend. We can be neighbors, but you can't run through my yard. Now turn around and get out of here. I have work to do."

"I'm going to check on this."

"There's a lot of things you ought to check on. You ought to check on how come you bought forty acres of cow pasture with no trees and no water on it."

"If you are bullshitting us," said the pinched man, "you are going to hear about it."

Ad said, "Right. Now turn around the way you came and have a nice day." He turned and walked back to his log work as the convoy revved and backed and filled and threw gravel.

It was obviously not the end of anything, and Ad thought, I got to learn to be easier on those dummies. They don't mean any harm.

The next day Ad was up on the wall drilling a one-and-a-quarter-by-eighteen-inch hole down through two logs and into a third to set a peg when the Jeep with the SELLIT license plates drove up and stopped. He had expected this. He didn't get down or stop turning the brace, and sweat dripped from the brim of his hat.

The guy was coming to talk; a visit was not trespassing. Ad watched out of the corner of his eye. It was the man he'd run off for electronic prospecting. He wore a Western-cut shirt with a turquoise bolo tie, jeans with a silver-and-turquoise belt buckle the size of a dinner plate, alligator boots.

He swaggered behind a protruding belly that reminded Ad of someone pushing a wheelbarrow. He wondered if the guy had ever been on a horse, doubted it, and wanted to say, You ought to get a wheelbarrow for that thing, but remembered he'd decided to be nice.

The man was bareheaded and wore aviator mirrored sunglasses. "Dr. Trent?"

Ad stopped cranking the sweep and looked down. "That'd be me."

"Can I have a word with you?"

Ad hung the drill brace on the top log and climbed down the ladder. The man caused a grin to appear on his face and extended his hand. "Merriweather Snipes."

"OK." Ad took his hand and noticed the guy was trying really hard to grip Ad's hand in a forceful manner. "What can I do for you?"

"Well, Dr. Trent, I tell ya. Things are changing around here. They're gonna keep changing. It's progress. It's what America is all about. Now I can sympathize with how you feel. After all, I'm a rancher too. Fact is, I've owned several ranches."

Snipes squatted down, picked up a sage stick, and started to doodle in the dirt. Ad looked down at the sunburned pate. He rolled his eyes. It was clear the man wanted him to squat down and doodle with him in some trite ritual of cowboy bonding.

Ad thought, I don't think so, and stayed standing, looking down, saying nothing.

When Merry realized that Ad was not going to squat with him he felt suddenly self-conscious. He was stuck, stranded in his gesture. He decided he hated Adkisson Trent. But he pushed on, relieving his awkwardness every so often by looking up sidelong.

"Yep. Things are changing and there's nothing anybody can do to stop it. You can't stop progress, now, can you? If you get in its way it'll swallow you like the whale swallowed Jonah." He looked up. Ad looked down. "There are a lot of new folks moving in up here. A lot of folks who just want their own little piece of heaven. You can understand that." He paused.

Ad said, "So?"

"So these new neighbors you are going to have just want to get along."

"How many new neighbors are you getting me to get along with?"

"Before it's over?"

"Yeah, before it's over."

"About four hundred."

"Holy Jesus."

"You can't stop progress, Doc."

"Don't call me Doc."

"It's possible you'll be called on to help these folks from time to time."

"Right."

"And the other thing is about the road."

"What about it?"

"These folks need a way to get to their parcels."

"Their parcels?"

"That's what we call 'em. Parcels."

"Parcels."

"Yeah, they need a way to get there and they'd sure appreciate it if you'd be neighborly and let them use this road."

"All four hundred of them?"

"Oh, it wouldn't be so bad. Mostly on weekends to get home."

"No."

"What?"

"I said no."

"That's sure not very neighborly of you."

"Do you think I'm stupid? If I open the road to any of them it's open to all. They're not just going home all the time. Once there's a precedent of access I'd forfeit the right to close it ever. The last thing I need is four hundred deeply confused refugees ripping through my yard in their Jeeps."

"Well, I wish you'd think it over."

"I did."

Merry felt like it was safe to stand up. He sighed. "I've observed you let *some* people drive through here."

"Friends. People I know. People who come to visit or check on cattle."

"Well, what if I was your friend? Could I use the road? Just me?"

"No."

"It would save me having to drive all the way around and getting stuck in that swamp. My forty is right where your road comes out."

"No."

"That's not very neighborly, let aside friendly."

"I'm not very friendly. If I let you use the road I have to let all of them use it. If you were the only one moving in it would be different, but you brought a whole city in here to keep you company. The answer is no.

"Listen, Mr. Snipes, it's nothing personal. I'm a physician. If anyone needs medical attention in an emergency I'll help them. But the reason I come up here is to get away from people and their noise. The road stays closed."

Merry removed his sunglasses and blinked in the light. His gaze was vaguely menacing, but he looked like he might cry, too. He rubbed the lenses on his shirt and turned to leave. "Suit yourself."

Ad watched him waltz his gut over to the Jeep. He called after, "You building something down there?"

Over his shoulder Snipes said, "Oh, yeah. Yeah, I am. I'm going to live up here full-time. You'll have to come over."

Ad didn't have to come over. After his shift in the emergency room he came back to the ranch and slept for ten hours. It was late morning, and the June sun was hot wax on the prairie. He had work to do. Mike's cows would be there in a week, and he had fifteen miles of fences to fix.

Ad liked fixing fence. It was a good excuse to get out and walk. He returned home midafternoon for a snack. When he cut the motor of his pickup he heard it, an unidentifiable rumble, not unlike thunder, not unlike a jet or a Union Pacific diesel. It was some kind of engine, or engines, getting closer. Road grader? Bulldozer? He walked to the middle of the road and looked. He looked toward the east cattle guard and waited. The rumble grew louder. Whatever it was was big and it was coming. He waited.

When he saw it he couldn't have been more surprised if it had been a whale on wheels. He said, "Holy Jesus Readymix." A cement truck was seething down the road toward him. Understanding fell into place like a window unshattering. He felt the rage come into his shoulders and blossom into his head, and he would have gone inside for a rifle if there had been time.

Then he saw the second cement truck following. Then the third, fourth, fifth, sixth. They were bearing down like huge stampeding insects. Ad stood in the middle of the road and they came on. The closer and louder they got, the smaller he felt, but he stood.

He was too angry to feel relieved when he heard the gear jamming and brake squealing. When the lead truck sighed to a stop, he walked around to the driver's door and looked up at a man in a smeared polka-dot red cap. He had big ears. He was eating an unlit cigar. His face was flushed. They both yelled at once: "Get out of the goddamned road!" and "This is a private road!"

Ad said, "Where are you going with all this shit?"

The driver looked ahead, then looked back at Ad. "Some guy named Snipes. Are you him?"

"Hardly. You're on the wrong road." Ad thought, My fight is not with this son of a bitch.

"Yeah. I know. The road they told us to go on goes right through a swamp. We already got one truck mired and needed three others to pull it out. It was a mess. Can we get through here?"

Ad looked down to the crossroads and considered not letting them pass. This was an obvious setup. "This road is closed."

The driver spat out his chewed cigar butt and said, "Do you know what happens to a truckload of cement if you keep it spinning too long?"

Ad knew but said nothing.

"The friction from turning seizes it up and the concrete hardens in the barrel. I got six trucks here that that's about to happen to. I got no beef with you, mister. We can't get through that other road. So either you let us through or we dump six truckloads of cement right here in your front yard."

Ad knew he was beat. "Get out of here. Straight down there. Use the gate, not the cattle guard. Turn left at the crossroads."

He stood back in their thunder as they passed. He watched them diminish down the road. Snipes wasn't pouring footings, he was pouring a solid pad. It would be there forever. The guy had a lot of damned money.

He went into the house and poured a glass of single malt. He thought about what he was up against.

JUNE 1993

MIKE WAS PRACTICING on his current best horse for an upcoming cutting in Laramie. Though Liv was no rider when he met her, Mike was getting her to be more relaxed and confident in the saddle. She wanted to learn so she could help more outside, take on decision making, feel less wifey and peripheral.

Mike gave her a green-broke three-year-old to bring along herself. Liv was more accomplished and more confident every day. The filly was coming along nicely, and Liv was starting to feel pretty good about horses.

They walked out to the corral together. The sun was hot, and the whole day and everything in it was drowsy. They groomed and saddled and brought some calves into the arena.

Liv's job was to hold the bunch against one end of the arena so that Mike could sort out a calf and let Freckles go to work— head down, haunches under, feet like Muhammad Ali—keeping the calf from dodging back into the herd.

They worked five calves and Freckles was looking sweet. Mike was concentrating on sitting the horse's moves, flowing with the electric reflexes. He didn't hear or see anything until he saw Liv's horse bucking, riderless, at the end of the arena. He reined up and rolled back and saw Liv, like a length of chain on the ground.

He jumped down and ran. She wasn't moving. She was lying on her side with her face turned skyward. Mike knelt down and said her name. There was a crumb of corral dirt in her eye, and he tried, delicately, to brush it away. He said her name. When his finger touched her open eye she didn't blink.

There would be no funeral service. Even days later Mike couldn't feel the pain he knew, eventually, he must. He was trying to think of a way to tell Liv's mother, who lived in a home for Alzheimer's patients.

The mother spoke only Finnish. Before giving her up to the home, Mike and Liv had tried to take care of her themselves. Mike noticed that every time he entered the room the same phrases were exchanged between mother and daughter. Mike asked Liv what her mother had said.

Liv said, "She said, 'Who's the big guy?'"

"She says that every time I come in the room."

"Right."

"And what do you say?"

"I say, 'That's my husband, Mike.'"

"And then?"

"She says, 'I don't like him.'"

Remembering that brought it all down and he wept. It was the beginning of the low light and the long nail.

There was no funeral, but friends came by to visit, bring food, talk about everything but. They'd mumble a parting condolence as though they thought it was their fault. All except Jim Thomas, the Mescalero, because Mike asked.

"Did you ever lose anyone real close?"

"Yeah."

"What did you do?"

"What do you mean, what did I do?"

"To get rid of the feeling?"

Jim looked at him deadpan. "Oh, that. I just did a sweat, burned some sweet grass, did a sun dance, talked to the Shaman, and then I felt fine."

"You're kidding."

"You think I'm a fool?"

But the sun dance idea stuck. He'd thought about it before, a little abstractly, but now there was an imperative that compelled him. He thought he might have survived the grief, but the guilt . . . he wouldn't make it. He needed help. There was a lot of tradition in the world to suggest the efficacy of flesh mortification.

A guy in Montana ran sun dances for money, like they were raft trips or something. He had a big following. Mike needed help, but he didn't think he needed a priest.

Maybe punishment would purge the guilt. Maybe he could at least replace his grief and guilt with physical pain for a while.

He climbed a grassy hill and set a pole with two nylon ropes attached to the top. He took off his shirt. He pinched the flesh above his left nipple and pushed his clasp knife through it. It wasn't too bad. He made another pinch next to it and pushed the knife through. As though he were doctoring an animal, he felt distant from what he was doing. Blood wept rivulets down his chest. He made two more cuts above his right nipple. On the right and on the left he ran wood dowels through the slots. He tied the dowels to the nylon ropes. He leaned back, hanging by his flesh from the ropes, which looked like they were disappearing into the sky. Because of his size, though, the flesh ripped almost immediately and he fell on his back. He didn't get anything out of it but scars.

The ashes came in a bronze urn that said CREMAINS on the lid. The lid was held on with a hex nut. Mike hated that. He needed a crescent wrench to loosen it. He emptied the ashes into a leather pouch and hung it from his neck. He saddled Potatoes Browning.

It was three miles to the Poudre River, where it writhed through a deep canyon. Mike rode down and in until he found a good sandbar where he could enter the current. He kept riding in until the horse started swimming and he slid from the saddle and hung to the side.

He loosened the opening of the pouch and emptied it of ashes. It was as if his throat were cut and he was bleeding ashes into the river. As he and the horse drifted downstream they left a cloud of ashes in the water. Then Mike turned the horse's head and let him swim to where he could get his feet under him again.

JUNE 1993

A WEEK AFTER LIV, everyone's days were still stained. Ad saw Murphy, the ditch rider, coming down the road. They pulled their pickup windows up even and turned the motors off. They talked. Ad interrupted what he was saying and pointed. Running down the hill toward them were a man with a rifle and a little boy. They came up and stopped. The man was flushed, pouring sweat, breathless, hysterical. The kid was just scared.

The man panted out how he'd shot a deer and wounded it and it ran off and they followed it but then it jumped a fence and dove down a ravine. He couldn't track it. He needed help.

Either he didn't know he was poaching, or he thought everyone was a poacher.

Ad took the keys out of his truck and hopped in the back of Murphy's truck with the mighty hunters. The man looked doughy, citified, out of shape.

"Where did your bullet hit this deer?"

"In the stomach, real low down."

The boy, who had no rifle but carried an enormous pair of binoculars, was calming down and starting to look around. They drove to where the buck had entered the draw.

Ad and the man went into the draw, Ad tracking, the man following with his .30-'06. The man was puffing again. "Can you carry my gun for a while? It's really heavy." Incredulous, Ad took the rifle.

Murphy and the boy drove around and down the side of the draw on the open slope so they could see the buck if he came out. Ad followed the small explosive tracks and occasional gobs of blood. They came to a wire fence where the buck had jumped over. A six-foot length of intestine adorned the wires. Ad was amazed the buck had made it this far, dragging his guts on the ground, losing the last of his blood.

After a mile of following at a trot, the spoor led them up out of the draw. Murphy was waiting where the tracks crossed the road. The exhausted man straggled to the truck and heaved himself into the back. Ad handed him his rifle.

Ad said, "He'll go down to the creek now. Go over to that rock where you can see down into the creek bed and wait. I'll go behind him and he'll come down."

Ad crested the hill and saw the man crouched behind the rock, taking aim. Ad thought he wouldn't give two cents for that meat now. Then he saw the buck for the first time, a hundred yards distant, on the far side of the creek. The animal was walking forward, head up, dragging his intestines. His tongue lolled. He couldn't run anymore but he walked with precision and grace. Head up, he walked serenely forward.

The .30-'06 crashed and the bullet struck the ground four feet in front of the deer. Another shot, again to the right. Another.

"Jesus Christ," Ad screamed. "Give me the rifle!" He knew if the rifle was not sighted in, as it appeared not to be, he could correct for it. A fourth shot hit the deer in the shoulder and he went down.

Ad turned away, then turned back just in time to see this: the man was down on his knees trying to cut the buck's throat, but his knife was too dull. He grasped the haft in both hands, raised the knife over his head, and began stabbing the deer in the neck over and over like a movie murderer.

Ad walked back to his truck feeling like hell. He wondered what that kid had learned.

TUESDAY

INSIDE THE GREAT DIVIDE BASIN is a deeper basin, the Red Desert. Red baked earth that turns to dust at a touch, squirreltail grass, low-growing flora halfway between moss and flower with green foundation and light pink tops that, to Mike, were nameless; same ocean pebbles, all colors, carefully arranged. No rain, no springs, no drainages, barely any ups and downs, featureless as the surface of a frozen lake.

There were bright blue and orange and green splashes of lichen on the vermilion sandstone, bright green and red cacti like spilled paint on a studio floor. They made Mike dizzy. He could see semis on the distant interstate, gliding silently along, like destiny, a destiny he'd missed. The trucks were happy colors, like the cars of a mile-long train that went by too and was gone. The highway was lined with huge snow fences like pews full of praying hands. The hills were the same color as the red cacti and were speckled with silver sage that shimmered even at night. The desert roared away from him like sleep.

At night he crossed the interstate through a fenced underpass meant for cattle and antelope. The traffic exploded over his head like white water he was under, and gradually faded behind him in the night.

1990

MIKE AND OSCAR SAT on the corral fence watching two twelve-year-old neighbor boys practice team roping on some steers Mike had provided for them. The men were comparing their debts. Mike had missed so many payments on his ranch he was a hair away from being evicted. Oscar was living in town, renting pasture. His entire vet practice got vacuumed into his ranching habit and he was still hopelessly in debt.

Between go-rounds the two boys talked. "My dad makes me eat everything I kill: I've eaten gopher, toad, rattlesnake—it all tastes like chicken. What's the worst thing you ever ate?"

"Raw testicles. Mike said I wouldn't but I did. How about you?"

"I ate a live cockroach."

"Why did you do that?"

"Meghan dared me."

"Did it taste like chicken?"

"Nope. More like cockroach."

Mike said, "Oscar if you ever got free and clear and could do whatever you wanted, what would you do?"

Oscar looked at Mike as though that was the dumbest question he ever heard. When he was sure the question was in earnest, however, he answered flatly, "Buy more cows. What would you do?"

"There's only two more things I haven't done I really want to do before I die."

Oscar waited.

"A sun dance, and ride a horse through the Sinks."

A sigh. A shake of the head. "I always knew you were yonder."

WEDNESDAY

HE WAS ASLEEP in the saddle when the sun rose, and he woke to a desert almost white, grass the same color as the sand, creosote brush clumped like survivors after a shipwreck, bobbing in the swells.

He could see the Wind River Mountains to the north. The low undulations in the desert floor were like sea waves, and he liked the way this horse moved under him, floating over the brush. The horse was a little cracker-assed, but leggy, a traveler. At a walk she had a good six-inch overstep, and Mike thought of a camel because she was so high-headed.

Cloud shadow was the main feature on the land now. He felt like a flea on a Frisbee. Bands of antelope shimmered through the distance like apparitions, like those mountains to the north that promised they weren't really there. Small ground-nesting birds. No water for forty miles now.

The afternoon sky darkened and a brushstroke of clouds drew down. The rain evaporated before it hit the ground: virga. Two drops touched his face, and the clouds pulled up again.

JUNE 1989

AD WAS ON TOP of the wall hewing the last log flat on the outside with a broadaxe when he heard the petulant whine of a three-wheel ATV being pushed to its limit coming up the grade. He didn't have to turn around to know who it was. When the screaming motor ceased, he sighed and levered the blade of the axe between two logs, so it hung, and climbed down the ladder.

There was that polyester grin and the pale blue leisure suit to match it. There were no hellos. Merry handed Ad a little yellow card, which Ad took and read.

It was a pass to enter the Bull Mountain Proprietors Association. In the space marked EXPIRATION DATE it was marked N/A. It was signed *Merriweather Snipes*.

Snipes kept grinning. Ad went to hand the card back and said, "I don't need this to drive through the Association. I've been using that road to get to town since before there was an Association."

Snipes said, "With that card you can go anywhere you want. There's going to be a lot of new roads down there. You can use them all. See, every member needs to get to his parcel."

"That's about a thousand miles of roads."

"Pretty near."

"Really carving the country up, huh?"

"People got to get where they want to go."

"With four hundred owners and no fences, how do I know whose land I'm on?"

"With that little card you don't need to know. You can go anywhere. It's written in the Covenants. Besides, we were hoping you'd help us keep the cows away."

"Only way to keep the cows out is build fences. Even then you are going to have the occasional cow."

"Covenants say no fences. We like the feel of untrammeled wilderness."

Ad didn't know what to say.

"Will you help?"

"I'll help my friends take care of their cattle like I've always done. You giving me this card even though my road stays closed?"

The grin stretched wider, brighter. "You are just protecting your rights. I'd do the same thing."

Ad was thinking, This guy is slicker than owl shit.

Merry kicked his motorized tricycle to life and zipped down the road. The insect whine of the ATV had no more than begun to fade when Ad heard, from the opposite direction, the approach of a big truck. More cement? No, it was a lumberyard truck carrying prefab materials. It was Merry's new geodesic dome.

Not in spite of the card but because of it, Ad considered sending the driver into the swamp, but because the driver, like the others, was not to blame, Ad let him go through.

He said, "Tell Snipes he'd better put a culvert under his road. He can't keep running trucks through my yard." But even as he said it, he knew there would be no more trucks. That game was over and Adkisson had lost. He could only guess what the next game might be.

Neighbors and friends. Fate and free will. Elemental dynamic. You choose your friends and treat them right. Some neighbors become friends. Others you treat right regardless. Some neighbors are a kind of weather on feet.

There is something vaguely dishonest, usurious, pragmatic about neighborliness. It's a necessity, like branding. Anyone who grows up outside a city speaks this language. But four hundred of them? Didn't that change things? Didn't that make it like a city where you don't have to know your neighbors? Couldn't he ask them to leave him alone in exchange for being left alone?

But it wasn't a city. The city was far away. The nearest hospital was thirty miles away, the nearest sheriff was sixty miles. These newcomers seemed fearful of the land they lusted after. He was a doctor. They'd be calling on him. Come winter they'd get stuck in the snow and not have the wit or means to take care of themselves. This was a new game and nobody knew the rules.

Adkisson had cut and set his rafters. He was nailing on the roof when Snipes whined up on his ATV. He was wearing the blue one-piece suit. Jumpsuit. Ad wished he would jump. Merry invited Ad to his housewarming the next afternoon. Snipes had finished his dome in ten days flat.

Ad thought *neighbors* and agreed to go. To demur would be too loud. They'd turn his absence into poison.

It must be said Merriweather had chosen a good dome site. The creek that ran by ran dry by June, but water wasn't far down. It was the stream that issued from Ad's spring, which never, even in drought years, ran dry. Below the spring the stream stitched mysteriously up and down, disappearing and reappearing, a cold clear embroidery.

It was underground where it ran past Snipes's, but a quarter mile downstream shone a string of beaver ponds.

Merry had built in a rock outcrop dotted with scrubby limber pines. His misfortune was to build on the windward side of those pines, so he'd have a better view. Actually, he had no choice. His dome was spitting distance from Ad's fence line and the leeward side of the rocks was Ad's.

Anyway, Merry had one hell of a view and, come winter, would have a hell of a wind: 180 degrees of clear sight that took in everything from Bull Mountain to Casper, with the Medicine Bow, blue, and the Snowy Range, frosted glass, in between. At night the city of Laramie dazzled in the middle distance as though some stars had leaked onto the prairie.

Whatever was happening on the Laramie Plains, especially with his spotting scope—all the wildlife, the human doings, all the weather and world-class sunsets—Merry had it in his window frame. The famous wind would wait.

Ad could have driven straight over to his northwest corner, stepped through the wire fence, and been in Snipes's yard. But the idea of sneaking up on people didn't sit well, so he drove the Proprietors' road two miles around.

The sight of a building, especially one so aggressively mathematical, on that site would never cease to be a shock to Ad, since he'd spent so much time in those rocks as a kid. To that kid those rocks seemed wild, magical, nature's province.

They'd called it Indian Rocks because it had clearly been an ancient hunting camp, replete with arrowheads, scrapers, and flint chips. The family had camp-outs and cookouts there. They had a circle of rocks for fire.

When Ad was nine he spent his first night camping out alone in those rocks, a mile from home. He'd built an Indian-sized fire, rolled out his army surplus Dacron bag, and lay unsleeping, terrified, under the sighted stars with his old dog, Argo. The coyotes sang.

He found out only years later that his father had followed him, keeping hidden at the timber's edge, and had stayed awake all night, watching.

So he was thinking about one of the few good memories he had of his father as he rounded the curve in the new-cut road and the Indian Rocks came into sight. Seeing the dome there wasn't as bad as the nightmarish apparition of fifty or so cars and pickups and a hundred or so people in a place where he'd never seen anyone but his parents and his sisters.

He fought a wave of nausea as he added his pickup to the rest, made his face into a cordial mask he thought would later have to be surgically removed, and descended from his vehicle.

He didn't know a soul there. People looked at him blankly, unconcerned, as he approached. There was little conversation.

Apparently they didn't know each other either. There were long tables rigged from sawhorses and planks, laden with potato salads and crab dip, people edged along. There was an American flag that was actually a sponge cake. There was a gas-fired grill where a man in a cowboy hat whose hatband was a bandolier of curio-shop arrowheads flipped burgers and dogs and quipped with those he served. Folks helped themselves to a barrel full of lemonade. There was a huddle of teenagers under a limber pine who had been taking, Ad guessed, Quaaludes.

A hitching rail made of lath in front of the dome wouldn't have restrained a pulling poodle, let alone a horse nosing a fly from his withers. Next to that there was a fancy carved and painted wooden sign that proclaimed this WILDERNESS RANCH.

Ad thought, That's two lies right there.

Behind Ad, Snipes's sonorous voice boomed. "Welcome!"

Ad turned, and there was a sight that would have given him a heart attack if he hadn't already been in shock. Merriweather Snipes was dressed up like an Indian: buckskin shirt and leggings, happy breechclout, leather moccasins, a beaded headband with a single hawk feather sticking up in back, and streaks of red and orange lipstick war-painted on his face. "I'd like you to meet my wife, Eunice."

Heart attack two. A fantastically large-breasted woman in a yellow pioneer bonnet, long calico dress, and a frilly white apron was squinting at him and holding out her hand.

"Adkisson Trent. Nice to meet you."

"Oh, I've heard all about you," mouthed the round and inno-cent face. "Merry says you're real old-fashioned. I like that." She beamed.

Indeed there was a sweetness in her face that Ad found quite stunning. She wasn't pretty at all—may never have been. Her face was moonlike and smooth and her blue eyes seemed to be looking through him to the distance at his back.

He was just thinking how she looked like a sunflower in her bonnet when she turned her face heliotropically toward the sun as it emerged from behind a cloud. Then it hit him. She was blind.

She laughed as though she'd read his mind. She said softly, but with a touch of pride in her voice, the way a child would tell her age, "I'm blind, you know." She reached out with both hands and anchored herself to Snipes's arm. "Diabetes. I used to be able to see just fine—well, I can still see light. And I can tell you're there even though I can't tell what you look like."

"It's OK. I don't look like much."

Snipes boomed a jovial hello to a new arrival and strode off in his Indian suit, leaving Eunice smiling into the sun.

She said, "Would you like to see our dome? Merry's so smart. He builds everything."

She took Ad's arm and led him, as though he were the blind one, up to the porch, where she felt for the railing, and through the sliding glass doors.

Inside, Ad had the distinct impression of being in a Winnebago. It was wall-to-wall simulated everything, from the purple acrylic shag to the plastic mahogany paneling and cupboards. All the appliances were dwarfish, sink, electric range, propane refrigerator. Ad swallowed to keep the nausea down. By accident, he thought, Indian Rocks.

Eunice effused. "Isn't it beautiful?"

Ad nodded, remembering she wasn't *completely* blind.

She told him how, after Merry got out of the service, he worked for—no kidding—Winnebago. "He actually invented a lot of the ways they do things in RV science today. He's a pioneer, that man."

"Right. Where do you get your electricity?"

"Oh, there's a cute little generator out back. You'll hear it when it goes on. Probably you could hear it over where you live!"

"Probably, depending on the wind."

"We've got TV."

"Great."

"Merry fixed it so he can rotate the antenna without getting up from his La-Z-Boy. We get five channels."

Ad was starting to sweat. "You sure have a nice view from here." Too late to take it back.

"That's what Merry says. To me it just looks milky, but I can feel the distance and I'm not sure I like it."

Ad wanted to ask her what she did all day long, unable to read or watch any of the five channels on the TV, no place to go, and rarely any visitors. He spaced that question and asked, "Ever been up here in winter?"

"Oh, yes. I love the wind in my face. And I can even drive the snowmobile when we get out in the open. Merry tells me when to turn." She turned away and her voice trailed off. "Only thing is I miss my friends I used to talk to. And Merry spends so much time with his hobbies."

She crossed the miniature kitchen and reached out her hand.

"See this bread box he made? Right out in his own little shop. He's the cleverest man I ever did meet."

"Nice."

Ad stepped out into the sunlight a little dizzy. He went over to the guy with the arrowheads in his hat and took a hot dog.

"Say, are you Doc Trent? I bought a forty right next to your fence. I want to build a cabin up here. You sure have a lot of trees. I was wondering—you wouldn't miss a few trees, enough to cobble up a little cabin. I—"

Ad cut him off more sharply than he meant to. "I don't have as many trees as you think."

Undaunted, the man continued, "—see you got a whole section. . . . Well, how about the road? You know, we're neighbors and it would sure save me some miles if I could—just me, mind you—"

Ad didn't wait for the rest. As he turned and headed for his pickup he heard the man say to someone, "Stuck-up rich asshole."

Ad got all the way home before he realized he still had the hot dog in his hand. He threw it as far as he could and watched it sail over pine tops into purple ether.

ONCE

WHENEVER AD FELT himself getting too judgmental about the rest of the human race, he thought back on his own disastrous attempt at normal life. He'd met her in med school. His failure to make a good husband was, he could now see, fated.

As a youngster he had been his father's good son: flesh of his father's flesh, shadow of his shadow. Ad's father's self-image was postwar American, the Hemingway model. He valued the basic dynamic of struggle and survival. He was atavistic, Luddite, claimed to be a Druid.

Unquestioning, Ad did what sons do. He modeled himself after his father, submitted to his father's authority. He shot his first antelope at eleven, buck deer at twelve, bull elk at thirteen. They downed pheasants, ducks, quail, doves. They fly-fished together. Ad embraced the artistry and the snobbery of the fly fisherman.

But starting at the age of fifteen and on a crescendo into his twenties, rebellion insisted upon itself. Though he never lost his passion for good horses, Ad became disdainful of ranching and cows. He took up alpinism and extreme-standard rock climbing, which he perceived to be a European pursuit.

After years of training, he got good. He lived for first ascents that sometimes took weeks to pull off: Yosemite, Rocky Mountain National Park, the Canadian Rockies, Canyonlands, Patagonia.

When he turned eighteen his father pressured him to enlist and fight in Vietnam. That was the breaking point, the last disappointment for both of them. Climbing reassured him that his reasons for shunning that disastrous and vain involvement were not, at bottom, concerned with cowardice or self-preservation.

He was in college, reading Blake, studying Zen. He was smoking pot and growing his hair and losing himself in high-standard alpine routes. Looking back he saw himself as a slave to the idea of freedom, a bearing no marriage could withstand. While all his old friends were polishing their roping skills, he was using rope to a different purpose.

Jean was beautiful and resilient. Fiery, Irish, too much like him to be married to him. She liked climbing and skiing and riding. He even took her to Yosemite for their honeymoon and pulled her up a couple of grade V's.

Then began the series of irrevocably wrong choices, the miscues, the refusals, the paralysis of affection. His commitment to climbing came between them. His devotion to freedom made him resent her. Whenever he wanted to do something truly serious, she got left behind.

He was incapable of compromise. So was she. Intransigence became the only thing left they loved in each other, outside of sex, which proved commensurately extreme and made them stay together much too long.

Jean liked life on the ranch just fine. When they took their school breaks that's where they went. Ad began the house to get away from his father. He got Jean a quarter horse, and she learned to help with cattle. But when she started asking for changes in the Trent family Luddite tradition—an indoor toilet, hot running water, electricity, telephone—he refused, citing the loss of values in modern America, alluding to Amish wisdom and economy.

Now he thought he should have done those things. Now, from the perspective of his desolation and loneliness, those seemed trivial, foolish, self-consumed concerns. He had also come to realize that he was rebelling against the power she, as a woman, had over him. All he'd wanted was to disappear into the mountains.

They let the black rose flower between them.

Climbing was his obsession and his escape. He asymptotically approached his limits. Then came the invitation to Denali. The Cassin Ridge. He'd be training all winter, then gone two months. Two months or forever. She asked him to call it off . . . for her. When he returned from Alaska she was gone. She told him she was pregnant and he had to get a lawyer.

The upshot was a daughter whose nurture he held higher-than any other calling. He quit extreme-standard climbing. He took huge amounts of time off to be with her in the summer. He taught her to ride and work with horses and cattle. She was all that mattered in his self-made wasteland. They were sidekicks. When she was with her mother and in school he slogged through his days and nights like couloirs in deep powder.

Given it to do over again he would have sacrificed everything—

climbing, the ranch, medicine, marital tranquillity—to be able to raise his daughter. Most miracles go unnoticed, but Ad sure noticed the miracle he'd missed.

Jean never forgave him his selfish choices, and he didn't blame her. He wished he could tell her he'd changed. No more adolescent immortality complex. He'd seen too much random death by now for that.

He was allowed two months each summer with his daughter, and a few odd weekends and holidays. Jean never asked him for money. Ad saved for Althea's future. If he died she'd be one rich little girl. Outside of that, his expenses were minimal. On his physician's salary he could take plenty of time off. The ER gig allowed for it. He could have spent half the year climbing, but he had quit climbing. At forty-five his shoulders, knees, elbows couldn't take it anymore, not at extreme standards, and he wasn't interested in "fun" routes. Besides, those honeyed days riding the prairies and canyons with his girl were worth all the climbs in the world put together.

Since the divorce, Ad kept his relations with women casual and brief. Was he gun-shy, or was he thinking of Althea, who now had all his love and, he thought, deserved more? He lived, for the most part, like a monk. He logged solo time. The nurses who threw themselves at Ad were like women leaping off a cliff.

He took a pull from the Laphroaig. He watched the cloud shadows skidding across the prairie toward him like emergencies. Aloud he said, "God, this whisky is good."

He watched the beiges of grass and the greens of forest turn into the blues of mountains. The colors blended and reblended, changing minute by minute. Terrible beauty. The cloud shadows raced over him like provincial histories: he'd be in sun, then shade, then sun again. The sun was constant, absolute. The shadows were relative, fashionable.

He waited for sun when cloud shadows swallowed him in cold. A herd of elk leaked from an aspen grove. He could see the range grass beyond his fence aroused in soft breeze.

SUNDAY

EUNICE'S BEST FRIEND, May, a thin stern woman, sat rigidly on a metal chair, hands folded. Eunice, in a rocking chair by the picture window, a looking glass in her lap, wept softly. The silver mirror was her first anniversary present from Merry. The picture window glared its white constant silence. She felt as though she were lost in a blizzard of light. She lifted the mirror as if to look into it. It made a dark hole in the white light. "I was a girl. He provided, took care. In sickness and in health. He could have had any girl, but he chose me, stayed with me. I was never afraid. I know he sometimes lost his temper with others, but he never raised his voice or his hand to me. In sickness and in health. Now what do I do? I'm alone. I'm blind. I don't know what to do. Merry always knew, and now he's gone." She rocked and wept. She faced the milky light everyone said was a view.

JULY 1991

FIRE WOULD BE ALL RIGHT, thought Ad, unless it was your own pasture, timber, and hand-built house that were going up in it, and your own short time on overpopulated earth spent looking at burnt toast for landscape.

So he ran cows, which also gave him something to do with his horses besides going around in circles or on trail rides. Horseback, he liked to feel as if he was *doing something*. With a purpose in mind besides just putting miles on a horse, a ride was more likely to take ten hours than one and provide some of the kind of roping Ad found more interesting than what you see in rodeos, where the calves and steers just run in a straight line across a tidy arena. He liked it when they broke through timber and killer rocks.

To Ad, a horse was halfway to wildness, halfway to gentleness, an interpreter between the rider and the landscape he rode. A Virgil. Besides that, it put you in touch with a tradition six thousand years old and still relevant. Another sip of Scotch on his rock and he caught something down on the prairie he knew was wrong before he knew what it was.

Two miles off across open sage and grass was a black dot like a period escaping from a typed page, beelining at a good clip. Ad thought *bear* because he often saw black bear down there, and they were usually hightailing it over coverless ground.

But it didn't move like a bear. Then he saw another one, smaller, and he knew. Then he saw more. A dozen or so big ones and a like number of small ones. All black. They were cattle— pairs of cows and calves. Nothing wrong with their being there, really, despite the Proprietors; what was wrong was the rate of speed they were covering ground.

Sometimes calves gamboled. Sometimes steers and heifers trotted or loped for no apparent reason. But cows are not built to run flat out, and they don't unless they have to. Given their weight and short legs it's hazardous to them.

These were galloping for all they were worth over brushy, rocky, prairie-dog-drilled ground, stubby legs flailing to stay under unwieldy bodies, calves, more agile but smaller, struggling to keep up.

The uniformity of their color meant they were Oscar's Angus cows, and something had spooked the bejesus out of them.

Ad murmured, "What the hell?" He watched the herd scatter and stampede down a steep draw and up over its far rise. He watched for what was spooking them, but he couldn't see a thing.

He jogged into the house (if there's no such thing as an emergency for people, there's damn sure no such thing for cattle), grabbed his felt work hat, took a halter and lead rope off the nail by the door, and jogged down to the corral.

When he came in sight of the corral, the three horses jerked their heads up in unified surprise. He slowed to a walk to calm them, and after eyeing him for a moment, one by one they lowered their heads to the hay and ate.

He went through the gate and haltered the lanky bay that was, of the three, the best traveler. He led his horse to the barn to saddle up and realized he was still wearing sneakers. Never mind.

Once saddled he trotted up past the house, then touched his horse into a lope. He pulled up in front of the wire gate between his land and the Proprietors. Then he set the bay into a lope again and headed for where he'd seen the cows flounder over the hill. He passed Snipes's dome and noted that an American flag had been added to the yardscape.

He crossed the last ravine he'd seen the cows cross, loped up the hill, and reined in to have a look. The last thing those mamas needed was another good scare.

The first pair he saw was not a hundred yards off, standing. He walked his horse over to them and rode in a circle studying. The calf looked fine, though it was drooling and its tongue was lolling.

The cow was holding one forefoot off the ground. He rode right up to her and she still didn't move. He pushed his horse against her and she trip-stepped twice away and stood, never putting her hoof down.

Her leg was sprained or broken, he couldn't tell which. She had probably stepped in a hole while running, and in any case she wasn't going anywhere now.

He looked around for the rest of the bunch and found them in some willow bushes by a creek. He stepped his horse among them, looking. They were all fine except for one cow that, like the first one, wouldn't move.

They were Oscar's stock, all right, with the 2A brand. Ad would have to call. They would have to rope and load the calves, then haze the injured mothers into the trailer after their calves. If legs were broken the cows would be slaughtered, a considerable loss of money on a good calf-producing cow. That would be money Oscar didn't have to lose. Ad scanned the empty horizon.

1964

OSCAR'S HAT LAY UPSIDE DOWN on his lap as he sat on the porch listening to his grandfather's voice. The stars seemed to be flying away. The old man looked up at them as he spoke.

Oscar had heard the story a thousand times. More. His grandfather never changed a detail. But it never got boring. Oscar knew that site, below a ridge on Fish Creek, near Tie Siding. He could visualize the scene as the old man painted the narrative onto it, or he could look at the pasture itself and imagine the events as vividly as if he had been there, as if it were his story blossoming before him.

"It was April of aught-four. I knew something would happen because of building that fence. I told him not to do it, but he was arrogant. If it was anybody else's idea, Maxwell didn't like it. He went through life like there was no easy way. He didn't know people can get along. He just didn't know it.

"Still and all, I never thought it would have got so bad. I should have, what with Tom Horn hanged for murdering a sheepman a week before. In my own mind, I don't think he did it. A man like Tom Horn doesn't shoot somebody in the back from that far away. That was over in Cheyenne.

"There was no snow and about half a moon. It was past midnight. The three of us were asleep in the sheep wagons. I woke up when the door thumped. When I sat up I was looking at the little hole in the revolver.

"At gunpoint they ordered us out of the wagons. It was odd the ground was bare, it being April. We didn't have our boots on. It was cold. They wired our hands together with bob wire. I guess that was supposed to be a message. We could have got out, but they held the guns on us. The wire hurt but I didn't think about it. I thought they were going to kill us.

"All of them wore masks. There were sixteen by my count. I recognized some of them by their voices: Will Keyes, Frank Carroll, Will Keyes's boy Harry, Wesley Johnson. Three of them held their horses. One of them held us to the loud end of a thirty-thirty. They set about pouring coal oil on our wagons and lit them off.

"In the light of the fire a gust came up and lifted one of their bandannas. I recognized that mustache and goatee. It was Will Keyes, all right. Then they took out pick handles they had slung in their belts.

"The sheep were all balled up, and they milled away from the fire and began to bleat. The men fell on them with the pick handles. The sheep never ran or anything. They just balled up and milled and bleated.

"The sound of the pick handles falling on the sheep skulls was partway between a thud and a crack, only a hard rain of thuds and cracks amidst the bleats. I'd say it sounded *like* something, but it didn't sound like anything but pick handles on sheep skulls.

"There were a dozen men bludgeoning. There were two hundred and fifty sheep. I don't know how long it took before the last bleating stopped. The men never said a word then.

"Now, I don't mind seeing a sheep slaughtered. Don't mind doing the slaughtering myself. But something about that many all at once. It was ungodly bad.

"They let us go. We walked back to the ranch. I crawled some because my feet got so tore up. The next day we spent shearing dead sheep."

THURSDAY/FRIDAY

HE RODE THE HORSE all night and again slept riding. The dirt was soft as flour and ankle deep. The horse covered ground like a cold front. He didn't care what that Indian was riding. Mike

knew he was putting down miles between them. There were no
more fences anywhere.

He had imagined the Red Desert the most uninhabited place
in the state, a place no one lived outside of a few Basques in
sheep wagons who wouldn't even wave if he rode by. What he
found was not what he expected. While it was true no one lived
there, by midmorning he found himself in the middle of a
labyrinth of wide dirt roads, so many he knew if he'd been trav-
eling roads he'd have got confounded. As it was, he had the Wind
Rivers to head for and a horse doesn't need any roads.

But there was traffic on those roads, lots of it.

The Red Desert, as it turned out, was pocked with gas wells,
peopled by pumps and tanks, all connected by arteries of dirt,
serviced by pickups, tank trucks, semis; vehicles like big termites
running around tending to their queens.

The problem was staying out of sight of the roads and the
vehicles running them. He listened for the approach of engines
and shied away from every causeway, looking for low hills to put
between himself and them. He had to make a break across several, quickly getting small in distance before the next insect
came rumbling down on him.

Once he found the wreck of an old sheep shed by a dry well
and an abandoned sheep wagon, where he rested awhile in the
shade. Once he thought he was well hidden in an arroyo when a
pickup with two guys in yellow hard hats blew past him at sixty
miles an hour on a road he hadn't seen coming. Luckily the guys
in the truck weren't looking for anything, having already found
what they were looking for.

Dusk came and he was beginning to relax when he heard the
whump of the first helicopter. The tarp was loosely folded across
the horse's flanks, ready for just such an eventuality. Mike reined

up and drew the tarp over his head and the horse's. The horse didn't move. The helicopter flew directly overhead and the tarp wasn't the right color. Mike didn't know if he'd been seen or not.

Anyway, it was coming on night and he rode. By morning he came to a creek and the horse drank long. The creek began somewhere on the rim of the basin and died in the flats. At noon he crossed the rim, the Continental Divide. He was back on the east side. The Winds were closer, looking more possible. The low mesas and the upthrusts—steep on one side, sloped on the other, like broadaxes—began again.

He topped a gentle rise and saw a low ring of mountains. Issuing from one of these mountains was a steady stream of giant haul trucks. They looked like toy trucks, Tonkas, but their wheels were twenty feet high. There were huge Cats with front-end loaders swarming at the mountain. The trucks were carrying the mountain away.

He turned back over the rise out of sight, but he could still hear the engines, their communal groan.

He crossed another creek. The grass was thickening, the sagebrush deepening like a carpet rolled out toward the mountains. A single windmill by a stock tank spun and turned its daisy face toward him, as if in accusation: *You weren't supposed to make it out of my hell.*

July 1991

EMERGENCY WAITING ROOM said the sign over the door. Oscar thought about that. It was consistent with Doc's philosophy: "There's no such thing as an emergency." Oscar knew what he meant, yet Ad saved lives routinely that waiting would have lost. "I guess it's just not an emergency if you're the doctor."

The painkillers were making him feel euphoric. His right arm, cradled in his left arm, was the shape of one of those little squiggles they put above *n*s in Spanish. He'd been lancing an infection on a fancy cutting horse when she struck him with her front hoof. He'd heard it go. He walked out into the waiting room of the vet hospital, cradling his arm. A man came up to him holding a white miniature poodle.

The man said, "My poodle keeps puking."

Sure enough. Oscar said, "I can't help you now. I have an emergency."

There'd been no one else on duty. The man was left holding the poodle, arms soaked in poodle puke. Oscar headed for his pickup, thinking, I'll have to call someone to take care of that horse.

Oscar laid his broken arm in his lap and picked up a magazine. Radiology was taking its time. The magazine was called *Montana Monthly*, a glossy, expensive product. He started thumbing through it with one hand. The first several pages were wall-to-wall ads: ranches for sale, developments, paradise this, and heavenly that, nice pictures of the properties. There were some ads for golf courses, ski resorts, restaurants, dude ranches. And clothes.

There was an article about fly fishing, one about skiing, one about grizzly bears. Then Oscar zeroed in on an article entitled "The Future of the West."

Funny, Oscar thought, I grew up thinking that was me.

The piece was written by a woman from the Department of Feminist Sociology at the University of Colorado at Boulder. It was written in an aggressively obscure style, as though the author had no confidence in the size of her ideas. Oscar had to read every sentence three or four times and keep remembering back to the gist when the next hypothesis came up.

As near as Oscar could make out, the author was saying that in the popular imagination there existed a romantic, mythic concept of the West, and of the cowboy in particular. In reality, however, the image of the American cowboy was a complete falsehood invented by the R. J. Reynolds Company to sell cigarettes to gullible urbanites.

The reality of the West, the author insisted, was an emasculated, culturally impoverished, agricultural wasteland, where men who had fallen prey to the Marlboro myth were afraid of urbanization because urbanization was essentially female.

Oscar thought about his cultural emasculation. He said out loud, "Huh." Then, "I guess she don't get out much."

Oscar thought about myths and legends. From Homer to the present, it seemed to him, myths portrayed people and gods who acted a lot like people. Either they performed great and heroic deeds and/or they fell into great and heroic folly. Either way, the purpose of myth was to encourage ordinary people to live up to extraordinary standards, thereby transcending the shabbiness of what would otherwise have been their natural behavior.

Legends. Often embellished for narrative interest, but based on real heroes and their bigger-than-life exploits. Like Jesus or Hugh Glass. Oscar thought of Jesus as a genius and a great philosopher. The son of God stuff was beside the point. And there was absolutely no question that Hugh Glass, mauled by a grizzly, his face torn off, left for dead by his companions, had crawled four hundred miles, surviving on insects and rodents, to St. Louis.

Knowing that superhuman levels of compassion, courage,

endurance, and morality were possible served to raise people's behavior to a higher standard. Imagine what people would be like without stories to guide them.

Closer to home, Oscar had found inspiration in many Western men and women, from his own father to Louise Schaeffer, Old Oscar, and Lyle Van Waning. Knowing you *could* be better made you try to be better.

The Marlboro Man. Oscar prided himself on his abject honesty, on his toughness, on certain skills. On being a good father. He didn't give a damn about any Marlboro Man. But he knew a rancher down south near Colorado Springs who'd been plastered on those ads, and the truth is he was a real cowboy, not invented by anyone but himself and his heritage—the tradition that formed him. Bob was in his sixties now. He bred and trained some of the best cutting horses around and showed them himself, all the while running two big ranches. He was soft-spoken, modest, and he damn sure knew what he was doing. He was an inspiration *even though* he'd let R. J. Reynolds help save his ranches.

Mike said that when you walk down Broadway in New York City you are surrounded by colossal versions of those ads. Cowpokes riding and roping and smoking everywhere you look. No doubt about it, your average urbanite liked cowboys, admired them, aspired to . . . nah. Oscar could take his worn-out 501s down to the pawnshop and get fifteen bucks for them. They shipped them to New York and sold them: "Worn by real Wyoming cowboys."

He didn't do it. Better to throw them away.

If they admire us so much, why are they trying so hard to stamp us out? Oscar wondered. It made him feel like an Indian or a redwood tree.

A nurse said, "Are you feeling photogenic, Dr. Rose?"

Oscar stood and thought, Besides, if it was female, I'd like it more.

JULY 1991

AD SAT THE BAY GELDING and watched Oscar's dust trail eat up the county road. Guy drives like he's afraid the trailer is going to pass him, he thought, as Oscar lashed around the turns.

Oscar pulled up and rolled down the window, off arm in a cast. "Ready to do some ropin', Doc?" Oscar hadn't brought a horse. He called Ad *Doc* because he knew Ad didn't like it when other people called him that, but he didn't care what Oscar called him.

Ad untied the riata from his saddle and hung it on the saddle horn. Oscar turned down the ball game on the radio. Ad got down and tightened his cinches.

Oscar said, "Say, Doc, before you go, mind handing me that arrowhead you're standing on?" Ad lifted one spurred boot and then the other, and there it was, a white side-notch bird point, barely broken off at the tip.

"Smart-ass." He handed it through the window. He turned and swung into the saddle, shaking his head. Here was the champion team roper watching him, a poor-to-middling roper, rope.

He walked his horse over to where the cow and calf stood together as he laid the split reins off to the left and threaded them between the index and middle finger of his left hand, took the coiled rope up between the index and thumb, and with his right hand shook out a couple of coils and built a loop.

The cow had her forefoot down but wasn't weighting it, and it was swollen all to hell. The calf turned and started putting distance between himself and what, on some level, he sensed was about to happen.

Ad knew that, no matter what, the calf would keep circling back to the cow. Walking his horse behind the calf, Ad held his loop out to the side. When the calf broke into a trot, Ad launched his horse into a lope and was right on top of the calf, who made his cut back to his mama. Ad threw and missed. The calf trotted smugly up to the cow and stood. The horse slowed and craned his neck around as if to say, What the hell.

The process was repeated, and this time the throw was good. Ad dallied; the horse set up and bounced twice; the calf hit the end of the rope and spun. Ad took a turn off the saddle horn and walked his horse around the calf so it could go, still roped, back to its mother.

Oscar opened the gate on the trailer. Every time the calf made a break, Ad dallied and the calf hit the end of the line. Ad dragged him the last few feet to the trailer and said, "If you see any animal rights activists around, tell them I'm not here."

Oscar took a second lariat, twisted the loop into a halter, and put it on the calf so they could drag him without choking. He took the free end of his rope into the front of the trailer and slip-knotted it to a stay, dropping the end outside. Ad dropped his rope, rode to the front, untied the slipknot, dallied, and dragged the calf inside. The cow limped up, jumped in after her calf, and Oscar slammed the mid-gate on them.

The operation was repeated for the second pair, only the cow, whose hind leg was bad, fell to her knees trying to load up, and both men had to hunker down and lift her, front end, then hind end, to get her in.

Oscar thanked Ad for the help, but he wasn't happy. He'd felt both damaged animals and they both had broken legs, meaning they were hamburger. Both mama cows done for.

"You don't suppose that Snipes son of a bitch is stampeding my stock on his three-wheeler, do you?"

"I don't know."

"Kinda puts a guy in mind of firearms, don't it?"

Ad looked at Oscar. "Don't even think about it. Not until you see it. Even then. He's got guns too, as you found out, and, worse, he's got nothing to lose. You got a family. Don't even think about it."

FRIDAY

THE DESERT GRADUALLY RELENTED to prairie and scrub pine, more mesas, red ridges, and bluffs. When he heard the second helicopter he rode into the shade of a juniper not much taller than his horse and pulled up the tarp. This time he was pretty sure he hadn't been seen.

He turned a ridge and looked down on the bright, bright green of an irrigated hayfield protected by sagey hills and a rim of red sandstone. He rode into it and crossed it just to be in green again. From the far side, on a broken spine of granite, he could see the teal Wind Rivers begin to blacken in dusk. He unsaddled and hobbled the horse and slept under a juniper tree, all night breathing its edgy scent.

In the morning he rode on. He followed the red rimrock of a mesa furred with sage. The sky clouded over and he hoped there'd be rain before evening. The mesa was a bald clearing in the scrubby foothills. Up ahead he saw something, something like a cross. He came up.

There must have been a single ponderosa growing on that mesa a hundred years or so ago. Its tangled mass of roots showed above the ground, though the tree was long dead. A block of granite, angular and big as a bale of hay, had been lifted by the roots clear of the ground and gripped. It looked like the trunk was impaled by the rock.

Above the rock, even more impressive, someone, undoubtedly an old Basque, had taken an axe to the tree, removing every limb but two, which, with the trunk, formed a cross. Then, further, he had axed a Christ right out of the tree wood, crude but clear. There was even an expression on the face, the usual sorrowful acceptance. At the base of the tree Mike found a mule shoe, which he dropped in his saddlebag.

AUGUST 1990

SMOKE WAS COMING from the old Wurl Ranch, which, as part of the Camel Rock Ranch, had been sold to the Proprietors Association. It looked like a grass fire. Ad pushed on the accelerator, thinking, At least it's an east wind.

From a mile away he could see that the whole hillside, about twenty acres above the old log buildings, was black and smoldering. The wind had shifted, bringing drizzle, and the fire was blowing back on itself, putting itself out.

With no grazing on the land, neither wild nor domestic, the grass grew tall but then dried and died. Several years of thatch had turned to hazard. Just someone pulling off the road with a catalytic converter could cause a prairie fire. There had been six fires since the advent of the Proprietors Association. So far they'd all been minor. It was just a matter of time before the right wind made a major one.

This particular burn was no problem. Ad got out and started snuffing small blazes on the leeward perimeter. His eyes were watering from smoke and he was starting to sweat when he noticed a red pickup drive up and stop. A man and woman got out and approached.

The cherubic, bearded man introduced himself and his pleasantly smiling wife. Ad lost their names. The man said he was a volunteer fireman out of Laporte. He'd driven down to the ranch and called in to Harmony Station. He got a shovel from his truck and fell in beside Ad. Then the pump truck arrived and started dousing the edges of the burn. Ad leaned on his shovel and they talked.

He worked at the Budweiser plant. She worked at Safeway. They'd bought forty acres and asked if Ad belonged to the Association. He said he'd lived there forty years.

The woman said, "Well, if you know this country maybe you can answer a question."

"I'll try."

These people seemed completely decent. Ad liked them.

"We paid forty thousand dollars for our parcel. It was our entire savings. We wanted to leave something for our grandchildren, not just money, something better: a piece of wild land with a heavenly view—fishing, picnicking, a beautiful, mysterious gift. We looked at all the land up here, all that's not been taken. We picked a parcel with water, a couple of cottonwood trees, near Sand Creek. You can see everything from there."

"Where is it exactly?"

"Well, you know the bridge across Sand Creek? We're just a quarter mile north of there."

"Oh," said Ad. "I know where you are. I know those trees in the draw."

"Well, what I wanted to ask is, when we bought the place in June there was a stock tank with two pipes running into it. It was full of the sweetest water. But now, here in August, it's dried up. We have to haul water from town. We want to build, you know? Do you think the pipes are clogged up?"

Ad knew that tank. It never had water in fall. The old ranch pastured that ground early. The tank was there to keep the cows from trying to get water down in the canyon where they might get stuck or hurt. He said. "Well it *could* be plugged. Not very likely both pipes are plugged. It's worth checking. You could probably drill a well. The cottonwoods are a good sign. They need water. I bet it's not far down."

The woman looked about to cry. She said, "We don't have much money. I thought there was water."

Ad hated pity, but driving home he felt pity for the couple. Duped by land pimps. Robbed of their savings. All they had to leave their grandchildren was a dry stock tank and two cottonwood trees. Forty thousand dollars for a stock tank and two trees. Their legacy.

SATURDAY

AT NOON HE SPOTTED a small band of wild horses. He regretted his shod horse, but then thought, Hell, if I can get in the middle of them and run with them awhile, the ones behind me will erase my tracks. Even if they have an air search aloft, I know that Apache is still after me."

The wild horses jerked their heads to attention almost in unison when they saw him. He approached them obliquely and they all watched. He circled nearer. The foals and yearlings moved toward their mothers. The stallion snorted. Mike's horse whinnied.

Mike pushed to a gallop and they were off. His saddlebags were flapping and the whole band ran in front of him. They drummed the hard ground. Mike urged his horse forward, and, tired as she was, she gained. Mike leaned forward in the saddle, his long hair flowing.

This mare of Oscar's had some world-class speed, and soon she was passing mares and young horses. They were right in the middle of the herd. Horses swerved off as he passed them. He was galloping over the sage in a band of wild horses.

After a half mile he quit. He didn't want to play out his mount. He watched the spotted horses disappear, still at a run, but slower, over a hill. He walked the mare out, both of them breathing hard. He felt joy.

ONCE

FALL, WHEN THE FIRST big wind comes up and hits the incandescent aspen leaves, the air fills with flurries of gold.

Weather patterns have inner cycles, variable and predictable. Ad wondered if it was just him, but once he'd talked to Lyle about it and Lyle said the same thing.

Summer seemed eternal and never forlorn. But at summer's

end when the sky goes chalky and the prairie washes out in a tawny haze, the loneliness comes on. Ad's theory about loneliness was that it is just fear with no trigger, no helpful adrenaline. Worse than fear. Loneliness crescendoed until the aspens turned, the first snow fell, and it withered like a creek going dry.

Winter was not lonely, strange to say, but solitary.

Spring was a rebirth of loneliness. It came on the wind.

Each spring and each late summer day had its corresponding cycle. Mornings you know what you have to do. You get up and do it. Loneliness invades the soul late afternoon. Sundown can test you with its flood of color, but once it's full dark you're fine.

SUNDAY

TEN MILES EAST of South Pass City, where thousands of pioneers had famously made their way west, the summits of the Wind Rivers were hidden by their own foothills. Anybody following Mike would think he'd choose one side or the other of the Winds to follow north, make the Absarokas, Montana, maybe Canada. But that's not what he was planning. Jim thought his job was just about over, since there would be no way to thread the long granite-sided valleys without being noticed by several thousand hikers, climbers, fishermen, and outfitters, not this time of year. Mike would get reported, surrounded, arrested. Game over.

Mike let his horse put her nose down and pick her way down a steep slope strewn with granite talus, mountain mahogany, and juniper trees, toward the sound of a fast, tumbling stream. He had a highway to cross soon. As usual, he'd save it for dark. Though he hadn't seen any sign of Thomas, Mike sensed he was close.

He was watering his horse, watching the light move under the water over the stones when he heard a voice. "About done with that horse?"

Adrenaline flashed. The horse raised her head and nickered. The familiarity of the voice took a moment to sink in. Mike said, "Goddamn." He scratched the back of his neck and blew a bubble. "You shouldn't do that, Oscar."

"Anybody see you riding that horse?" Oscar was sitting on Potatoes Browning on the far bank, forearms crossed on the saddle horn. Potatoes was pretty close to the color of the granite boulders.

"Not that I know of."

"Good. In that case I'll take her back."

Mike and Potatoes made their way up the far side of the canyon as Oscar made tracks upstream before doubling back. Mike crested the ridge and found a little ring of boulders to bivouac in. He was close now. He wondered how far back Jim was.

He sipped from a bottle of Scotch that Oscar had said was a present from Ad. He wondered where Ad was. He thought about what now seemed a lifetime of running, riding deserts, mountains, crossing rivers. He thought about the lifetime before that, with Liv, the one with a ranch and a future that was imaginable. It was all so abstract he couldn't muster any emotion about it. All that remained was the end of the story.

JULY 1991

DESPITE THE EVENTS with Oscar's cows, Ad was feeling pretty good as he walked his horse up the lion-colored gravel road home. Oscar said, "Doc can rope 'em if they're sick enough."

Ad was savoring the sand rocks' hues—blood red before the blue ranges—same color the sun felt on his shoulders. Also, he enjoyed the familiar way his horse moved, never plodding but stepping with snap, overstepping with his springy legs and high head.

He dipped through the draw where the cows had crossed the day before. He stopped at the lively trace of water and gave his horse the reins to pull a long drink.

He was crowning a rise when he spotted where a three-wheeler had torn up the earth making a hard turn. There were deep divots the cattle had made at a dead run. It was hard not to put two with two. These ATV guys had a knack for trashing fragile grasses and topsoil, for muddying the creeks. Maybe it was just a coincidence that the cows had stampeded ahead of unrelated pimply tire tracks, but to believe it would be a stretch.

He reined his horse toward Merriweather Snipes's dome, thinking it might be worthwhile trying to explain a few things before someone got shot.

He was rounding a bend in the freshly bladed road to Snipes's when he heard, then saw, a vehicle approaching. He stepped his horse over the furrow of dirt that lined the road, soft dirt that still held, ripped up and tumbled, sagebrush, grass, and withered wildflowers. He touched the brim of his hat as the sheriff passed in his little four-by-four, and the sheriff waved back.

When he drew up he thought about tying his horse to the "hitching post" Merry had built in his yard but thought better of it and just dropped the reins. He knew his horse would stand and graze. If he was tied to Merry's idea of a hitching post he might try to scratch his nose on it and knock it over, spook, drag it off, and get hurt.

Merry came out on his porch and boomed a big-grin howdy.

Ad said, "What's wrong?"

"What do you mean?"

"I've only ever seen a sheriff up here once."

"Oh, that. He's a friend of mine. Just stopped by for coffee. As Chairman of the Bull Mountain Proprietors Board of Directors I wanted to talk to him about how things are going to change around here. He agreed it would be a good thing to show some police presence now and again. He's going to deputize me so I can keep an eye on things, being I'm here full-time. You know, what with all the new folks moving in, we wouldn't want any crime. We wouldn't want any—you know—burglaries, vandalism."

"I guess not." Ad lifted his hat off and studied it. "You seen any strays around lately?"

"Yeah, there was a bunch of those stinking bastards here yesterday. Came right into my yard. I ran 'em off on the ATV. I hate cows. This is supposed to be a wilderness."

"How can it be a wilderness with you here, Merry? We need to talk about this. The law in both Colorado and Wyoming states you have to fence livestock out, not in. If you don't want cattle on your land, legally you have to put up fence. Or you could rent the pasture to local ranchers. Make some income and lower your taxes."

"No cows. I hate cows. And my taxes *are* lower. I told the county I was running sheep."

"I don't see any sheep."

"Right. You think I'm stupid?"

Ad stared, amazed. "Well, Mr. Snipes, you are going to have some cows from time to time unless you fence them out and convince your pals to keep the gates closed. Those cows you ran yesterday belong to a friend of mine. They were on a school section with good fence, but somebody left a gate open. Cows are going to get out if people are in too much of a hurry to close a gate behind them."

"If they do I'll run them off."

"That's what I came here to talk to you about. The guys who pasture cattle up here know what they are doing, know how to move them. We found two animals with broken legs, likely because you ran them that way."

"It's not my fault they can't run."

"I just want to ask you a favor."

"Ask."

"If you see strays, come over and let me know. I'll gather them and take them back where they belong. That way there won't be any trouble."

"What trouble? I already told you I hate cows."

MONDAY

THE MORNING SKY was tattletale gray, then alabaster, then cloudless royal. At this altitude it was never hot, and he could see snow from the ridge before working his way down through the rims and cliffs and elephant-sized boulders of the South Fork of the Popo Agie River.

At one point he found himself rimrocked and considered backing his horse down the cliff *en rappel*, not unlike Oscar's move that time on the horse chase. It would have made a nice touch, but he thought better of it and doubled back.

As he rode he reminisced and tried to find emotions to attach to what he remembered. Isn't that what people do near the end? He remembered Lyle's last days, staying in bed for the first time in his life, happily fondling memories—"all the things we done."

Everything seemed vaguely good. Eventually the grief fell off things like old paint. He and Potatoes were posthumous now. He remembered all the adventures they'd shared and it didn't make him sad, the way it usually does with horses you say good-bye to.

He was not in any hurry. It took him till midafternoon to descend to the frothing river, ford it, belly deep among boulders, and climb to the far rim. When he topped out, something made him turn around. He looked across to the other side. What had taken him half the day to accomplish, in a straight line, from rim to rim, was only half a mile.

On the far edge of the canyon he saw a horseman. The horseman was watching him through binoculars. He couldn't really see the binoculars, but there is a posture of people looking through binoculars that can't be mistaken. It had to be Jim, watching him up close from far away.

Well, now Mike knew exactly where he was. He waved. Jim waved back. Mike turned his horse and started down into the next canyon.

He rode down through old growth timber and among boulders like junked cars. Between the trees, a quarter mile down, he could see the Middle Fork. It was pure white and moving so fast it appeared to move slow. It made Mike think of an ancient woman undoing her long braid.

He wondered what Jim was planning to do when he finally caught up. The Indian didn't seem to be in any more hurry than

Mike was. Like someone had told him to follow, so he followed. Like he was just curious about where they were going next. Maybe by now he knew where Mike was going and was just coming along to watch the escape.

By dark he reached the river and stood contained in its roar, like a train going by, about five hundred cubic feet per second, about sixty miles an hour. Mike didn't plan on sleeping that night. He sat leaning against a tree, lost in his past, trying to put things in order, trying to give thanks.

He spent the night three hundred yards above the visitors' center on the other side.

JUNE 1989

THE FIRST TWO DAYS of the drive were straightforward, punching them up the county road, which was well fenced on both sides. Ad rode a two-year-old he was training for Althea when she was ready for more horse. The filly was still unpredictable, full of youthful spooks. The best thing for her, Ad knew, was to bore her to death behind a herd of cows and calves. That was the best place for a six-year-old girl, too, though Althea was pretty solid on her old gentle gelding.

So the two of them rode drag, went all day without seeing Mike, who rode point, rode hard, blocking holes in the fence, lining the cows out in the right direction.

Nights they made a big fire, ate stew out of a cast-iron pot, and Mike told funny stories and sang old Bob Dylan songs so out of key it made everybody wince. Liv finally made him stop.

•   •   •

Mike said, "Althea, you ever been in on calving? You ought to come out some winter and watch the little calves get born. It's a hard time of year for weather and sleep, but that's my favorite time on the ranch.

"One night last winter I was riding a young horse about like that one your dad's training for you. I wasn't expecting much to happen—it was just the beginning of January—so I thought I'd put some miles on a younger horse.

"We had our herd pastured near Tie Siding, so I had to go in the horse trailer to check the cows. Sure enough, I found a cow that looked pretty close to calving out, and I figured I'd better load her up and bring her in.

"Only trouble was, I couldn't rope off the horse I was riding and I didn't have any help. I had to figure out some way to get that cow into the trailer out in the middle of nowhere—no place to pen her or anything.

"She was a pretty gentle cow, so I thought maybe I could coax her close to the trailer, rope her from afoot, and then figure out something—I wasn't sure quite what. I eased her near the trailer with the horse. She just stood there looking at me, as if she was curious to see what my plan was.

"I got down, hobbled the horse. I opened the trailer door, got a lariat out of the truck, and, hiding behind the trailer door, I made a loop. The cow was only a few feet away, waiting.

"I thought maybe I had enough rope to hitch one end to the side door handle. I tied it off and wafted a loop out over her head. She bolted and ripped the door handle clean off. But I grabbed it as it went by, and the next thing I knew, I was getting a pretty fair tour of the prairie from a snake's-eye view. At least I had that door handle to hang on to.

"Pretty soon, though, I saw a telephone pole coming up, and I thought maybe I could dally her on that. I got my feet under me somehow, and for a minute it was like I was water-skiing behind a cow—just without the water or the skis. I jumped sideways when I got to the telephone pole and kind of rolled around it and dallied the cow. I had her.

"She came up short and was breathing hard from running and choking herself on the rope. She was looking at me like I was unusual or something." Mike grinned.

"Well, I tied her off good and went up to her and cranked her tail so she stepped forward and quit choking. That gave me time to run back to the truck and trailer.

"I backed up to her and found another old rope in the truck bed. I knew it was a real old rope, but it was all I had. I made a halter out of the loop and put it on her. I tied the end of the second rope to the front of the inside of the trailer. I untied the good rope from the telephone pole and took the loop off her.

"I cranked her tail again and whooped, and she jumped into the trailer. I had her. I jumped into the trailer to slam the midgate on her, but she turned around fast and came over me like about three football teams.

"When she hit the end of the old rope, it snapped and she was gone. Off into the night. I was starting to get a little frustrated." He grinned. "She only ran off about a hundred yards or so and turned back to see what kind of genius idea I was going to come up with next.

"I got down on my hands and knees and tried to sneak up on the end of the broken rope, but she kept pulling it away, just out of reach. I bet I crawled two miles with the frayed end of that rope wiggling along about three feet in front of me.

"Finally she stopped to graze like she knew I didn't have any way to stop her even if I did get the end of the rope. I grabbed it and she took off again, full-tilt boogaloo, dragging me through the brush.

"I was considering the pathetic nature of my situation when I saw the fence line and a cattle guard coming up on the horizon. One good thing about being on your belly is that it makes the horizon closer. Aha, I thought, now I got her.

"I was kinda surprised, however, when she cleared the cattle guard with an inspired vault. And while she was flying through the air the calf came flying out of her and arced through the night and hit the dirt.

"I often wonder what that calf thought, flying into life. I was about halfway across the cattle guard when I let go of the rope. I thought, Whew. I thought, guess I got that done, and I loaded up my horse and went home."

Althea stared at Mike as though she had no idea what to make of this adult and his story. Mike chuckled a friendly chuckle and stared into the fire. "Yeah, Althea, you ought to come out for calving sometime and see how the pros do it."

The last day of the cattle drive, things complicated. The fences bordering the road were just bad memories of themselves. The road followed a creek bed that was gagged with beaver ponds and willow bushes. During the night, cattle had drifted over the last pass and were strung out five or six miles in straggly groups along the road.

They struck camp and Mike and Liv started gathering the cows that remained in the meadow where they'd overnighted. Ad and Althea made a sweep of the timber surrounding and kicked up three pair and a dry cow belonging to someone else. The dry cow had to be cut out and turned back, which was tricky because she was leading the others and she liked to run. She liked to run in the direction all the others had gone.

Ad found himself galloping alongside his daughter through thick timber with a lot of deadfall. Whatever happened to riding drag and keeping things conservative? He didn't want to pamper his kid, give her a lollipop version of reality. On the other hand, if she got hurt, he knew whose fault it would be. This was a situation, Ad knew, where the worst could easily happen.

His two-year-old got excited and unloaded a few bucks, but he was just worried about Althea, who was mounting a heedless, headlong assault on the dry cow, trying to cut her off at an old downed fence line. She seemed to have no instinct for self-preservation. Ad thought, The sins of the fathers. . . .

The filly's bucks were easy to sit and Ad soon had her lined out in a gallop again. She needed a spinning lesson, but there was too much going on. Ad watched the cows clear the fence, and Althea, who probably wasn't strong enough to turn or stop her horse at that point if she wanted to (she didn't), followed over with a yip of excitement. They just ran the cow till she gave out.

Ad faced off with her, a good cutting lesson for the filly, while Althea picked up the pairs and turned them up the road after the herd, which was, by now, miles ahead.

Meanwhile, Mike was short-handed. Liv had ridden on to stall the front of the herd and keep them from leaking into side canyons. There was a section of National Forest leased by someone else, and the herd had to be moved through that other herd, bulls and all, without mixing the animals together. Mike had brought his best cutting horse for the job, but given what happened, nothing could have helped.

Mike gathered all the cows that needed to be bypassed, and choused them, with their two bulls, into a side canyon off the main drainage. Coming back to pick up his lead cows, he found six heifers belonging to yet someone else about four miles back down the road. They had just been dragged along like iron filings on a magnet and they needed to be sorted out and put somewhere before the drive could proceed. Mike cut them out and put them through a fence that was barely there, the kind of loose and leaning barbed wire affair that cows have no trouble crawling through but that you don't take a horse anywhere near.

Bulls have only one job in life, outside of eating, so they get very curious when they hear or smell strange cows. It wasn't long before cattle were spilling out of the canyon, led by the enthused bulls, who had come down to see what there was for them to do.

Mike spurred his horse and headed them off, but the bulls ripped through the fence like it was cellophane at Christmas. The cows dutifully followed them, twanging the fence wires like banjo strings, and joined the six heifers. Then about twenty pair of Mike's poured in and Mike couldn't follow them without risking damage or death to a valuable horse.

All the mixed-up cows were pouring downstream through thick willows toward the Poudre. They were going the wrong way toward the wrong river.

Mike galloped his lathered horse back toward the truck, where they'd camped, for some wire cutters. He was fuming, and his horse was getting a lot of steel out of his rider's mood.

Mike blew around the corner where Ad and Althea were by then peacefully driving their measly three pair. Mike pushed his horse into a sliding stop like a freight train derailing.

"Can I get some help around here?"

Ad just looked at him, thinking, Who in tarnation does this guy think he is?

It was clear a situation had soured, but it was hard to divine the specifics. Mike booted his horse and was gone.

Ad said, "Guy's nuts."

He said, "Guy's nuts," just as Althea's horse started bucking for no apparent reason. A horse that never bucked. A gentleman. But there he was, not just kicks and crow hops but sunfishing, whirling, flying. He was all rodeo, and Althea hit the ground with a *thwap* and started crying.

Ad swooped off his horse, throwing the reins away, and set her on her feet. "Are you crying 'cause you're hurt or 'cause you're scared?" He looked her over, his heart booming.

"I'm scared," she said, through sobs.

Ad hugged her till she quieted, thinking, Holy Jesus. Then he said to her, "You know you have to get back on."

Althea wiped her tears and nodded. She asked, "Pop, did I make eight seconds?"

"You bet, Sidekick."

He lifted her back into the saddle and they rode on after the cows. Soon they heard Mike galloping back, and Liv was coming down the other way, wondering where everybody was.

Mike cut the fence. The four of them caught up with the cows, sorted them, and started the right ones up the road. They saw one of their bulls standing in the middle of a beaver pond. They left him there. He'd be along.

Things were not going well, but they were going better. They got the herd lined out and everything went all right for a while, which is to say normal—cows and calves diving into impenetrable willows, scrambling up talus slopes, each one having to be ridden after and kicked back to the others. They rode ten hours that day, even Althea.

Nobody knew where the Appaloosa came from. She was broom-tailed, goosenecked, and squealy. Maybe one of the fenceless ranchetteers had let her get away. She was racing up and down Ad's fence line, where they were going to put the herd through. She was all in a tizzy because of the approaching horses and the commotion of cows. She whinnied like a hot pig.

Liv trotted ahead and opened the gate and sat her horse to count the cows through. Mike went to run the Appaloosa off, but she kept doubling back over him. The cattle were worried about the worked-up stray horse and wouldn't start through the gate.

Four times Mike shooed the horse down the fence line, but each time she rolled back squealing and scattered the cattle, sending some of them trotting back down the way they had come. Ad galloped to get around the deserters, leaving Althea to push the others through the gate.

A few pairs went through, but then the Appy thundered back. Mike's temper flared. Again. He threw his hat on the ground and tied his hair back in a ponytail. He unhitched the rope from his saddle and went after the Appaloosa as if he meant to kill her if it came to that.

The loose horse was mean and swerved through rocks. Mike's horse was exhausted and had trouble closing. Just as it was about to set up and spin back toward the gate, Mike rifled his loop, not at the horse but where the horse would be. It was so perfect Ad thought it was just dumb-lucky.

The Appy came up short as soon as she felt the noose tighten. Mike just glared at her, and the two horses stood and blew while Ad and Althea pushed the herd, and Liv counted them through the gate.

Taking up slack, Mike stepped his horse forward and took his rope from the stray's neck. The Appy rolled her walleyes and bolted. Mike rode through the wire gate and closed it. Then he started riding through the herd looking for the calves he had already noticed were in need of doctoring.

There was no question of luck anymore as Ad watched Mike

put a syringe between his teeth like a pirate's cutlass and rope six calves without missing a loop. Ad said to Althea, "I think we better rethink this guy."

Mike went back for his hat. They let the cows and calves mother up before pushing them off the ridge and down to water. Thunder started to rumble its promise. The cows went down and it started to slash rain. After some hasty, half-audible so-long's, Mike and Liv pulled up the collars on their yellow slickers, pulled down their hats, and loped toward the trailer.

Ad and Althea were only a mile from home. Though her wrist was sore and swollen, she suggested a race for it. Ad didn't argue, since the road hugged the ridge top and the lightning was becoming more frequent.

They blasted off. There was a bright flash, a simultaneous crash, and Ad, who'd had his head down to keep his hat from blowing away, saw a spark jump across the ring on the breast collar of his saddle. He felt a medium flow of electricity go through him and his horse, who doubled under. Ad's left eyebrow burned. For a second he could smell singed hair.

When they reached the barn and untacked their steaming mounts, Ad said, "Al, it might be just as well not to tell your mom about today." Althea tossed her long blond hair, laughed, said, "Aw, Pop," and carried her tiny saddle into the tack room.

TUESDAY

UNIQUE AMONG RIVERS is the Middle Fork of the Popo Agie. A white artery spurt, it rips its way out of the mountains, immaculate, white as bone, as boiling snow.

Then it disappears. It hits a limestone wall and dives underground like a white whale sounding. Then nothing.

The hole in the wall that swallows the whale is also like a whale's maw, capacious and complete with driftwood baleens. It's dark in there and loud as a falling sky.

The river disappears for over a quarter mile, swallowed at what is known as the Sinks. Then it reemerges in a placid emerald pool full of lazy, overfed cutthroats at what is called the Rise.

Needless to say, no one knows what happens between the Sinks and the Rise, though there are guesses. No spelunker in scuba gear has ever lowered himself down the throat of the river. He'd be torn apart. It's a mystery—a mystery with a visitors' center that opens at 6 A.M.

At 6 A.M., just across from the visitors' center, a very large, bearded, naked man sits on a saddleless, haltered zebra dun, waiting for visitors. He blows a bubble.

Admittedly, 6 A.M. is a little too early for visitors, but Mike Arans is in no hurry now. He's willing to wait, chest pressed against the finish line.

If he'd only turn around and look up at the ridge he'd ridden down the evening before, he'd see he already had a visitor, silhouetted against the morning sky, looking straight at him.

ONCE

IN THE FIFTIES, people started to acknowledge the wild horse problem. Without natural predators the wild herds were prolifeating into thousands. They were mostly grazing unfenced on remote and poor public lands, running the grass down, eroding drainages, and threatening the livelihoods of ranchers by making the pasture useless for stock growing. That, and they were starving.

Catching wild horses had been a popular pastime among nervy horsemen, ever since there were wild horses. In the fifties and sixties, when they weren't running horses for sport or catching them to break, they'd round up and corral them by the hundreds and ship them off for dog food and glue.

As an idea, horses for dog food is not attractive to anyone in America. It was seen as a necessity. Sometimes, outside of necessity, there isn't much.

Oscar's family never had wild horses on their land, but there were herds nearby. When Oscar was little, his father and his uncle ignored the pleas of wives and daughters and went off together to rope wild horses.

Occasionally they'd bring one home to break and sell for a saddle horse, but the success rate and the profits on that deal never justified the time it took, so they had to call it a sport. Usually they'd just rope them and let them go. They lost a good many ropes on horses that plain wouldn't stop. Once they couldn't find any horses, so Oscar's uncle roped an elk. Wisely, he didn't try to dally. He just blew his riata a kiss.

Oscar was twelve when the two brothers first let him tag along on a wild horse chase. They located a herd on a mesa of rabbitbrush and deadfall from an ancient forest fire.

Oscar picked out a two-year-old and played his horse out, running around throwing loops at it. When he finally gave it up he didn't see where his father and uncle had gone. He crossed an arroyo and rode into an area that was like a natural corral of rocks. Wow! he thought. This would be the place to catch them.

He figured his uncle was a jump ahead when he saw him out in the middle of the rock enclosure, squatted down, with his back against a stump. He had his head down like he was rolling a cigarette. His horse was grazing peacefully nearby. And there was a wild horse, a white stallion like a pure Andalusian, roped and snubbed to the stump, still pulling back hard, his haunches rared under him, shaking his head like a hooked marlin.

"Yippee!" yelled Oscar, and loped up to where his uncle was calmly waiting for the stallion to choke himself into submission, waiting for Frank to come help hobble him and maybe take him home. Oscar never forgot the beauty of that white horse.

It wasn't until he was about ten feet away that he registered the numb stillness, not napping, not rolling a smoke, that shadowed his father's brother's face.

He saw the three coils of rope that were holding his uncle up in sitting position. One around his bent knees, one holding his upper arms tight against his sides, one around his broken neck.

The stallion had Oscar's uncle wound up like a gossamered fly, and he wasn't laying back on the rope to get away.

Oscar stood there dumb until his father rode up and cut the wild horse free.

OCTOBER 1989

SO THE NEXT TIME Oscar and Mike got a free day they decided to chase mustangs. Mike made Oscar promise to bring a horse.

They were unloading before the sun came up over the mesa, which loomed like a sundered ocean liner.

Both horses were tense and prancing as they started up the red trail through the scrub. They could sense from their riders, in that horse-wise way, that this was no ordinary day of working and roping cows.

The men picked up fresh sign at a spring that wept out of the red side of the mesa and followed uphill through heavy brush and big red sandstone boulders. On steep pitches the horses' feet slipped in the scree, and their shoes sparked.

As they lunged and humped up the slope, Oscar riding behind, he told the story of how his uncle got himself hanged by a mustang. He still couldn't be exactly sure of what happened, but he wondered if the whole thing had been a trap, if a horse could have enough guile and meanness to lure a rider into what seemed like an easy place to catch him, then pull some premeditated whammy like that, and, if so, could he teach other horses the same trick or like ones. In any case, the long and small of the grizzly tale was *pay attention.*

Oscar talked about what kind of horse they wanted: a big skewbald stallion with a lot of rear end, a thin neck, not too big of a head or too small of a tail, as one associated with Appaloosa stock.

They followed the tracks of unshod horses up a well-rutted trail, but they soon noticed there were as many tracks coming back down the trail as there were tracks ascending. It wasn't making sense. They decided to split up, Mike continuing upward, Oscar forking off to the top of the mesa directly to get a better overview.

They determined to meet at the rock corral in three hours. Neither carried a watch. Oscar rode for over two hours without seeing anything but deer, coyotes, eagles, and desert flora without end.

He was easing his horse down a steep rock slab above a three-hundred-foot drop. He took his feet out of the stirrups completely, half expecting the horse to lose his footing and disappear over the edge.

Then the ground got even worse. He worked along a narrow ledge that got narrower and narrower, then quit. There was no way to turn around, and backing the horse would have been double suicide. Oscar muttered, "Story of my life." Then he mentioned to the horse, whose ears were rotating like radar scanners, "Well, Spook, at least it ain't boring. You wouldn't want to be bored, would you?"

The only thing that suggested itself to do was to jump over a four-foot void to where the ledge picked up again and widened. It didn't look like a good idea, but it was the only one handy.

Oscar decided the idea was weak enough to need a backup idea, so he shook out one of the two lariats he was carrying, and lofted the straight end over a point of rock about ten feet above and three feet in front of him. He cinched the loop end over his saddle horn and held the loose end in his right hand.

Spook was less than enthusiastic about the leap. Oscar collected him and asked. Spook backed and pranced a bit, then squatted down and sprang. Oscar let the slack run out, and the horse gained the far ledge. The footing was treacherous, though, and once over he began to slip and scrabble. That's when Oscar dallied and held on till the horse got his feet under him and stood.

Oscar unwound his dally and pulled his rope off the spike of rock. He loosened the locked loop from his saddle horn and patted his horse on the neck. He exhaled a long breath, realizing he never remembered inhaling.

He re-coiled his rope as the horse stepped carefully along the resurrected ledge. The ledge ended and the slope eased, and he lunged his horse to the top of the pitch.

When he came over the top he saw them: twenty or so mustangs full tilt, manes and tails assuming the wind. Behind them a great ruckus of dust in which Mike disappeared and reappeared. Potatoes Browning, nose out, ears back, gaining.

Oscar spurred his horse, half galloping, half backpedaling, through the sand repose and off to join the chase.

Mike knew which mustang he wanted, so when various members of the herd swerved into coulees, he let them fall back until his horse had figured out his target.

It was a big paint stallion that looked like it had stamina, not a young horse. Mike knew wild horses don't have the staying power, they aren't the athletes that ranch-worked quarter horses are. Mike figured he could run him out. Indeed, he was closing, though he didn't know Oscar had joined the chase about two hundred yards back.

There were three horses running ahead of Mike now. They passed a row of sandrocks like teeth on his left. The stallion made a hard cut and leapt through a low gap in the geologic maw. Potatoes cut too and almost lost his rider. When Mike got back to the middle of the saddle he saw the rock formation encircled him. He had never seen it, but he knew it was the place Oscar had described, where they were to meet up, where Oscar's uncle had got bamboozled and hanged by a wild horse.

Mike saw the temptation of the old stump and decided to stay in the saddle no matter what.

The skewbald stallion slowed as if unsure what to do next, as if he'd got himself into a trap. He was forcing Mike's hand and Mike knew it. Now or never. Mike swung his loop twice, and by the third time Potatoes Browning was less than a length behind the mustang. An easy throw. The question now was what to do next, since the stallion didn't stop when the loop tightened around his neck; in fact, he put on a burst of speed.

Mike made a dally but kept his horse following. Setting up would mean a wreck. They made a full turn inside the fairy ring of rocks. Then the stallion did something astonishing. He made a sliding stop, but before it was complete he doubled to the left and rolled back. Mike saw him charging as he pushed his own horse into the bit. Potatoes shied instinctively and kept the charging horse on his right side, turning to avoid a collision.

He rolled back as the stallion went by, which saved them but had the unfortunate effect of locking Mike's dally. Mike turned loose of his rope but it was too late. He was tied to the wild horse, who had made the same move again and was coming toward them.

Mike would have bailed but he felt the lariat clamp down on his thigh, tying him into the saddle. Potatoes again did the right thing, turning to face the mustang, again with disastrous results. The rope was now encircling Mike's waist, and the two horses were facing each other, hunkering down on their haunches. They were cutting Mike in half.

Then Mike felt the rope go slack and he could breathe. He slipped from the saddle and his horse stood. He saw Spook about thirty feet away, riderless, standing by his dropped reins.

Through the atmosphere of grit and his own grit-blinded eyes, he made out Oscar dropping his knife and building a loop from the rope he held in his left hand.

When the stallion raced past him, making for the opening in the rocks, Oscar wafted out a loop in front of the horse and roped the paint by the front legs, dropping him like a puppet flung to the ground, his momentum carrying him into a flip in an explosion of dust, legs, horsehair, and squeals. The mustang struggled to rise and run, and Oscar jerked him to the ground again. They did that seven times.

Oscar knew how dangerous it was for the horse, to be roped by the front legs at a gallop, but the son of a bitch had upped the ante and now Oscar wanted his ass.

Mike stood staring at the cut end of his own lariat, which was trailing from the stallion's neck. He wasn't quite sure what had happened. Oscar said, "Jump in any time, Mike."

Mike took a second lariat and a long cotton rope from his saddle. They scotch-hobbled the stallion, and he sat down in the dust to rest. Oscar picked up his knife, folded it, and sheathed it. They stood and watched for a good half hour as the stallion exhausted himself, struggling, falling, heaving by turns.

Nobody said anything. Then, when they picked up their horses again, Mike said, "Now what do we do?"

"I was just about to ask you the same thing."

What they did was tie the stallion's nose to his left hind leg so he had to hop with his head down.

Oscar led him with a rope around his neck, dallying and giving him a stretch when he fought. Mike rode behind with a line tied to the cotton rope that hobbled the stallion and kept his head down.

By and by they had an agreement, sort of. They loaded the stallion into the trailer with a steel cable and a come-along.

Mike said, "So now that you've caught this stallion, what will you do with him?"

Oscar said, "Turn him loose with some beautiful brood mares and let him screw his brains out."

TUESDAY

THE SHERIFF HAD GIVEN UP on his Apache tracker. True, the guy could tell you if an ant had crossed a sugar cube, but on this manhunt his eccentricities were showing. The sheriff had been reduced to tracking the tracker, who had contacted him only once from Rawlins.

They'd spotted the Indian twice from the helicopter. They'd never seen the guy he was supposed to run down. The sheriff had to guess from the direction the Indian was going, straight north across the Great Divide Basin toward the Wind River Mountains, where the fugitive was headed.

Once the tracker crossed from the South Fork of the Popo Agie, the sheriff decided that Arans had to cross the Middle Fork, no matter where he was headed. The sheriff knew something about the Middle Fork. You can't cross it. It's too swift and violent and boulder-studded. That is, unless you cross it where it goes underground, between the Sinks and the Rise.

That's where he was parked at 6 A.M., waiting.

AUGUST 1991

MIKE TELEPHONED Al Falb, a neighbor.

"Hello."

"Hello, Al? This is Mike."

"Say, Mike. How you doing?"

"Gettin' along. Yourself?"

"I ain't got no more get-along. I'm so old now I'm always the same."

"You couldn't be that old. I heard you just bought that big buckskin gelding from Oscar."

"It's an old horse."

"What do you want with an old horse?"

"Hell, I don't even buy green bananas anymore."

"Listen, Al, I was riding up on Boulder Ridge today and I saw a bunch of your steers."

"How did they look?"

"I couldn't get very close to them."

"Then they must be fine."

"Yeah, they're fine, but some of these landowners are getting hot under the collar."

"Oh, those chuckleheads. 'Squatters,' I call them. Not that they don't own those little postage stamps of prairie fair and square, just they *live* like squatters on the land they own. I don't get it. Yeah, I have what you might call a telephone relationship with several of them bozos. Especially that loud-voice son of a bitch. What's his name?"

"Snipes."

"Yeah, Snipes. 'Squatting Bull,' I call him. He seems to be their fearless leader, ain't it."

"Seems like."

"Oh, he calls me every few days or so and cries about cattle crapping in his yard."

"What do you tell him?"

"To fix his fence and close the gates. I hope he doesn't, though. It's good grass on that squatter land. Good feed for my steers. If they don't eat it, it's nothing but a prairie fire waiting for a match."

"Well, he chases cattle on his three-wheeler. Broke legs on two of Oscar's cows."

"Oscar told me. I don't know what to do, short of shooting the bastard. Anyhow, he won't hurt steers."

"So you don't want to do anything with them?"

"Well, how do they look?"

"I didn't see them up close."

"They'll be all right. How's the grass?"

"The grass is fine."

"They'll be all right. How's the water?"

"The water is fine."

"They'll be all right. Maybe I should put some salt out for them."

TUESDAY

ON THE EDGE of an overhanging boulder, looking straight down on the Sinks, Jim Thomas stood holding his horse by the reins. The sun had risen but had not yet honeyed the river valley. It had just begun its daily chore to redden the boulders strewn like dice and the tops of pines that grew near the canyon rim.

Until he saw him bareback on his horse and naked, staring into the white violence of the river, he hadn't been altogether sure Mike wasn't going to cross where the river ran underground. Now he was sure. He should have been sure before. If Mike kept going there was no place left to go. Jim watched. Had he called out, no one would have heard.

He felt a tug on his reins as his horse lifted his head and turned his ears. Jim looked. Oscar Rose was riding a skinny sorrel mare up the trail toward him.

"Howdy."

"Howdy yourself." Jim looked hard at Oscar's horse's feet. Then he looked at Oscar, a glance packed with meaning.

"What ya lookin' at?"

Thomas looked back into the canyon. "Big naked guy on a zebra dun horse standing by the side of the river."

"Really? What's he doing?"

"Looks to be petting his horse."

"Huh. Can I have a look?" Oscar stepped his horse up to the edge of the overhang, stood up in his stirrups, and looked. "Damned if he ain't."

"So what do you know about this?"

"Very damned little I know about anything," Oscar said, and tipped his hat back.

"He's your friend. Aren't you going to try to stop him?"

"He's your fugitive. Aren't you?"

"I just said I'd follow him and I've been following him for four hundred miles. If he does, of his own free will, what I think he's about to do, I can't follow him anymore. I can't follow him into that big Disposall."

"Yeah, geologists reckon the Sinks is so full of dead timber and rocks and limestone holes it's just a big strainer. That's why it comes up so calm at the Rise."

"So why aren't you stopping him?"

"You know, when I was in college I read this story by a French guy. About a schoolteacher who has to escort this Algerian prisoner to jail. There's an uprising, so the French are short of police. The schoolteacher doesn't want to do it. Seems the

Algerian killed a guy for stealing a goat, which in Algeria, I guess, is perfectly reasonable, but under French law he was guilty.

"Anyhow, the teacher takes him to a crossroads and tells him if he goes one way, he can escape to freedom. He'll be a fugitive all his life. The other path leads to prison, where in some sense he'll be free, at least of being a fugitive. The schoolteacher leaves the criminal at the crossroads but he looks over his shoulder just in time to see the guy head down the road to prison."

Thomas just looked. He said, "Well?"

"Mike's lost everything. I guess we all will eventually. Being a fugitive is not being free. What he's about to do is something no one will forget."

"I guess not. So why doesn't he just go to jail and be free?"

"I guess because he's not an Algerian."

OCTOBER 1991

MIKE HAD ASKED, but nobody could remember why the mountain was called Deadman. It was a big easy ridge, top not reaching timberline, where all this country's snow comes from. Did somebody find, early on, a dead man, and after that it just became the handiest way to refer to the place? Lost thread.

They found a dead woman this spring. Last November she and her husband made a wrong turn and got stuck in the snow in a blizzard. The man stayed with the car and was saved, but the woman headed out. They found her carcass scattered by winter-starved coyotes.

Mike had waited for elk season's end to ride this country. Shirley's brother had had his favorite horse shot out from under him, though the horse's mane and tail were flagged with orange fluorescent tape. The bullet went right behind his knee.

Mike rode up through the lush alpine grass of big tilted meadows. He rode through the seaworthy lodgepoles big-snow country grows. He rode to the ditch camp.

Nearly a century, now, ago, they began to build the reservoir and all the ditches that lift and divert the water. They built the ditch camp with axes and nearby trees and chinked it. A tight log house with a good stove. Next to it a barn and corral for the oxen and mules they used all day to slip out the ditches. The cabin could bunk a work gang of six, and in the spring a crew lived there in the deep snow, shoveling snow out of the ditches to start them.

He smelled it in the air, the redolent black bitter of dew-damp ashes. The barn was gone. A few wraiths still rose from the gray and black cinders. He rode to the bunkhouse and got down. The lock hasp was crowbarred off, the door ajar. Some-body'd had a party in there. There wasn't much they could hurt. Maybe that's why they burned the barn. In the middle of the worn tongue-and-groove floor was a tidy coiled pile of human excrement with a birthday candle stuck in it.

Mike took the fire shovel from its hook and scooped and flung it—shit and shovel—out the back door. He looked under the bunk. They hadn't discovered the trapdoor to the cellar where all the stores and emergency provisions were, including, Mike knew, a case of Canadian Club. He'd call Murphy.

If someone told you, you wouldn't think about it. You'd say, "The hell." But Mike rode away thinking about the person whose desire it was to burn that impersonal history of logwork walls. What was that *against?*

JULY 1993

MIKE TROTTED TWENTY PAIR of his own Angus and Black Baldies down a sagey slope into a verdant tall-grass meadow. He reined in at the top of the hill and let the cows dribble down and fall to grazing and milling. They'd stay on that grass for a while.

He decided to check the bottom by Sand Creek Bridge, pick up whatever, if anything, was there, and return with them for the cattle he had.

He followed downstream the drainage the cows were in, studying the willows for strays, down to Sand Creek.

The wind was full of willow smell and it tussled the tall grass. There were no cows, so he doubled back. This time he took the road, and turned off when he drew even to where he'd left the cows. He heard a two-cycle engine revving and whining under the wind, but he didn't think much of it. One heard buzzing and screeching all the time now, especially on weekends—an enraged hive of ATVs and motorbikes.

So he was surprised when his cows and calves poured out of the draw where he'd dropped them, running hard back toward the spot where he'd gathered them. They parted around his horse like a stone in a stream. Then Merriweather Snipes ripped up the hill behind the cattle and passed Mike like he wasn't there.

Mike got mad.

He noticed the pistol strapped to the handlebars. His horse jumped into a dead run. Snipes was pushing as hard as he could without dumping his machine in the sagebrush and varmint holes. The three-wheeler was tilting and bucking dangerously.

The horse easily outstripped him, and Mike made a wide sweeping arc to overtake and turn the stampeding cattle. He got around and turned the leaders and swung the herd around. He saw Snipes, having given up, sitting still on his machine, revving, exhaust fumes like a smoke signal of impotent rage.

Mike trotted the cows right past him. Now it was Snipes's turn not to be there.

The only problem was, they both were there.

The cows, tongues lolling and drooling, slowed to a walk and lined out in front of Mike and his horse, up the road toward the pasture where they belonged.

Ad trotted up and Mike told him what had happened. Ad said he'd talk to the man and wheeled his horse around.

Mike pushed the cows through the gate that had been left open. Then he started gathering cows off Ad's section; time to get them off the pasture. It was dark when he finished shoving sulfa pills down the throat of one cow, as Potatoes Browning kept the heel rope tight. Mike went home under stars.

"I thought you were going to call on me if you had any problems with cows over here."

"Problems? Yeah, I had about twenty problems at sunup right here in my yard. They broke the mirrors off my car again. I shooed 'em and went back to bed. An hour later the problems were back."

"You can't run them like that with your damned little motorized tricycle."

"I can't?"

"You don't have any fence. The law says you have to fence them *out*."

"This is a wilderness. I don't want any fence. Would you want to fence off Paradise?"

"Why do you feel the need to stampede them like that, clear down to the Running Water?"

"I like to run them. I hate cattle."

"You break their legs doing that."

"What do I care about their legs?"

"If you'll just come get me if you see any cows over here, we could avoid trouble."

"Who wants to avoid trouble?" Snipes grinned; then the grin vanished, switched off. "You gonna pay for my mirrors?"

TUESDAY

ALL NIGHT MIKE HAD WORKED hard at remembering. He discovered his childhood was mostly not memorable. Nothing got interesting until he became an idealist and got busted and moved west. He turned events over like that river tumbling bottom stones.

"It was all good, Potatoes, even the hard stuff, even the stuff that ended too soon. And, you know, I'm starting to think it never does end. Nothing ever does end. You and me had some times, didn't we? Isn't that good? Isn't this ending going to be good?"

He stroked the horse's neck.

"Listen, pard, I recently heard on the radio where these Portuguese neurologists discovered by mapping the brain that you can't tell the difference between the body and the mind, or the body and the soul, for that matter. I know I never could. Anyway, that means modern science has finally caught up to what William Blake said over two hundred years ago. Are you listening to me?"

The horse craned his neck around and nuzzled Mike's toe.

"OK. So if there's no difference there, where's there any difference? Now and then, here and there, I and thou, this and that. Are you following me?"

Potatoes looked around. His eyes were like moss agates, crystal balls of silence.

"Anyway. Past and present. You and me. No difference, get it? Whatever is waiting on the other side of the Sinks is no different from this side, except that it's not this side. No this, no that. Are you ready? All I mean is, really, bud, wherever I'm going, you're coming with me."

JUNE 1992

AD WOKE BUT HIS EYES STAYED CLOSED as he swam through that sensation of not knowing where it is one has waked. He liked the feeling and didn't try to figure it out. Then his mind slowly turned it over. He was home. He let well-being sink through him like falling snow before he opened his eyes and rested them on the cedar paneling of the gable roof.

He luxuriated in the warmth of the bed, the grain of the wood, the soft half-life of the pill he'd taken when he'd reached the cabin about midnight, the rich indulgence of the late hour articulated by the sunny trapezoid that planed across the single picture on the wall: a poster-sized reproduction of Piero della Francesca's *Resurrection*: the woeful sleeping soldiers, the triumphantly standing Christ, whose pallor is still that of the morgue. Ad thought Piero's Christ was a dead ringer for Eric Clapton.

Slipping further into the indulgence of not rising, Ad tilted his chin upward, his head back to see out the window behind the bed. The sky was blue and full of sun, but there were fat snowflakes like milkweed falling through it, too.

He propped himself on one elbow. June snow. An upslope had fetched in overnight, a low layer of moisture washed up on the Front Range. When the clouds touched high altitude, they turned to snow, blue sky above, and swept low over the open ground like soldiers under fire.

The snow fell to earth and vanished. But it knotted in clumps in pine branches. Ad sat up and looked out the window at the prairie, soft green with a misty gouache. The white pines on the ridge postured like priests. Weather that might have been murderous in another month was deeply calming, like another, safer world would be. Ad lay back down and rode out the rest of his pill.

Half an hour later he was laying kindling in the firebox of the cookstove. When the fire had a good pull he put the water on and climbed back to the loft and bed, not to sleep, but to keep his mind blank for as long as leftover sleep would let him. Nothing was going to screw up this day. Nothing lurid or horrific had happened at work the night before. No one would drop by. No phone. No mail.

If something bad was happening out in the human world somewhere, which surely it must be, he wouldn't know about it till later. When the kettle whistled he went down and had coffee.

He dressed and went into the day. He wanted to walk. The moist east wind was carrying beads now instead of flakes. He stood on the stoop and considered 360 degrees of alternatives. He considered distance. He plotted out a course that began in deep timber behind the house. He picked up a deer trail that contoured the side hill. Clumps of snow were plopping off the trees all around him like silly artillery. He spooked a cow elk.

Without really meaning to, he drifted onto a trail that had been his mother's favorite, where they had often walked together when he was little. Evening walks. The path slinked through a stand of Douglas firs, then dropped down to follow the hem of the woods, so you were in the trees, out of sight, but you could see out over the whole wide plain swooshing below.

He'd just gotten down to that part of the trail where he could see it all. His eyes caught something that didn't belong, it was like a cold wind blowing through him, a primordial fear deeper than self or survival.

About a hundred yards down the hill was a six-by-six square post about two feet long planted in the earth. When he stood over it he had to admit to himself what it was. A small aluminum tag stamped with numbers and stapled to the post declared a mining claim.

The fear forestalled ignited into rage and he was trying to pull the thing out of the ground, saying, "Son of a bitch!" He couldn't uproot the post so he pushed it over with his boot. It had been driven into the rocky soil by a length of rebar anchored to its base. He levered it out and threw it into a currant bush.

He was breathing hard and holding his arms out from his sides when he saw another identical post a hundred yards off. He paced over and worked it out of the ground.

He was sweating now, extracting the sixth wooden tooth he'd found, when someone shouted behind him, "Hey! What are you doing? That's a federal offense! You can't do that."

"Can't? Watch this, motherfucker." He flung another marker into the air and away before he turned to face whoever it was he could hear crunching the gravel at a trot toward him.

Ad felt murderous, already bloody, beyond recall. The man approaching him was still yelling about federal offenses. He was decked out in camouflage. He sported a pistol on a military web belt high on his waist.

"I'm telling you to stop." He unholstered his pistol.

Ad never looked at the pistol but glared at the man. He said, "You are trespassing."

"No, I ain't. I'm staking claims. Is this your land, parcel thirty-six–twelve–eight? Are you Dr. Trent?"

Ad sickened at the description of his land as a parcel, just like all the other parcels, ready to send. "Yes."

"Well, then, I'm right where I'm supposed to be." He holstered his pistol.

Ad said, "I own this ground."

"That's what you think." The man reached into his breast pocket and extracted a computer printout. "Says here you don't own the mineral rights to this property. You only own the surface. And to tell you the truth, Doc, you don't even own the surface if there's something under it. It says here the homesteader, a Mr. Patrick Sudeck, could've paid a twenty-five-dollar fee for minerals in 1923, but he didn't."

Ad's rage swung like a weather vane back to sick and helpless fear. He knew the man was right. Twenty-five dollars in 1923 was a year's income for the old homesteader.

Ad said, "You have to get permission to come on a person's land."

The man grinned triumphantly. "You weren't home."

Ad was sure he was lying, but there was nothing to do. He said, "Look, miners have worked this country for a hundred years and not one of them found anything. There's nothing under here but rotten granite thirty miles down."

The man looked sidewise, left and right, as if afraid of being overheard. "We're looking for new stuff: molybdenum, titanium, uranium. We got new methods. And besides, I just do the surveying. I don't care if they find anything or not. They found diamonds at Tie Siding. If the company I work for wants to tear up this section with backhoes and bulldozers they'll do it. They can tear down your goddamn house and there's not a thing in hell you can do to stop them. See, this is America. You don't own a goddamn thing. You just pay taxes on it."

"Who are you working for? I want to call them."

"No problem, Doc." The man reached into his hip pocket and handed over a card: SAND CREEK MINING COMPANY. There was a telephone number, a fax number, and a list of executives. The first name on the list was Merriweather Snipes.

TUESDAY

THE RIVER WAS LIKE A COIL of concertina wire. Potatoes stood ankle deep at the edge of a rare eddy by the bank, which slipped off precipitously and married the white violence.

Mike looked down to the whale mouth in the limestone that inhaled the river. Huge spars and boulders ribbed the sides of the cave. Above it rose forty feet of overhanging limestone cliff, gray-green streaked with black and striated by eons. Above the cliff, a pleasant grassy slope fell back and up to the edge of a spruce forest, which rose to the sky. The skyline tips swayed in the dawned-up clouds.

The sound was constant, a roar like standing behind a jet taking off.

The other side of the river, where the visitors' center and the highway were, was backed by another canyon pitch, but gentler, not unlike a hundred canyons Mike had crossed in his last days.

Granite cliffs like giant stairs with grassy flats interspersing. You could ride it but there'd be a lot of switchbacks, threading cliffs like a shoelace. There was also a small population of low junipers, like squat green cousins, watching him. He thought, Visitors.

The top of the canyon was bald-looking, just sage and grass but with another little family scene. A dozen dead spruce spars, probably fire-killed but still standing, huddled. Above that, clouds going somewhere.

Mike thought stepping into the river was like riding into the clouds.

Left of the burn was a single stunted ponderosa jutting into the sky, rounded off, asymmetrical, itself like a green cloud but with roots in the granite cliff.

He twisted around and looked up to the top of the timbered ridge behind him. He saw two men, one mounted, perched on an overhanging rock, silhouetted. The rider waved. Mike waved back.

"Guess I've got my visitors," he said, and stepped the horse forward into the rush.

The horse began to swim against the current but Mike turned his head downriver. From the ridge above they were visible for a maximum of one second. Then they were gone. It was just the river again.

SEPTEMBER 1991

MERRY LIT A LUCKY and kick-started the three-wheeler. He whined off down the dirt road and, after a half mile, geared down to a crawl and steered over into the sage. He was hunting arrowheads but he didn't like to walk, so he crept along on the ATV, looking off to the side. If he saw anything that might be flint, he had a large cooking spoon splinted to a stick, so he could fetch it up without dismounting.

To concentrate peripherally, that's what Merry tried to do. The gravel slipped past like it was on a conveyor belt. He picked the ground on one side of the ATV to search as it idled along at a walking pace.

As a kid in Nebraska he'd hunted arrowheads in plowed fields on bluffs above the Platte. Once he'd brought a spear point home that his father said was a Clovis point, ten to twelve thousand years old. It may have been used to slay woolly mammoths, saber-toothed tigers, giant sloths.

The vision electrified him—skin-clad hunters surrounding the mud-foundered behemoth, darting in to sink their spears and jumping back before the tortured monster could obliterate them.

He had envisioned these men, so like him and so foreign, as he'd coddled the artifact in his hand, fingering the concave base, the flute, the ground edges where it was hafted.

Here in the high plains it was different. Points were harder to see in the gravel than in the dirt of a bean field. The points were mostly smaller, true arrowheads, often the same color as the gravel they lay in.

So he concentrated on the corners of his field of vision, and when he glimpsed the shiny flint he got a jolt of excitement. If, on inspection, it wasn't just a chip or fragment, but a whole artifact, he retrieved it reverently, sustaining the thrall.

Back home he'd hold the point in his hand and meditate on the identity of the man who held it last—his courage, his audacity, his cleverness, his freedom from sentiment. The animal world in which he was an animal.

• • •

Oscar was atop a high knoll, on his horse, arms crossed, leaning on the saddle horn, studying. Addressing the horse. "What in hell is that knucklehead doing?" It took a minute of studying to figure it out. "Well, at least he isn't stampeding cows." Then he got an idea.

Grinning, Oscar spurred his horse down the hill in a head-long gallop, a maniacal set to his teeth. When Oscar was a kid they played this horseback game called counting coups. . . .

Because of the motor, Merriweather never heard the hoof-beats until Oscar was on top of him, galloping fast, leaning way over in the saddle. Snipes got a jolt of pure adrenaline as Oscar clapped him on the back and rode by, whooping and circling. Oscar rode back up the hill, thinking, Maybe he'll have a heart attack.

He stopped and wheeled his horse, stood skylined. He was raising his arm to wave when he saw, for the second time, the pistol pointed at him. He heard the report, but saw no bullet hit. He turned and loped away, said to the horse, "Maybe that'll give him something to think about. It does me."

TUESDAY

THE TRUTH IS THAT until he was in the river he actually thought there was a slight chance he might come out alive. As soon as the water took him, however, he knew there was no hope. He let go of the lead rope. The current played him like a straw in a hurricane. It tossed him up once completely out of the water and turned him around. He was inside the black mouth that was swallowing the white river, the river rushing toward the darkness with him in it, and the darkness taking it all.

He went under again, not just under the surface but pulled straight down, like falling off a cliff, like the river was diving straight for the center of the earth.

He had heard from kayakers that when you go under the water you instinctively hold your breath until the fire in your lungs tears your insides out. They said that when you give up and inhale the water it is a sensation of blessed peace, relief, and grace. The people who said these things had all been saved by someone else. The point was, though, hard as it was to imagine, drowning's not so bad.

Mike tried to expel the air from his lungs, but he couldn't. Down there in the darkness he was all lungs and felt filled with broken glass. He was battered and tumbled as he fell, but all he thought about was his lungs.

Then he was rising. The current had made a U-turn and was geysering straight upward as fast as it had been falling before.

He rose like the bubble of air he had become, and when he surfaced he bobbed up a bit out of the water. There was no sky. He was still in total darkness.

But he could breathe. He sucked in gasps of moldy air. He treaded water. He was inside a cave.

He heard the sound of the horse paddling madly in circles, breathing hard, snorting. The horse would swim in darkness until exhaustion took him under.

Still treading water and breathing hard, Mike began to feel himself circling, too, spiraling through the dark like a lost planet. The circles became smaller and smaller and he knew he was about to be sucked under again. He was going down the drain. He gulped for air and was gone.

TUESDAY

ADKISSON LEANED ON THE TOURIST RAIL overlooking the Rise. The water was lime green, and a school of lazy trout were fanning into the mild current like wind socks, waiting for goodies to float into their mouths. The sign said NO FISHING, which explained the almost grotesque size and sluggishness of the fish.

No way in hell, thought Ad. The water was calm and shallow. There was no ascertainable origin it issued from, though clearly all the water that thundered through the Sinks came up sanguine at the Rise. The water seemed, though, to be seeping through fissures so fine as to make it placid and sourceless.

Ad's pickup was the only vehicle in the small lot at the overlook, so he turned around when a car went up the road and noted with some interest that it was the sheriff.

He turned back and gazed at the green, inert water.

Then something amazing. From a jagged tumble of boulders ten feet above the surface of the water, out from a toilet-sized hole in those boulders, a bushy head and bearded face emerged. Then the whole man crawled out and stood in the sun.

Ad watched, awed, as Mike staggered down the slope, waded into the shallow water, and, naked and bleeding, staggered across the Rise, up to his knees in emerald water.

Ad slid down the bank and splashed toward him. Mike was bleeding from the nose and ears, he was mapped with lacerations, his left arm hung mangled at his side.

Ad grabbed him and hung his better arm over his own shoulders and made for shore. Mike was clearly in shock. He mumbled, "Where's my horse?"

Ad didn't answer. He whispered "Jesus" and eased Mike toward the truck. Mike kept mumbling nonsense, but, Frankensteinlike, he kept his feet under him.

Ad rolled him into the cab and spewed gravel getting out of the lot, gunned down the road. When he reached the town of Lander he forced himself down to the speed limit.

In a clear voice Mike said, "Where are we going?"

He still had to be delirious, but Ad answered him straight. "We're going to put you back together with some splints and stitches and plaster (I'll just pretend you're Oscar), and then we're going to take you over to a ranch near Garrett, where you can go to work and no one will ever find you."

Mike turned toward Ad, a bloody Medusa. In a clear voice he spoke. "Can I ride the horses?"

TUESDAY

OSCAR DRAGGED HIS SLEEVE across his eyes, straightened his hat. "That was something, wasn't it?"

"Yeah," said Jim. "That was something."

"My trailer's not far from here. You want a lift?"

"No, I'd better ride down below that banshee and see if there's any remains."

"Suit yourself."

"Yeah, I'll just call from the visitors' center and have someone bring my rig."

"Right. Oh, one thing. When the sheriff gets done with it, can I have Mike's saddle?"

"I think that could be arranged."

Jim rode down a diagonal tack and crossed the river where there isn't any river. He was surprised to find the sheriff there, sitting in his car.

"Where in the hell have you been?"

"Tracking the fugitive."

"Yeah? And where is the fugitive?"

"Right now I'd say you're sitting on him."

"What?"

"Yeah. And by the way, as of now I don't work for you any-more."

Jim told Cummins what had happened, that he'd been hired to track a man and he did, and now it was over. He tied his horse to the rail along the tourist path, and they drove in the sheriff's car down to the Rise. They stared at the inscrutable green water for almost an hour.

OCTOBER

THE PROBLEM WITH RIDING THE BUS is that most of the passengers, except the kids, have already run out of luck. So when the bus marked PHILADELPHIA opened its door in Ogallala, Nebraska, and the redheaded, round-faced, peach-fuzzed teenager wearing a Patagonia pullover and carrying a color-coordinated backpack boarded, he scanned the seats for the least terrible option.

There were no empty rows. Without being too obvious or deliberate, he assessed the passengers for one that looked survivable. He passed a reeking drunk and then a man who was not drunk but reeked anyway. He passed an old pinch-faced woman clutching a laundry bag whose expression as she glared at him said, Don't even think about it!

Several of the rows were already double-occupied—a mother and daughter, a couple of jocks from Cheyenne. Soon he was at the back of the bus and out of options.

The man he sat beside was a little scary, but he didn't smell and he didn't look up threateningly. Mainly he was big. He was chewing bubble gum, gazing out the window blowing bubbles. His hair was black and buzz-cut. He had full lips and a hawk nose. His arm was in a cast. He had recent scars on his face.

The redheaded kid threw his pack up into the rack, plopped down, and said, "You going to Philly?"

"What?" The big guy turned from the window and looked at the kid for the first time.

The kid said, "I'm going back to visit my folks. What are you going for?"

Mike's voice sounded uncertain, like it came from a long way away.

"I'm going to blow up the Liberty Bell."

The kid forced a chuckle.

THURSDAY

AD SAT ON THE ROCK WORSHIPING HIS COFFEE. The sun was just beginning to flash the Snowy Range like a tiara on the brow of the Medicine Bow. Ad was thinking how *times change* meant *time changes*. Once the world was water. Everything was sea-level. Then the mountains were islands. The sandstone rim below was blood-colored proof of an absent sea. If he held his gaze due north, the prairie still looked like an ocean, away to the lift of Laramie Peak, there on the curve of the world, over a hundred miles, with nothing but uninterrupted watery grass.

Something pushed the Rockies up, but at first they weren't real mountains. It was just a big hill, six hundred miles of incline. Erosion made the granite faces, the river valleys, and left topsoil thirty feet deep in Iowa. "Nobody likes erosion anymore," mused Ad, "now that all the scenery is made."

The Snowy Range is made of quartz. Of ranges it was there first, not too high, bone white. Then the Medicine Bow drifted in from somewhere, maybe Yakutsk, slid under the Snowies, and lifted them into the sky. Ad wondered if the Medicine Bow would stay put or if it was on its way somewhere else. Would it take the Snowies with it, like a bride, or leave them behind, bereft and diminished? Hard to tell, but it's good to get a little perspective now and then.